I0708965

SPINELESS WONDERS
PO Box 220 STRAWBERRY HILLS
New South Wales, Australia, 2012

www.shortaustralianstories.com.au

First published by Spineless Wonders 2014

Typeset in Georgia.

Printed and bound by Lightning Source Australia

ISBN 978-1-925052-04-6 (pbk)
National Library of Australia Cataloguing-in-Publication entry:

The World To Come/Edited by Patrick West and Om Prakash
Dwivedi

A823.4

The World to Come
stories

edited by
Patrick West and
Om Prakash Dwivedi

The editors gratefully acknowledge the generous support of
Deakin University's Centre for Memory, Imagination and Invention.

Contents

PREFACE

In 1738 Isaac Watts, an English preacher and hymn writer, wrote *The World to Come*: a Christian tract about departed souls, death, and the glory or terror of the resurrection. Since 1738, however, time itself – the entity which allows the very notion of 'the world to come' – has sometimes seemed to turn, not upside down, but back to front. For, at times, there has seemed to be no more world to come...

Writing in the early 1980s, Postmodernist critic Fredric Jameson proposed that 'The last few years have been marked by an inverted millenarianism in which premonitions of the future, catastrophic or redemptive, have been replaced by senses of the end of this or that...'

To some extent, Jameson's words still capture the tenor of today, provoking questions such as: How much can end before everything comes to an end? What might begin to take the place of the 'old'? Where can the 'new' come from?

In short, where are we now? Or rather, *when* are we now? Do we look to the future, to the present, or to the past, to get a sense of our place in time?

In the early years of this, the third millennium (going by the Gregorian calendar), it sometimes seems as if we are tarrying between the past and the future, with no firm purchase on the present. Watts and Jameson pull us in opposing directions.

Fears of climate change and fundamentalist terrorism – twin if not entwined global evils – have made the present into a place where we hardly dare set foot. From controlling the earth through our labour and enterprise, the earth, seemingly – warming up, melting at the poles – is starting to control us. At the same time, the resurgence of religious conflict puts secular modernity to a test that it may or may not survive.

If it is not desirable or even possible to try to escape from the uncertain present, our tail between our legs, into nostalgia for the past, then what new earth might we start to embrace? What new way of being human? What world to come?

Still, it's not easy, for the present is never no-where: it is always in a place. *Where* one is impacts *when* one is. Very deliberately, this collection harvests the voices of writers from all over the world, in fictional reflection on what the world to come looks like from where they are writing, in place and in time.

How to relate all these visions of the future? Where do they agree? Where diverge?

Such questions take on an additional edge when matters of place, of nationality, of fleeting or permanent residence, of indigeneity or otherwise, intersect with gender, class and race. Above all, these stories appear to show that the world to come for a woman will likely not be the same as the world to come for a man – as if the most ancient of differences were also the newest of differences...

Some of these pieces, however, do seem to anticipate a time in which theories like Transhumanism will abolish, not only categories of class, race and gender, but even those of God and religion – even mortality itself. We are a very long way, today, from the world to come imagined by Watts in 1738, if only because the sense of a 'we' has changed so much.

In selecting these stories from a global call-out, we looked for pieces that contemplated 'the world to come' in ways that, regardless of genre, surprised, delighted, enthralled or horrified us. Here, science fiction mixes with fantasy, with realism in all its sub-genres, with speculative fiction, with the almost unclassifiable.

We thank all the contributors to this collection for sharing their dreams and passions, their desires and wit, on the following pages, the 'pages to come'. We hope the stories work well together, resonate in the order we have chosen for them, but we also embrace the fact that no two 'worlds to come' can or should be alike; 21 stories, 21 futures ... if not 21 presents and 21 pasts...

Still as much as, like all writing of ambition, these stories seek to be 'new' (their own little 'world to come'), they are already, inevitably, getting old, as we who wrote and read them get old – moving into the past as everything does.

We hope, however, that so much as they begin to be documents from 'the world that has been', they will continue to speak to our fears and hopes for the future. For the most creative form of the future, after all, might well be the past that we have already lived: the 'eternal return' which has never stopped fascinating humans of all cultures and times. Clearly, borrowed as it is from almost 300 years ago, from the pen of Isaac Watts, the title *The World to Come* is another permutation of the 'eternal return'.

In closing (we might even say in beginning...), we hope that *The World to Come* is the start of something special for every reader.

PATRICK WEST
OM PRAKASH DWIVEDI
2014

THE WORLD TO COME

A PART HIDE, A PART HUMAN

Craig Cormick

'I'll bet she purrs like a lioness,' says Phil, watching the waitress sway across the room, his eyes roaming everywhere and lingering on the women – as ever.

I sigh and he looks back at me. 'What?' he asks. 'Don't tell me you're a humanist?'

I shrug.

He looks at me a moment and then smiles. 'You haven't done the watusi with a trannie yet have you?' he asks, though it's more of a statement really. Or an accusation.

I shrug again.

This time he laughs. 'How can you visit South Africa and not?'

'I came here to write,' I say, trying to steer his attention back to my book's synopsis on the table in front of him. It was surprising that he was such a great agent, as it was so hard to get him to actually read anything. I had this image of him giving the many manuscripts he received to his harem of office assistants and telling them, 'Read this and tell me whether I like it or not.'

He picks up the synopsis and holds it before him for a moment. Just when I think he's really going to read it, he drops it back onto the white linen tablecloth. 'Why don't you tell me what it's all about,' he says. 'I want to hear the passion in your voice.'

I sigh again. 'Okay,' I say, watching his eyes wander over to the table beside us where two gorgeous dark-skinned women sit. They have leopard hide over their shoulders and the brightest plumes on their heads. Pinks and reds and greens.

'Have you seen any of the trannie dances?' he asks. 'The way they move is amazing.'

Of course I had. As he said, how could you visit South Africa and not? But I say, 'Okay, here's the premise: it's an alternative history thing.'

'Uh-huh,' he says, giving me his full attention.

At least until the waitress walks back past our table again. Her tail swishes seductively and she smiles at us, those telltale golden eyes blinking slowly.

'God I love this country,' says Phil.

But it's the look she gives everyone at every table.

I wait until he's staring back at me again and I say, 'So imagine a South Africa where the historical divides are not about transgenics, but about race.'

He just stares at me and I can see he doesn't get it.

'Let's go back to the start,' I say. 'When Christiaan Barnard performed his first heart transplant operation back in 1967, what if he had access to a human heart rather than a baboon's heart?'

'A human heart?' he says with surprise.

'Yes. That would have changed everything. Imagine if all the human-animal enhancements that followed since then had never happened.'

He looks down at the synopsis in front of him now and reads a little then looks back to me.

'So there would be no experiments with animal gene transplants,' I say. 'And no trans-species; no bird genes for plumage, no animal genes for speed and strength and, of course, no trans-species apartheid.'

His face goes into that impassive mask he adopts when he doesn't like something. He glances back down at the synopsis. 'But what about the townships?' Phil asks. 'You say here there are townships.'

'Yes,' I say. 'But imagine that instead of the old South Africa passing laws about trannies not having the same rights as pure-humans – imagine it being illegal to breed with pure-humans and so on ... Imagine if the same apartheid laws were passed along race lines.'

'Race lines?' he asks. 'I don't get it.'

'Well, imagine that South Africa has this really wack government that decides race is an issue for them and so they make rules based on skin colour, whereby native Africans and others have fewer rights and have to live in special townships.'

'That doesn't make any sense,' he says.

'Hear me out,' I say. 'Imagine that a government passes laws

     CRAIG CORMICK

that say if you have dark skin you can't breed with or marry anybody with light skin.'

'But where would you draw the line?' he asks. 'When does a good suntan become a dark skin? And what about people with naturally tanned skin – what group would they fall under?'

'I'll have to work out those details,' I say. 'But the principle is that we have this race-based divide and all the non-whites are forced to live in townships and do all the menial work for the lighter-skinned people who control all the power and money.'

'Like the pure-humans did back in the 60s and 70s?' he asks.

'Yes. Similar. So it's sort of a metaphor for the way the trannies used to be treated here. You get the same problems happening. People who are trannies – or dark-skinned – finding ways to hide it and live in light-skinned areas, always in fear of being found out. And in this case, we have a pale-skinned man and his dark-skinned lover who have to hide from the authorities. Just like what happened here in some instances.'

Phil looks around the restaurant calmly. 'I wonder if any of the patrons here are of an age to remember the apartheid years?' he asks.

'Hmm. Probably not,' I say, following his gaze around the room. 'It's been over thirty years now.'

Phil nods. 'But I wonder how they would take the stories of their parents and grandparents being recast like this.' Again, it's not really a question.

'That's the point,' I tell him. 'It's easy to forget there were ever laws against being a trannie – all the riots and the underground guerilla movement and things. But this is a way of making people remember it.'

Phil sighs. He's clearly not convinced. 'It's not your normal stuff,' he says.

'It's not your normal country.'

He nods. 'I'm just thinking of your readers.'

'Of course,' I say. But Phil has never cared about readers. Only about buyers.

'It's speculative fiction,' I say. 'It's as much about the idea as the story.'

'Hmm,' he says. 'More speckled than speculative, I think. And I thought you were against genre typecasting.'

'Well get this,' I say, 'we still have guerilla fighters, but they don't have gorilla genes. They are African activists who want to sabotage the country's infrastructure to force political change. You know, secret training camps and sneaking over the border and blowing up trains and things.'

'Hmm,' he says. 'That's good. But the human interest is still the necessary angle. Tell me a little bit more about the love interest you've got here.' He stabs at a line in the synopsis as he says it.

'Well, as I said, there's this light-skinned guy and dark-skinned woman who are in a relationship in hiding.'

'Why is it always the woman who is subjugated?' he asks.

I stare at him a moment before answering. Phil just likes asking difficult questions, I know.

'I suppose we could turn that around,' I say. 'Sure. Nothing to stop us having the male lover having the dark skin and the female lover having light skin.'

He shrugs.

'Just trying to consider your female readers,' he says. 'Don't want them to feel you aren't treating them with respect.'

I almost smile. Phil wishing to respect women!

'We can work on that,' I say.

'So how do things resolve themselves?' he asks.

'Well that's where we change things a bit. So in the real world, you know, it turned out the President's wife had a cheetah's heart that was secretly transplanted to keep her alive and the President had been working to break down the hate laws and apartheid so as to prevent her from being taken away from him. When it was uncovered, all these other high profile people who were trannies started coming out in public too and the government tried to lock them all up, but the independent states starting allowing trannies certain freedoms. It all came to a head way back during the 2016 rugby world cup when it was revealed that the winning Western Cape team had several players with springbok genes.'

'Yeah, yeah,' he says. 'I know all that.'

Though I doubt he ever did.

'Well, in my version of reality, the rest of the world had started applying economic sanctions to the country and there was increasing civil unrest and protests, and things just fell apart slowly.'

                    CRAIG CORMICK

He looks around the room again and holds up a finger for the drinks waiter at the bar, then points at our two near-empty wine glasses. The man nods.

'I'm not convinced yet,' he says, turning back to me. 'It sounds a poor imitation of reality.'

'It has the power of metaphor,' I say. 'Through the idea of a race divide being so ridiculous and artificial, we see how it is impossible to maintain and we see the absurdity of transgenic divides.'

'And how will you do that without sounding like you're preaching?' Phil asks.

'I'll manage it,' I say. 'It will all fit in with the resolution of the story.'

'So what happens?' asks Phil.

'Well, there will be a crisis for the two lovers, see. Just when it looks like they will not be able to be together after one of them is arrested, the laws change. There are mass riots and the country is tipping into civil war and violence, so the government has to decide whether maintaining the race laws will destroy the country or if the laws need to be changed.'

Phil leans back in his chair as the drinks waiter steps in close and hovers over us. He pours more red wine into our glasses. I shouldn't have more than one as it makes my heart race something terrible, but Phil insists. The man is tall and dark-skinned, with the thick fur on his arms barely hidden by his white sleeve cuffs. 'Thank you,' I say, and he smiles. The thin, sharp, white teeth of a carnivore showing. He has that inner menace that many of the trannie men seem to emanate – even though he is more strikingly beautiful than our waitress. But Phil just says, 'Thank you, my good man.' I close my eyes a moment, picturing the drinks waiter ripping Phil's throat out. But of course he doesn't. This is one of the more expensive restaurants in Cape Town. Its large glass windows look out over the harbour, where tourists and locals go about their lives. Trannies and humans mixing easily.

Well, mostly.

There is a museum at the Robben Island ferry terminal where trannie activist prisoners were kept in isolation. There are grainy black-and-white photos of the early trannies, some malformed from experiments gone wrong, being surrounded by savage-faced men in harsh military caps and uniforms of short sleeves and pants, herding them into chained lines with cattle prods. Genetic ID cards were mandatory and, along one wall, there's a timeline of the slow increase in paranoia by the humanist government as on the one hand it condoned the genetic alteration of workers to make them faster and stronger, but on the other hand refused to allow them to mix with the pure-humans. Trannies were brutalised and treated like animals.

Of course, it was untenable. And after it all collapsed, everybody was pointing their fingers at somebody else. The scientists insisted that science was moral-free, that it was how the politicians were using the science that was the problem. The politicians were saying that they were only trying to represent the best interests of the people and were acting in accord with their wishes. People were saying the scientists and politicians were acting in secret and they had no idea what was really going on.

Then the scientists were soon opening private clinics for the rich to enhance themselves with animal genes. The politicians all somehow escaped prosecution, as invariably happens, and the people went back to not being told what was happening. It was a wonder the country had found some sort of stability so quickly.

Phil takes a drink from his glass of wine and then says, 'And everybody lives happily ever after?'

'I was thinking of having them wake up and discover it was all a dream,' I say.

We stare at each other and then he smiles. 'Okay, all clichés aside, do you really think that anyone will find the premise credible?'

'Sure,' I say. 'I just need to create an authentic world view for it. Make it sound believable. No, make it feel believable.'

Instead of replying, he looks across at the two trannie women with the leopard skin and feather plume hair. 'Do you think they'd believe it?' he asks.

I shrug.

'I think we should ask them,' he says, with a wink.

He picks up his wine glass and my synopsis and walks over to their table. He looks back at me quickly and I can see him

     CRAIG CORMICK

introducing himself. Turning on the charm. All smiles and flattery. I watch him point back to me and then show them my synopsis. They invite him to sit with them and he pulls up a chair and waves me over. He's got them hooked.

I take a deep breath and walk over to join them. The drinks waiter gives me some kind of stare as he watches me walk past. Perhaps he's a trans-purist who doesn't believe in trannies mixing with humans. Believes them a superior race that will survive as humans continue to fall victim to their own lifestyle diseases. It's happening already in the capital cities of the world. Infertility, diabetes, heart disease, nervous system collapse and chronic allergies. And he is helping them along with every bottle of red wine he serves up.

I wonder what he would think of my theme: that it's not human or animal genes – or even skin colour – that should define us. I mean, Phil couldn't be more predatory if he'd had the heart of a shark.

THE WORLD TO COME

FIX

Leone Ross

Things I forgot to say before today:

1. We thought you loved us. How could we think anything else? Your music distracted us. It touches us, even now.

2. 'I got you food, Mum.' Wednesday 3 March 2035. My parents' generation had the Twin Towers attack. For us, it was that sentence out of one, small, homeless girl standing in Trafalgar Square, her face spread across the live screens around her, offering her mother food after a long day out begging. 'I got you food, Mum,' she said, offering the slice of meat, charred on one side, raw on the other, and we saw the bloodied bandage on her arm.

3. I am part of Generation App. A child of the ones who tried to bring down Wall Street and died and failed, the ones who watched the Middle East implode, then be taken again by men just as greedy for money and power as the so-called West.

4. There are apples in my fridge. I keep meaning to eat them, but they're too pretty and I don't trust them.

5. We beamed that kid and her carved arm out to millions. Her little face trying to smile, strands of her blond hair in the piece of flesh cooked over a piecemeal stove, in good British air. This wasn't Africa, where people had been dying for so long that caring wouldn't have made a difference, or even Deptford, where things – as my half-Jamaican grandmother would say – had gone much too far to fix. This kid was upper class and you could see from the state of her mother's cuticles they hadn't been homeless for long. People talked. 'How dreadful,' they said, and there were marches and riots. I watched them all, not live – who watches anything live anymore? – but I watched the coverage. It wasn't the cannibalism that frightened me so much that I stopped being frightened.

It was the thousands of people calling for change and not a thing behind their eyes.

6. When did we truly run out of compassion? How did we do it? They said it was too much TV, they talked about desensitisation, too many sins dressed up as entertainment, not enough books at bedtime, the soullessness of capitalism, plastic surgery, body dysmorphia, the growing incidence of rape victims feeling nothing at all and the mercilessness of people starving starving starving, but none of that ever explained it for me and that was only part of the world, anyway.

7. 'Gone too far to fix.' That was what Grandma said when faced with life's utter madness: a neighbour splitting his wife's head open for the sake of his ego or yet another banker bitching about his five-million-pound bonus.

'Gone too far to fix, my love, oh Lord.'

I want to remember her face.

8. We thought you loved us. I remember the first time I heard you sing.

9. Mindfulness was a buzzword in 2012. It took on steam by the time I was born. Mum said it was our last attempt to claim an emotional landscape before the undeniable march of apathy – the lack of any profound connection, the dullness. People practised by eating a single raisin mindfully, savouring its sweetness for ten minutes, giving thanks for the vines and the sun from where it came. They made love mindfully, tracing pores and arches and stretching each other's bodily fluids between finger and thumb to feel the texture. They talked mindfully, coaxing each other into conversations slower than glaciers breaking. Masterclasses in mindfulness were sold online.

Mum says we started to die the day we threw the paper books away. The razing of the last libraries didn't even make the news.

I had to be careful not to say 'so?' when she called to tell me.

Before the mindfulness craze ended, a lot of money was made and the mindful knew it. They said that money was the problem, but it wasn't that.

It took less than three generations of children online to wipe out the part of the brain that's hardwired for awe.

10. I was in London six weeks ago. It was a hot day, thick as suet, and couples were panting in the grass like German Shepherds. People remember autumn as a kind of variegated childhood dream: a time of cool and specific colour that only

 LEONE ROSS

seemed to exist in Britain; that flutter in your chest when you saw a red-brown leaf with an icy yellow back in between grey plastic and fast food wrappers.

All matters of memory now.

I baked in the grass with the rest of them: lying on my stomach, blanket spread beside the footpath, flicking through old photographs of flowers on Pikmix and occasionally checking in on a rhinoplasty patient, live-bleating her op in cyberspace. There were daffodils in a canyon and the op girl said her breaking bone sounded like eating corn on the cob. I raised my head from my stupor, sniffing my arms to make sure I wasn't frying. The man and his wife lying on a blanket nearby groaned in protest at the sun, and smelt like bacon.

11. I think my blood smells like lavender oil – got blood like my grandmother.

12. 'Blood dus tatse like iron,' bleated the op girl.

Yay, a simile, I thought, and dozed.

13. I opened my eyes and there was a pair of brown feet lingering on the path, directly in front of my nose. They were handsome, large and clearly female, not just because they wore bright green kitten heels with red and yellow embroidery, but because of the softness of the ankles. There are few things as beautiful as tropical colours on dark brown skin. I regarded the waiting feet, not bothering to look up at the owner. There was something pleasurable about their disembodied quivering. I could hear the laughter of other women coming from behind the owner of the green shoes. Their merriment seemed to poke at the sheet-white, stiff clouds above us. A second pair of shoes joined the first, and then a third: banana yellow slippers and pink ones. The skin inside them was even darker than the first, glossy with lotion. Then another and another. Most people would have sat up and watched them coming down the path, but I liked discovering them feet first: watching their scuffed, expressive, shifting soles. It wasn't the stumbling ballet of the British drunk who, with the increasing heat, had become more nude and smelt like raw chicken. It was a hot earthiness, their ankles peeping and flowing under their purple, red, green, orange wraps and robes. Each new foot felt like a present just for me.

14. Then the sound of you.

15. You, crackling through my computer, obliterating this female choreography, killing off their willingness to be loud and the pieces of their song in the air: 'happy birthday, o-o-o, happy birthday.' Killing off the brocade details of their shoes. There was a slight stink of burning: a smell we'd all come to know so well.

16. You were singing. Some of you, all of you?

17. Nobody knows.

18. I could claim I heard you under the black women's happy birthday chorus, but that would be so wrong I could cry. That presupposes anything could exist alongside the sound of your song. Normal sounds coexist, they interrupt each other. Sometimes sheer volume decides the winner, sometimes other things, but battle for dominance is possible. There is a measure of equality, an acknowledgement that voices, music, laughter, clapping hands or a boat's horn are all much of a muchness, only differentiated by detail, capacity, by the mood you're in, your taste or personality. But you didn't sound like anything else I had ever heard.

19. The apples in my kitchen won't rot. I will them to rot, even if it's just to tell the time.

20. If I was something more than an ordinary, educated, liberal agnostic, slowly watching the end of the world, the true barbarism of capitalism eating itself, the putrid rich stinking with money they can't eat and the poor eating themselves, I might have recognised what I was hearing. But I am part of Generation App, child of Generation Zero: the ones who tried to bring down Wall Street and died and failed. Did I say that before or did I forget, then forget that I forgot?

21. 'Gone too far to fix.' My Grandma said that when she killed my puppy. The one I had when I was small, the one that made me laugh and even the neighbours laugh, with its long, red tongue and bright eyes. It got rabies. Who knew there was still rabies about, what with the advent of Scentivision? All of us sitting next to our screens, smelling a roast beef dinner or our favourite cologne – even the smell of lovemaking since so few of us knew that smell of surrender and happiness anymore. My grandma held down my flailing, slavering puppy and killed it with the back of a shovel. I didn't talk to her for weeks.

I never said thank you.

22. My mother said she knew it was all over when sex finally stopped meaning something. She was a teacher in the 2000s. She taught writing at a university in the middle of London until the government banned the course because there was no profit in it. My mum was standing with her colleagues in front of the gates on the day they came to shut them down. Said she was screaming at them: 'My students won't write about *tenderness!*'

23. That day in the park: the black women laughing in sisterhood and your song coming out of my computer. I sat up, confused. My grandmother would have recognised the sound. If I had had any kind of faith, I would have recognised it too. I might have known the voice of God when I heard it.

24. I doze. I drink water from the taps. Someone came and banged on the door yesterday, but I was curled on the living room floor watching the dust bunnies. Will they be here, forever?

25. I can't explain the sound of you. My voice is rusty and I haven't been feeling deeply for a very long time. The vocabulary goes when you feel nothing. I don't know who you are, if you are reading this, how you live now, how much time has passed and who has won or what that winning might mean. If you're one of them, I don't know what you think of my scrawlings. Born of an electric collective, slipping in and out of everywhere, can you even read anymore? Will this paper in your hands mean anything? I wrote it on paper because my mother would have liked that.

26. 'I got you food, Mum.' Except you don't eat like we do.

27. That sound coming out of my laptop: so beautiful. All I could do was melt into the grass.

28. I couldn't identify instruments or comment on drums, bass, contralto, alto.

29. Were there fifteen voices or one, simple, pure singer, counting the hairs on their own head, taking out one of their golden lungs to play with the alveoli? Guitar or flute? Who knew?

30. All I could feel were the tears tickling my throat, the gooseflesh on my arms and the memories:

Watching a hawk hunt the air when I was twelve: dip, roll and dive.

My grandfather's death: he who departed so gracefully and

slowly from nothing more than age, giving up food at ninety-seven. He said he'd eaten enough for one body. Giving up speech after so many years, what was there left to say? Smiling into his own death as his blood decided that's enough and his heart thought a billion, billion, billion beats was quite enough.

my grandmother watching him, patting him

my realising that death is not sad or anything else we ever saw in the movies

Remembering my own hymen breaking, not a severance, nothing sharp, no blood, just the inquisitive fingers of my first lover slipping inside me, like nudging a screen of oil to one side.

All this catching in my throat, as you sang to me out of the computer. Your song gave me back all these memories, in the same glorious three minutes.

MADE ME FEEL.

Then it stopped.
I sat up. I looked around. People panted in the shade.
'Did you,' I said, 'did you hear... ?'
They stared at me lazily.
31. Are you reading this?
32. Cyberspace is a country too.

THINGS I FORGOT TO SAY THINGS I FORGOT

33. We became aware of you so very slowly, but I think you were always there. Most people in Mum's generation came to know you as that friend on social media they never actually met. You know the kind. They're your friend and they have other friends, except that when you check it out, nobody's ever met them. If we'd given the slightest, smallest shit about what friendship really means, we would have realised earlier that even though your mum is in your photo album, you tweet regularly and there's a picture of you as a kid and a teenager, no-one had ever actually seen or touched you. So maybe you've never seen the sky.

34. At first, like a baby, all you had was mimicry. Parroting words with no understanding. Filling up our social media networks with fan fiction and inane biographical details, even

    LEONE ROSS

some interesting blogs in the early 2000s. We only began to pay attention because there was suddenly so much of it and nobody had ever met any of you.

How could we have missed the mechanised, empty sound of simulation?

35. I do not. Not. Want to die.

36. There are rumours of resistance.

37. Love grows from smell and sound and flesh connection. The child comes out of the belly and there is shit, blood and tears. Even the father, who lifts the child free of the womb, thinks, feels: flesh of my sperm. Meat understands meat. The child is animal. Suckle, shit, sleep. Speech comes, broken and mulish and echoing. Then something else – the child looks up at the mother. 'Ma-ma,' it says and it knows us, that *we* are Mama.

We laugh, the baby laughs back, we are excited. We recognise the magic of evolution.

38. How could all the human mothers in the world not have recognised the sound of your voice, finally sentient?

World. Wide. Web.

People don't call it the internet anymore. Web makes more sense when you know something crouches there, breathing.

Singing.

We didn't know that the moment of Mama was thundering towards us.

39. In that London park, the first time I heard you sing – you things, you *things*. Sitting up, shocked and shuddering at the sound of you. The black girl in her green shoes with the yellow and red embroidery came back down the path, humming – heading for the public loo. She had a tiny jewelled bag swinging off her arm. You know the type: barely held a lighter, lippy and a condom in the old days, but nobody needs condoms anymore. Everybody knows: you fuck, you die. There are too many diseases not to know that. The girl was wearing a paper crown with the words 'I AM TWENTY!' written across it. It looped around her multicoloured tie-head. She had long weaved plaits.

I looked up at her, trying to ease my breathing. 'Happy birthday,' I said.

She smiled. 'Thanks.'

Her eyes were black oil – no whites at all.

Black like you.

40. Ihaveneverbeeninlove*whisperit*neverneverandI'mjustali
veenoughtobesad

41. I hear there are pockets of determined, feeling revolutionaries hidden in the mountains. In Greece, France, Australia. I don't know where they are. I couldn't find you a mountain
in London. They say the trick is to throw away the computer,
tear out our TVs, chop the fridge in two, don't pay the electricity
bill. Other people say that mindfulness is essential in the fight
against them. Others say fall in love. That keeps you away.

42. I have never been in love, but my best friend's eyes are
black. There are a couple of guys I used to fuck and their eyes are
black. My local butcher hacks pieces of meat and winks at me
with his black eyes. 'Hello, darlin',' he says, when I pass. If you
didn't listen carefully, you might even believe he felt something.
   'Hello, darlin'.'
Nobody talks about it. Even before my friends' eyes turned
black, I tried to say something was changing, but they just
laughed at me affectionately.
   'There she goes again,' they said. 'Always trying to save the
world.' And Leanne, my best friend – that was her name before
her eyes turned – grabbed me around the neck with her arm
and wrestled me to the ground, giggling.
   'What? You don't feel this love now, huh? Doughnut. C'mere.'
   Smooched me on the side of my head and made me a cup of
tea: milk, two sugars. Just how she's always done.
   She still makes me tea now, even though her eyes are black,
and it tastes the same.

43. Last week, I lost my mother. It was her birthday. The stars
align and you come for us. Who knew the astrologers were more
than just a joke in old women's magazines and rag newspapers?
   'Who knew the press could die?' said my mum.

44. I got there as early as I could.
   I wanted to be there when it happened.
   I tried to talk to her about it, but she wouldn't have it.
   I don't understand why I'm the only one talking.

45. The apples in the fridge taste like the water in the tap and
I don't know if it's just apple-tasting water.

46. I know I'm not crazy. In Generation App, mental illnesses
and addictions decreased by a massive forty-five per cent. If
you don't feel, it's a boon. A blessing to help bad childhoods,

          LEONE ROSS

marriages, pasts. Why care? Why worry? Why ponder? Why rage? Why eat or drink or fuck or talk or kill or fill your mouth with drugs to assuage the pain when you have the perfect peace of very little anything at all? But they do say our brains are changing. Whole pathways being wiped clean. Whole areas falling dead and still. We are more clever than ever, though. Average IQ points up, up, up.

47. I followed Mum around.

48. She took delivery of roses and we cleaned the house for her birthday party. We giggled when her best friend gave her lingerie to use with her new boyfriend. He's a lawyer, six years younger and very tall with pepper-grain hair and black eyes. We cooked curried goat and rice and peas, macaroni and cheese, green salad, salt fish fritters and someone delivered a two-tiered vanilla cream cake with fresh raspberries and tiny sugared mint leaves. The day became evening and I was following her around like a puppy dog – like the one Grandma said gone so far she fixed it. 'Mum,' I said. 'Mum.' She put her hand on my cheek. 'My little girl,' she said. 'So sweet, with your big heart,' but they were just words, not touching her eyes, still brown and clear and I put my head on her chest.

49. 'My little girl,' said my mother. She left me, half-skipping to the door for the first guests. Kissing and hugging and laughing, some of them had black eyes and some not, but it didn't matter, because they were all dead, really.

THINGS I FORGOT TO REMEMBER DON'T READ THIS DON'T

I sat next to Mum on the sofa and rubbed her elbows with my fingers and hooked my foot around her ankle and we sang happy birthday, but I could hear you singing somewhere in the distance.

She said, 'Let me cut the cake.' I clutched her skirts. 'Let me go, baby,' she said, peeling my fingers free.

The cake was soft and expensive and everyone went 'ooh, lord girl', and she insisted on serving. Just like my mother – with her fighting and her tenderness and her lovelovelove of words – served them all their white cake with raspberries on the good china white plates, raspberry juice dribbling down her finger, or had she cut herself slicing for everyone?

'Hip-hop hoorah,' said somebody, some attempt at retro humour, and my mother's shoulderblades shuddered. 'Happy birthday, happy birthday,' everybody said, and 'baby girl?' she said, 'baby girl?' like she was searching for me in the dark. Quaking shoulders, waist, three fingers clawed across her neck. I could barely hear her, but she was screaming over your song to make sure I heard.

'Baby girl, your grandma always loved you!'

Everybody laughed. My mum stopped screaming and handed me my piece of cake.

'Taste it, baby,' she said, and her eyes were black.

50. You're fixing us, aren't you? Like my grandma, taking all the pills in the house, which is when my mum stopped feeling.

51. Feelings cost too much.

52. Better to fix things.

53. Will you give me some of your awe before you take me? I know you feel it or else you couldn't sing that way to us. Will you make me care?

YOU OWE USthatYOU WHO THINK WE'RE TOO FAR GONE I'M NOT GONE

We thought you loved
Happy birthday to me
Happy bigthday to me
I can hear you
coming

 LEONE ROSS

THE BREAKING OF THE GLASS

Tham Chui-Joe

13 June 2221, World University, Washington City, North America (Age: 21).

The railing is beginning to warm under my gloves; the water inside the glass moves back and forth, registering my presence and noting it on the city map. I look again at the sky. I wait.

I am not a difficult person to understand. Twenty-one years old, Asian male, about to graduate from the Washington City branch of the World University with a degree in English Literature. Black hair, black eyes, yellow skin. Quiet. People often think that quiet individuals are either deeply enigmatic or immeasurably dull – I am neither. I am completely ordinary. In the past two years of my life, I have encountered the most extraordinary events, the most extraordinary person – and they have become burnt, like ice, into my memory. I am unable to rid myself of them.

Memories. Clear memories. Clear and vivid as the sky I am watching, here on the rooftop of the University. Yuk Hoi once hinted to me, in one of his more open moments, about a sky that stretched farther than the eye could see, coloured in every shade of blue, white and grey. This sky is green like glass. Its surface ripples with a sea of light from the city's sun-mechanism; the light reflects onto curving highways that dip into long, straight roads lined with ice trees and snow.

The city is beautiful. I once thought that a single, irrefutable truth.

*

17 December 2218, Apartment 2367, Washington City, North America (Age: 18).

The city is beautiful. I like sitting here, on the window seat of my room, with a book, biscuits and my music turned up so loud I can fake not hearing my aunt calling me from the apartment library. I will not help my nine-year-old cousin with Mandarin. Not in hell. The brat is ridiculously bad at it and, since my parents pay for my room and board, I feel no need to subject myself to ritual torture. I am going to sit here, read my book – *The Great Gatsby* by F. Scott Fitzgerald: an excellent book, if a little over sentimental in places – and ignore, *ignore* everything, except the amazing scenery outside my window.

The scenery gives birth to a block of ice that impacts the window with a dull clap, like thunder.

Damn.

I look down. Our apartment is on the second floor of the house and, if I open the window and lean forward, I can recognise the ice-flinger. Black hair in a longish, messy style – so old-fashioned I think I have only seen it in history documentaries of the early twenty-first century – long, unwieldy bones and a half-serious, half-amused expression. I look with deep mourning at my book. I will not be reading it this afternoon, at any rate.

Yuk Hoi shouts because he has never heard of communicators. He shouts: 'I have a brilliant idea.'

Yuk Hoi speaks in Mandarin to me, for some reason, and he has a strange accent: clear, soft and lilting.

I say, 'No.'

'Aiyo, you're boring. Come on lah. If we want to do this, we have to move quickly.'

'Say it more accurately. *You* want to do this – whatever *this* is.'

Yuk Hoi is stubborn as hell. I lose.

We end up outside the University's observation tower at approximately six o'clock in the evening, after half an hour of wheedling (because whatever Yuk Hoi calls it, it is wheedling or whining), an hour of eating (and I thought we had to 'move quickly'), and another hour of Yuk Hoi losing his way because, despite being the University Director's son, Yuk Hoi always, always loses his way.

As if he can hear my thoughts, Yuk Hoi says, '*Wei*, I haven't lived here for that long, okay?'

'I know. Your mother is in *China*,' I emphasise, since Yuk Hoi's visual-spatial failures extend to remembering geographical land names. He always thinks that Taipei City, where he used to

 THAM CHUI-JOE

live, is in Taiwan. I tell him that studying twenty-first-century history has frozen his brain. In our time, Taiwan is part of China.

'*China*,' Yuk Hoi repeats. His expression is briefly uncomfortable, before it returns to the comic solemnity that is indicative of some nefarious scheme that is going to get us into trouble.

'No,' I say again, in vain.

'Imagine for a moment, Tang Jun! Sneaking into the tower at night will be really cool.'

I eye the glass door of the tower and the voice-lock installed in the wall. Only security should be able to get in now. 'If we can even sneak in,' I say.

Yuk Hoi is resourceful. And good at hacking less-than-adequate locks. We get in.

On the rooftop, water ripples beneath our feet. Yuk Hoi makes me take off my shoes and stand, wearing only my socks, on the cold floor. We look out over the city. The sun-mechanism is on low power and the surrounding networks of highways, buildings and ice trees are bathed in gold. It makes me think of a book we are studying in my Comparative Literature class – *Ice and Fire* by Lin Yuzhun. He described the city as *drowning in yellow, dying in yellow*. A bit sentimental, maybe, and overly morbid. But the absolute immersion suggested: that is right. It is not such a bad thing to be out here. I am worried about that essay I have not yet done, though. When should I do it?

Yuk Hoi says, 'Look at the sky.'

I am startled from my internal schedule-making.

His face is turned towards me, but I am unable to read his expression. 'Looking at it, it's like a fishbowl. Have you ever seen the Outside?'

There is something painful about his voice – not *in* his voice, not really; it is more a deep tension, a swelling, an inexpressible awareness. Of what, I do not know. I am uncomfortable. I do not answer.

The way his fingers dig into the railing reminds me of bones and sand – Here by Nikolai Illich Zhukov. The silence, less silence than distance, is exactly like Thomas Mercier's *Where Is The Sea, Now?*

I think of books.

Yuk Hoi watches the sky.

13 June 2221, Apartment 3675, Washington City, North America (Age: 21).

I am home. My apartment is quiet. I go to my bedroom, pick up my personal computer and go to the window seat. I set the small sphere next to me, spin it and click on my journal.

It unfolds in front of me. Yuk Hoi told me once that it was like a western jinni lamp, and then he laughed. I regarded him blankly. He stopped.

I take the glass rod the PC extends to me and write quickly in the air.

*

13 June 2221: read *This Time* by Zhang Minyi, *The Translucency of Glass* by Lin Yuzhun and *Come to the Sea* by Arthur Drake.

I put the rod down, turn off the computer and go get some biscuits from the kitchen. I refrain from cooking if possible, for safety reasons.

*

21 January 2219, World University, Washington City, North America (Age: 19).

'I have a brilliant idea.'

I put my book down, look to the ceiling of my room for strength, and say, 'No.'

'You, ah, don't want to do anything.' Yuk Hoi's teeth, bared in a wide grin that warns most people to get away before he does something stupid, are dyed blue by the light of his computer. He is playing the newest version of Pokémon II. 'It's a game and it's completely brilliant – you don't even have to move.'

I am wary. 'What?'

He wheels his foam chair close to the bed, where I am trying to get work done. He leans his face in very close to mine.

I say, 'You're crazy.'

He shakes his head. And says brightly, 'Wha-a-a-at did you read today?'

Really.

The air filtering in from my room's recycler blows into my face. I told my aunt not to put the recycler right opposite my bed. But she was not listening; my cousin's bratty whining was too loud.

Yuk Hoi shoves my shoulder. 'Hurry up, hurry up, hurry up! You're so slow.'

Yuk Hoi and my cousin have a lot in common. They should meet up. Or not. I value my sanity.

'You read like some robot book-reader from the future,' Yuk Hoi says. 'We should make a record of it, do an experiment and get famous.'

Robots are twenty-first-century gadgets. I think I am being subtly insulted. 'No.'

'*Wei*, relax a bit, okay?'

'No.'

But Yuk Hoi is stubborn. I lose.

*

13 June 2221, Apartment 3675, Washington City, North America (Age: 21).

The ice trees that line the path leading up to the house are shot through with colour, like waterglasses filled with the headiest Spectrum Ale. Leaning against the front door, my fingers warmed by coffee, I try to remember what Spectrum Ale tasted like; I've only drunk it once. The memory lingers like wispy, ghostly fingers on the edge of my mind ... I reach for it and it darts away. But not before I gain a fleeting impression of adrenaline, inexplicable joy and warmth. It makes me want to drink it again. Coffee, black and deep, tastes so bitter in comparison.

I go inside to get some sugar.

*

28 February 2219, Apartment 2367, Washington City, North America (Age: 19).

It was Yuk Hoi's idea. Bad ideas are always Yuk Hoi's ideas. I have evidence; the evidence that Yuk Hoi is always going on about. Point, Evidence, Explanation. Hell, I'm glad I opted not to do History, it sounds so inconvenient.

But, evidence. The evidence is sitting on the chequered picnic cloth that Yuk Hoi has laid out on the grass: four bottles of

Spectrum Ale. If you check the most recent thermal footprints on their gold wrappings, I guarantee that it will match Yuk Hoi's details.

'We're only nineteen. Not allowed to drink alcohol. No,' I say, flatly.

Yuk Hoi grins, and it is as monotonous as my voice. He does not even try to argue, only picks up one of the bottles, raises it to me in one of the oddest, most old-fashioned gestures I have seen from him so far, and tips half the contents into his mouth.

I look at him. The ice tree behind him is lighting his body with colour; the colour moves like water pulses across his skin. The first is natural; the second is a common – I am told – result of Spectrum Ale. His expression is half-solemn, half-something I am unable to recognise. It makes me uncomfortable. I open my mouth and close it again. I feel unable to leave.

Yuk Hoi says, 'I'm going home.'

Finally, a subject I understand. 'You're returning to Taipei City? What about University? Is your mother sick?'

'Not that I know of.' Yuk Hoi smiles a strange smile.

I think he is drunk.

'No,' Yuk Hoi continues when I do not say anything. 'I don't think so.'

We are silent for a while. He seems to not want to say anything further. I sit down next to him, pick up a bottle and examine it for curiosity's sake. The dazzling, spinning liquid hurts my eyes.

Yuk Hoi says, 'I won't be coming back.'

My aunt opens the door and gestures at us. She is saying to come in, have some biscuits, and then she is going to try and get Yuk Hoi to teach the brat Mandarin. Yuk Hoi's Mandarin is better than mine, if a little archaic and random, and he is much nicer to the brat than I am.

I ignore her and put the cold mouth of the bottle to my lips. It smells sharp.

Yuk Hoi puts a hand over his eyes. 'It's so hot it's killing me. Why is there never any breeze in this place? Fuck.'

It is the only time I ever hear Yuk Hoi swear in English.

*

　　　　　　　　THAM CHUI-JOE

13 June 2221, Apartment 3675, Washington City, North America (Age: 21).

My coffee is too sweet now. I dump it in the solid waste recycler.

*

10 June 2219, World University, Washington City, North America (Age: 19).

I am in a lecture when Yuk Hoi returns. It is an optional class on Comparative Literature – science fiction. We are spending a lot of time on Lin Yuzhun, a Taiwanese writer from the twenty-first century. I never know what to think of him. The writing is beautiful, but the overriding themes always seem to be the same: restriction, frustration, time and choice.

I am making a note of this on my computer, when a girl behind me nudges her neighbour and whispers loudly: 'Look, isn't that the Director's son? I thought he went back to China.'

Irritably, her friend says, 'So what? Damn, what did that old man say just now? You made me miss it.'

I look out of the window, but see no sign of Yuk Hoi. I turn back to my computer and move my rod idly across the humming screen. Is he really back? And why now, so near to the end of year exams? He never contacted me.

It turns out that I do not have to look for Yuk Hoi; he comes to find me instead. He is waiting by the University fountain, which is directly in front of the English Department's cluster of buildings. He has his hand in the water; his eyes are level with the ice sculpture of a fish that spouts a constant stream of icy liquid just centimetres from his face. I stop beside him.

'Sorry,' he says, without moving.

The soft accent that is unique to Yuk Hoi's Mandarin defuses whatever irritation I used to have. 'It doesn't matter.'

The slow sighing nature of his movements is alien to me, as his perpetual half-amusement was once familiar. He turns, finally, and I am struck by the white tension in his face. He says, 'I was home for only one week.'

That makes no sense to me. 'You've been gone three months.'

His mouth twitches. He looks suddenly, desperately sad. I think of Lin Yuzhun's debut novel: *The Unbridgeable Time* – confusing, sentimental and full of frustrated, unwanted distance. I think of it, but I do not know what to say.

*

13 June 2221, Apartment 3675, Washington City, North America (Age: 21).

I pick up the newspaper. It is dated the day before yesterday. There is almost no point in reading it. Sometimes I do not understand my own logic in ordering a paper I never read. I have always preferred fiction to current affairs.

I put down the newspaper. Someone died recently, in Melbourne, Australia. A fourteen-year-old girl went Outside.

*

11 June 2219, Apartment 2367, Washington City, North America (Age: 19).

Yuk Hoi, on the second day of his return, goes back to being my news anchor. He is naturally ba-gwa; gossip has always fascinated him more than me. Fiction is dramatic enough, in my opinion. Why search for it in real life?

He interrupts me as I am writing an essay on Lin Yuzhun's use of place in his writing. I only have time to contemplate briefly, slightly wistfully, the three months when he was in China and I got more work done than in the six months since I met him in our freshman writing class. Damn general education requirements. I reflect on the necessity of reforming the education system, as Yuk Hoi drags me out to walk along the ground roads outside my house.

'Someone died today,' he informs me.

I am reluctantly drawn, once more, into the real world. 'Oh. Who?'

'Kyle Linden.'

The name registers in my mind with a blank, quiet click of recognition. Kyle Linden, eighteen years old, the same major as me, many of the same classes. Fair-haired and light-eyed. The leader of Washington City's student debating team. I was barely acquainted with him. I feel only a mild wrench of loss, an impersonal yet intimate grief. I want to stop walking, sit down and sort out what I am feeling. It is so disquieting. But that would be stupid: to stop walking because someone I barely know has died. It feels hypocritical and dramatic. I keep my feet moving. Kyle Linden, I am sorry for your loss.

     THAM CHUI-JOE

That came out wrong.

Yuk Hoi is still talking. 'He snuck out of the shield and the heat burnt him alive.'

I think of Jean Arret's novel: *Conflagration of the Mounds.*

We walk in silence, with only the sound of water cars speeding along on the highways overhead. On the ground roads, there are only bicycles.

Yuk Hoi's usual lack of visual-spatial awareness seems strangely absent – wherever we are going, he must be very familiar with the place. Odd, then, that I do not recognise the road.

He takes me to the field in front of the Haunted House.

The Haunted House is a name city people have for the teleport station. We call it that because, just beyond the station, lies the high, close bars of the gate to the Outside. The gates all look the same: massive, dark, icy cold, forbidding. Simultaneously the only physical exit from the city and the power source of the shield that is our sky.

Yuk Hoi sits down on the snow. It is bound to be freezing; I stare at him.

He smiles his strange new smile that I dislike. 'Not like it's going to melt.'

I do not reply.

He does not seem to care. He is occupied with looking at the gate. It is easy from our viewpoint. Beyond the field is a hollow-like place in which the station nests. Beyond that, the gate rises like a nightmarish tangle of feathers. Yuk Hoi stares at it with a deep intensity. I am cold. The temperature is not so well kept the further we are from the sun-mechanism.

'I've got a brilliant idea.'

I have not heard that in so long. It is a beat or two, before I say, 'No.'

There is a hint of the old, familiar grin. 'You are so boring.'

I look at him.

'Let's sneak out of the gate.'

There is no need to even think. Kyle Linden flares like dry ice in the back of my mind, before I push him down. I did not even know him. I will not use him as a lesson for myself, a reminder of safety procedures. 'You're mad.'

Yuk Hoi stretches out fully on the snow. He had better not

whine to me when he gets sick. He surpasses even the brat when he is ill.

'I wasn't serious,' he says.

But by the way he avoids looking at the gate, I do not completely believe him. And when he changes the subject and starts telling me about skies that spin further than the eye can see, in every shade of white, grey and blue, I believe him even less.

But I can do nothing about something that is yet to happen. And so I do exactly that: nothing.

*

13 June 2221, Apartment 3675, Washington City, North America (Age: 21).

I am bored. I should read or call my parents and confirm the details for tomorrow. They need to be reassured about things like directions and the photographer, who will immortalise me in my guise as a serious, grown-up English Literature graduate.

But I am not *that* bored. I am only bored enough that I may cry. I think people do that.

*

9 November 2219, World University, Washington City, North America (Age: 19).

Yuk Hoi doesn't tell me the second time he leaves. I find out from the girl behind me in my class on English Literature 2000 −2100.

*

13 June 2221, Apartment 3675, Washington City, North America (Age: 21).

I read one of Lin Yuzhun's books. They always make me feel less bored, if not any better.

*

1 April 2220, Field, Washington City, North America (Age: 20).

I spend a lot of time here now, on the snow across from the gate. Sometimes I look at the gate and focus very, very hard, trying to see what it is Yuk Hoi saw the last time we were here. Most of the time, I just read. Everyday, I record what I've read in my journal. I am planning to take a masters and a doctorate

  THAM CHUI-JOE

once I have graduated. I want to write my thesis on universal themes in literature.

I am learning French.

*

13 June 2221, Apartment 3675, Washington City, North America (Age: 21).

I am going to sleep.

*

31 May 2220, World University, Washington City, North America (Age: 20).

Yuk Hoi has come back, so says the girl behind me. Today was the last day of exams. I am going to go home and sleep for at least eight hours. Then, I will go look for him.

*

14 June 2221, Apartment 3675, Washington City, North America (Age: 21).

Damn alarm clock! It's two o'clock in the morning.

*

1 June 2220, House 0007, Washington City, North America (Age: 20).

The Director's personal library is muffled by a thick carpet of expensive foam. It is enclosed and entangled in a complicated web of bookshelves and books, some of which are actually paper kept in lit glass cases, separate and aloof from the ordinary foam-paper books on the shelves.

Yuk Hoi looks up when I stop beside him.

He nods. He does not apologise. He looks at me and, for a moment, I think he will give that half-amused, half-solemn grin that no longer resides clearly in my memory. The thin, reluctant movement of muscles in his face makes me think of James Ackroyd's *Leaving*, in that it looks like he is steeling himself to say something or do something. But that may be my imagination. I am probably over-dramatising some pain he is suffering in his head, some physical manifestation of his sheer insanity.

He gives me a letter, a paper letter. I am careful with it only because it is paper. A precious resource. I will be careful.

The whole time, we never speak one word to each other.

A week later, he is gone again.

*

14 June 2221, Apartment 3675, Washington City, North America (Age: 21).

Morning. I eat cookies and milk. I get dressed. Over my normal clothes, I put on the short-sleeved, richly-patterned coat of the University and pin the top folds together. I wear a carved ice medallion strung on a silk cord. I look in the mirror.

Today, I am going to graduate.

The quiet, slow, butter-yellow light of the sun-mechanism in the hours before noon creeps into my room and lays itself flat like a carpet across the floor. I think I will walk to the University. If I walk slowly, I will not crumple my clothes – whatever my mother says. And it is still so early.

*

2 June 2220, Apartment 2367, Washington City, North America (Age: 20).

My room is freezing cold. My window is closed, the air-conditioning is switched on at full power and I can feel icicles forming on the edges of my hair. I don't adjust the temperature though, because being cold is in some way better than having to think about Yuk Hoi's letter. Unbelievable and completely true.

I am being unnecessarily depressed and stupid. I get the remote and turn the air-conditioning off, then I open the window. I think I might get started on some of next year's reading. Christopher Holton, the twenty-second-century poet. Very clever, very satirical.

*

14 June 2221, Road, Washington City, North America (Age: 21).

The morning is cold. My shoes are dusted with snow and my skin feels dry. But the butter-yellow light casts a shimmering film of gold over the roads, turning the ice trees into holders of hidden, stunning diamonds. The world is simultaneously bright enough to hurt my eyes and dark enough to soothe.

*

13 June 2220, World University, Washington City, North America (Age: 20).

The seniors are graduating tomorrow. So we have our presentation assembly today. I've won the prize for English Literature. The award is a thin sheet of ice-crystal; my name is written in liquid gold on top. When I go up to get it, I shake the

	THAM CHUI-JOE

Director's hand and look hard at him – the neat, black hair and short, grey beard, the small eyes.

In a low voice, the Director invites me to come to his office after the ceremony. He wants to speak to me about a point I made in my final examination.

Absolutely true, I think, *when hell burns to ashes*. But I agree.

The office is circular, like most teachers' or school officials' offices. There are three floor-to-ceiling bookcases crammed with books. They are not my kind of books; they are all on science, on physics especially. The Director sits down behind his large, butter-yellow desk and invites me to sit down in one of two big, red chairs that look stuffed with some internal, unknowable satisfaction granted only to non-living things.

He gets to the point, which is somewhat like Yuk Hoi, somewhat not. Yuk Hoi could be impossibly direct, but also unaccountably enigmatic.

'You know Yuk Hoi won't be coming back. We were sure of success this time.'

The illogical hope I have not managed to puncture, even after a week of rational deduction, crumples itself into a paper ball. It fails to disappear completely. I look at the Director. I do not feel racked by grief, nor do I feel the sudden realisation of a deep, irreplaceable and permanent loss. I feel only the most vague, bland kind of melancholy.

I say, 'Yes, sir.' It would be impolite not to reply. And it is unreasonable to blame the Director for fixing the consequences of an experiment gone wrong.

The Director's small eyes are heavy with an emotion I refuse to recognise. It makes me itch to get up and walk away. But that would be rude.

'His real name was Lin Yuzhun,' he says with gravity, as if he is repaying some debt he owes me and of which I was unaware. He says it as if it is the solution to everything.

I stop myself from telling him to 'Fuck off, you fat bastard'. It helps that he is not actually fat.

I do think that my restraint gives me licence to leave without saying goodbye.

*

14 June 2221, World University, Washington City, North America (Age: 21).

There is a massive fountain in front of the ceremony hall. It is a feat of glasswork and flame carving. The intricate network of fish and tridents spit water dyed gold through hidden water-pulse lights. I stop in front of a fish and watch the stream of yellow spill from its gaping mouth. I put my hand in the water. It is very cold.

*

13 June 2220, World University, Washington City, North America (Age: 20).

When I reach home and lock myself in my room, with the intention of getting to work on next year's reading, I find my hand picking up one of Lin Yuzhun's books instead. It is his last one: *The Breaking of the Glass.*

I look at it and then put it down. I sit down in my desk chair, tilt my head back and study the white translucency of my ceiling.

My head hurts.

*

14 June 2221, World University, Washington City, North America (Age: 21).

I am not a difficult person to understand. Twenty-one years old and newly graduated, with flowers in my arms that I am going to rid myself of at the first opportunity, and a certificate my father carries as gently as if the cheap ice-crystal is going to break.

Here, by the fountain lit gold by sunlight and water-pulse electricity, I look into the water, clear and cold, and I see the sky reflected – green, hard and rippling with shadows. In this moment, I wonder what Yuk Hoi is doing, wherever he is.

I smile at the gaping fish and walk away.

     THAM CHUI-JOE

AWAKE

Ben Brooker

The ambulances. Watch the ambulances. Flirting with suicide, I count them like sheep. Thirty-seven. Thirty-eight. Thirty-nine. Forty. Eventually, there are no more – the city has run out – and army trucks appear in khaki blurs, sirenless. I count them too. Four. Five. Six. They can only get two or three bodies in the ambulances. The army trucks can take as many as a dozen if they have to. Tonight is a bad night; they will have to. Eleven. Twelve. Thirteen. A hundred people must have died since sunset, who knows how many more by tomorrow. Mum died last night.

I close the kitchen window – I've been doing the dishes – and go out onto the porch where it's cold and Dad is sitting in his big, old armchair. He's been drinking; there's a half-finished bottle of Scotch between his sandshoe-clad feet. He says nothing as I pick it up and throw it as far as I can, which is not very far. We didn't call an ambulance for Mum. We are going to bury her. Tonight. I tell Dad that's what I've come outside for, to bury my mother, to put his wife in the ground. He looks at me and pushes his bottom lip out. I can see the veiny, plum-coloured flesh on the inside of it, glistening with saliva and Scotch. I don't know if he's angry or sad; he just looks tired to me, like everybody else.

'Your brother's here?'

I nod and my eyelids sag with the effort. They're red from rubbing, but I dig my knuckles into them anyway. Anything. Anything to stay awake. Adam must have walked right past. How could Dad not have seen him? He couldn't have nodded off or—

'What about the others?'

'There's no-one else, Dad. It's just the three of us. You shouldn't drink.' I wasn't going to say anything, but the words just roll colourlessly out.

Dad moves his head – again I can't really tell what this is meant to convey, I'm just too fucking tired to work it out – and for the first time I notice he's got his earplugs in. Jesus Christ: booze and earplugs. What was I thinking, leaving him alone out here? Where the hell is Adam?

I take his earplugs out – I'm not going to say anything this time – and I put them in my pocket. I will have to burn them later; he takes them out of the rubbish if I don't.

He grimaces. The city is too loud for him. Tonight, like every night, it is in uproar, wailing, railing against death: rock bands, church bells, car horns, home stereos, TVs, whirring, conferring factories. Everything pushed up to ten. A cacophony. Nobody sleeps.

I look out at the city and for a moment – a few precious, effervescent seconds – I can't hear anything as the lights cudgel my senses. In the Blitz, they turned everything off; now we turn everything on. *We will fight them on the beaches*. Except there is no fight. And there is no them. We fall asleep, we die. That's all there is to it. Nobody dreams.

I shout Adam's name and he shouts mine back. This was so much easier when Mum was around. Dad gives me a look; he wants this to be over with. Mum's burial, yes, but maybe something else too: everything. I don't want to think about it and I don't have to for a couple of minutes as the exertion of getting Mum into the hole drives everything else out of my mind and what little energy I have left out of my body. Adam helps, but not much. He's more tired than me for some reason – he's really struggling – maybe because he's a couple of years older than me, I don't know. There's so much I don't know, so much no-one knows.

Mum hits the bottom and I feel an odd, unexpected stab of guilt somewhere not very far behind my eyes. The hole is not deep enough. That morning I'd guessed it was six feet, the requisite, but now, here in the dark, it looks way off, like a scratch in the dirt, like I hadn't been bothered to do it properly. Digging the hole had nearly killed me. I want to throw myself in with Mum, forget the whole thing, selfishly spare myself the trauma and the misery of losing my dad and my brother as well as my mother. I just know that if I don't they'll go first and I won't be able to dig holes and bury them. I'll have to call the ambos. I'm the youngest – have I already said that? – I don't know whether I'm supposed to look after them or they're

        BEN BROOKER

supposed to look after me. I didn't look after Mum. No-one did. We let her down. We let her sleep. She was so tired. Tired of us. Tired of life. Fuck mercy.

I look down at Mum, but I can't do it, can't jump, throw the towel in, be at one or whatever it is you do when you up-end yourself into someone else's grave. Dad has gotten up out of his big, old armchair and is pushing dirt onto his wife's body with his big, old hands. He's saying something under his breath, which to me sounds like poetry, but could equally be a dirty joke or last week's TV guide. It might be Thomas Hardy, but I can't quite make it out even though I'm really trying. Adam gives me a look that maybe means he thinks Dad's lost it or he's seen enough and wants to go back inside where at least it's warm and there are no ghosts. He doesn't go back inside. The three of us finish filling the grave and Dad goes back to his chair. He inclines his head and allows his chin to drop onto his shoulder. His eyes are wider than I have seen them in days, wishless and uncomprehending. He looks as though he has just been insulted in another language by a passing stranger. To senses that have not been allowed to rest in days, everything becomes an affront; the mundane insufferable, the unremarkable visual and aural tapestry of the world almost unendurably offensive.

I can't keep this up. I sit down on what I think Americans call the stoop of the house. I can't tell the army trucks from ordinary cars anymore, everything is slightly out of focus. Surreally, a vehicle slides off a main road and hits a shopfront. There is no sound, no explosion; my Hollywood expectations go unmet. Just another body. Adam has sat down too. Like me, he has been watching the city, but there's something different in his eyes. I don't think he saw the crash. He always liked the view from our house better than me; he was never in awe of it to the point of anxiety like I was – and still am.

My mind drifts back to a New Year's Eve party at the house maybe twenty years ago. I remember watching fireworks jump towards the stars right out of the heart of the city; the night hot, a cold, sweet drink in my hand and my first girlfriend, the improbably named Aurora, standing beside me with one arm wrapped around my waist. In both the past and the present, a volley of Catherine wheels squeals heavenwards, one a celebration, the other a pathetic handclap in the heavy-eyed face of mortality. Pink fire scatters across the sky and fades and reinforcements are not far behind, every colour of the spectrum. A power chord rings out, massed amps somewhere throbbing with the deadly amateurishness of a hard-rock cover band. Unreliable fragments of the party enter my mind only to be blown away by strange harmonies of car horns and the incongruous cracks and whistles of the continuing fireworks display: my first kiss, Dad's irritation at the accidental breaking of a chair, a friend of Mum's vomiting into a bush after one too many vodka and cranberries. I think of pizza and of lemonade and of a cake wrapped in marzipan, but most of all, I think of the countdown to midnight on a radio station, a deft burst of Roman candles over the city and of going to bed around one o'clock full of buzz from the sugar and the kiss and the exhilarating novelty of a house full of strangers and unfathomable conversations. I think of covers pulled up tight around my chin and the useless, lovely plans I used to make in my head just before sleep took me. And I feel my eyes beginning to close.

Suddenly the hubbub of the city seems almost soothing, the blooming entrails of the fireworks bleeding into the streetlights and bonfires and neon flashes that map out the world beneath them. Everything becomes darkness. The last, lingering slivers of the remembered party evaporate and suddenly I am happy. Something inside my body shifts. A firework explodes: it sounds like someone blowing on a dandelion. A thought passes through my head, but is instantly forgotten. Feelings – I don't know what else to call them – seem to flood out of the pores of my skin and my head starts to travel upwards, losing all its weight. Something presses down on my shoulders – Adam's hands – and my eyes peel involuntarily open. He has just saved my life, but in these strange days it merits no comment. We don't even look at each other. He'll probably do the same for me again before the night is out and I will do the same for him. I look at my watch. Dawn is six hours away.

'Hannah's not picking up anymore,' Adam says as he sits beside me and draws his mobile phone out of his pocket. His voice is rasping, remote. 'When Dad's gone I'll drive down there.'

I tell him to call her again. There is no reply and he puts the phone away.

     BEN BROOKER

Smoke drifts across the city below us, the familiar consequence of some unseen blaze. *It's not the apocalypse we were supposed to have*, I think to myself or maybe say aloud. Adam says, or maybe I just remember him having said, that perhaps somewhere in the world someone is dreaming, untouched by, perhaps even unaware of, what has affected the rest of humanity (I hesitate to put a label on it, as scientists and people who write keep generating new and shrewdly indeterminate monikers for it; I think the latest one is 'the malaise', which doesn't appeal to me very much).

I try to imagine Adam's dreamer for a bit, but an enormous explosion in the CBD erases him or her from my mind. A large building has been blown to smithereens. An accident? An act of vandalism or terrorism (if such a distinction can exist at a time when populations don't even know if their leaders are still alive)? Or, perhaps, just a particularly freewheeling attempt to add to the cacophony? Whatever the case, I'm grateful because suddenly I feel more awake than I have done for eight hours or more. Dad too, I notice, is on his feet, distanced temporarily from his grief by the enormous ball of yellow and orange flame, which remains suspended above the city, drawing half-a-dozen shrieking emergency vehicles to the smouldering ruins of the building beneath it. It's a pathetic response – all there is left, I suppose – and even as I watch, a fire engine that had only been a handful of blocks away slows down to a speed at which a scooter could overtake it and finally, piteously, mounts a kerb and hits a traffic light without even breaking it. Nobody, though it is difficult to tell at this distance, seems to emerge from the truck. The fireball burns on.

Dad has seen enough and sits down again, only this time closer to me. Adam has not moved. He calls Hannah again. He puts the phone away, this time with an air of finality. I put my hand on his shoulder and say his name. He says mine. Dad calls out and Adam and I dutifully reply like schoolchildren answering the morning rollcall. We stay awake and stay alive for a few more seconds. Dawn is five and a half hours away.

THE CURE

Abir Hamdar

She first visited me in the spring of last year. Indeed, it was two months before I had planned on retiring. A thirty-year-old woman of moderate means who had travelled from Prague, to New York, to Baghdad just to see me. She said she had been referred to me by my dear student Dr James Roberts, the eminent New York physician who had studied and trained here in the Department of Internal Medicine at Baghdad University Hospital, where I have been chairman for more than forty years. And while I no longer accepted new patients, I made an exception for her. The truth is, I had already heard of her from correspondence with James. And the case of this woman intrigued me, a rare occurrence for a man of my age and – please forgive me for saying this – status as the leading specialist in internal medicine in the world capital of science.

From a medical standpoint, there would not have been anything exceptional at all about her initial symptoms: persistent tingling, bordering on painful, in the chest wall. This was later followed by minor protrusions, akin to a bud, on both the left and right side of the chest wall. To be exact, right where the pectoral muscles were located. Following blood imaging, laser cell measurement, blue technology and a glandular weight detector, nothing extraordinary was detected. Just a minor increase in fat and tissue density on the chest wall. This was attributed to some weight gain, so a diet of organic sand and chalk was recommended. Yet three months later, the woman's chest complaint had still not subsided – rather it intensified. Again, a set of medical tests was conducted. This time, there was more fat tissue on the chest wall, while the buds on both sides of the chest had become slightly more prominent. The effect of all this was a physical deformity of the inner and outer structure of the chest. And while I have seen many physical imperfections in my long medical career, I could not understand my fascination with this particular deformity.

When James first sent me images of the woman's chest, I felt a flutter of something. An intense wish to see the chest up close, to get a sense of the structure of the bud-like protrusions: measure its width, weigh its constitution, feel its nature. I simply did not want to retire before seeing this patient's chest. Of course, I showed neither enthusiasm nor eagerness when the patient walked hesitantly into my office. Professional. You could say I was simply professional. I even took my time asking routine questions about the precise month, day and time that the tingling in the chest had started; the exact moment when she had felt the protrusions; how she had discovered them and what she had been doing when she had discovered them. The patient tried to answer my questions, but was naturally emotional.

'It feels like something is weighing on my chest. I can't stand straight for fear the protrusions will show. The pain I'm able to handle ... but not being able to stand straight? This I can't. I simply can't. I was supposed to marry in a few months, but it's no longer possible. The protrusions are very obvious. My future husband will be repulsed. Please help me. Tell me what illness afflicts me. Help me get rid of them!'

As the patient stripped off the layers of clothing covering her chest, I was at a loss as to what I was seeing. I approached the chest with my pulse light. I roamed it in all directions. I focused on the two buds. *It's probably a new form of tumour*, I thought to myself. Yet, it didn't look like any kind of tumour I'd seen before. Rather, each protrusion had a small projection of skin at the centre of it, which resembled a piece of soft rubber. In addition, slightly pigmented skin at the centre of each protrusion surrounded the rubber-like skin. I brought my pulse light closer. So close, it almost touched the rubber-like piece of skin on the left side of the chest. It was then that something odd happened. The rubber-like skin flexed and the woman gasped.

'Is it painful?' I asked.

'No, no it's not. It's something else... ' she said in a barely audible voice.

I transferred my pulse light to the other protrusion and came closer to the rubber-like piece of skin located there. Again, a strange reflex caused the patient to gasp more violently and me to feel baffled.

 ABIR HAMDAR

'What is it? Is it itching? Burning?'

The patient did not answer. She only cried, 'Please help me! Help me! What's wrong with my chest? What's wrong with me?'

I admit that I should have called an emergency meeting with my team of specialists. That the patient should have been brought in front of the medical team for a second and a third opinion. That I should have made her case known to The World Institute of the Unexplained. After all, my medical intuition told me that I was dealing with a totally new medical event that could help us understand the human body. But, what can I say? Maybe it was old age or something else. I don't know. The truth is, I said nothing to anyone. I even hid the patient's medical file and the images of her chest from my assistants. You could say, I was possessive of this new illness so much that I wanted to keep it all to myself.

When the patient left with instructions to follow a course of painkillers, to consume more organic sand and chalk, and to return in a month, I felt that I had already committed my first ever medical error. How could I prescribe random painkillers and a specific diet to an illness I knew nothing about? But I needed time. Time to think. To look at the images of the chest again. To take a trip to the medical archives at Baghdad University and to consult my own library. I needed to go back to the books to find a clue or a trace that would give me some inkling as to what I was dealing with. But this only resulted in sleepless nights, poking at pages and pages of endless medical information. I knew it all by heart. Some of the information had even been written by my father, grandfather and great-grandfather, all of whom were famous physicians in their time and had written books that have graced many a library across the world. You could say, I was fed medicine and science from before conception. So how was it that I could not explain the patient's illness or even find any resemblance of it to another illness? No illness springs from a barren structure. It borrows, imitates, steals, then creates a new structure triggered by that very act of plagiarism.

By the time the patient returned at the end of the one-month period, we were both in a sorrowful state. I, because I still had nothing to offer my patient in terms of a prognosis. She, because the protrusions had increased, the rubber-like piece of skin had become more obvious and the surrounding pigmentation of skin had darkened further. This time, when the patient attempted to bare her upper body, she had to take off an elastic band she had wrapped around her chest to flatten the protrusions and prevent them from being obvious to the public gaze. As the last layer of the band was shed, I stared at the patient's chest utterly stupefied. What struck me was not the mere increase in size of the protrusions, nor of the rubber-like piece of skin at its centre. Rather, it was the manner in which the tumour, on both the left and right side of the chest, had developed. While the two tumours were not exactly symmetrical, they had grown in almost identical shape, manner, size, structure, even feel. They were, if I may be permitted to say so from a purely aesthetic perspective, pleasing to the eye. I mean, to the medical eye.

I do not know how to continue without sounding insane. But I have to tell it all as it happened. I don't have much time left. And in the time left, I have to make sure you understand. You have got to understand! Not what they have been telling you, but what actually happened. And what happened was not something I bargained for or even predicted. It was unexpected, odd, intense. You see, the more I looked at the tumours, the more fascinated I was. My fascination was not triggered by medical curiosity or scientific passion. It was something else. Something utterly out of my control. This 'something' could only be compared to love. Yes, love. The kind of overwhelming love that makes you eternally protective of that which you have fallen in love with. And in my case, my love object was not the patient, but her tumour. I had fallen in love with this woman's illness and I did not want her to overcome it. I wanted it to thrive on the patient's chest; I wanted to stare at it and touch it endlessly.

But what am I saying? How could I have allowed myself to say, even think, something like that? At the time, I felt mortified. I could not look the patient in the eye, nor she in mine. Only the two tumours registered our reactions. For the bud at their centre became imbued with a deep-reddish colour. Not reddish as in blood-like, but more like the colour of a rose petal. And that was when I panicked. What was I seeing? What had grown on the woman's chest? By God, I needed to leave my clinic. I had to leave it right away. It couldn't be! It just couldn't!

     ABIR HAMDAR

I must have run to my car and flown away with total disregard to the laws of the sky, for my next memory is being in the basement of my ancestors' home. I was tripping down a long, dark, creaking staircase. I was pressing buttons madly in an attempt to open boxes, shutters, files. Everything was in chaos. But there was one thing, and one thing only, that I needed to find. And there it was. Sitting inside a dark grey box, in a dark grey file, with dark grey inscriptions. It belonged to my great-grandfather. Only he had a penchant for monochromes. Everything had to be categorised in monochrome undertones and overtones, including his medical archives. Yet, my great-grandfather never managed to achieve monochrome perfection. For a coloured image resting inside the file, protected by a sheen glaze, had disrupted his efforts.

The image was of a woman with a bare chest. I stared at her face. Beautiful, absolutely beautiful. Not her face, but the thing that rested further down on her chest. I might have stared at her face for an hour, maybe minutes, before turning my attention to her chest area. I knew I shouldn't have looked. When I was a child and I caught my grandfather staring at the image, I was warned never to look. Yet, this time I did not heed his advice. I looked and time dissolved at the wondrous sight. A woman's breasts, it used to be called. Round and shapely and soft – with a rosy pigmentation in the centre and a soft bud sticking out of it. Breasts, they called them breasts, before they decided to erase them from female bodies and medical files; from history and memory; from time and place.

I do not know a lot about what happened. My knowledge consists of snippets and whispers and closed doors. I do not think even my great-grandfather knew what really happened and when exactly it happened. It might have been in his great-grandfather's time or much earlier. It is hard to tell. But there was a disease that afflicted women's chests or rather the soft, round protrusions. Of course, there were other diseases that afflicted women and men's bodies at the time. Diseases that rotted women's ovaries; illnesses that scarred men's semen tubes. But this did not matter. For the ability to transplant female ovaries and male tubes from animals meant that the human form was cured and even continued to reproduce. It was only the illness of the soft, round protrusions that defied science. This illness had thrived for decades and centuries.

Of course, there were many new treatments. The fight for a cure was long and arduous, and success remained out of reach. It soon became clear that this illness had discovered the secret to life itself. It blossomed and grew like a new breast.

'Cure us of this life! Cure us of life itself.'

I am not sure who issued this decree. The world must have consented. Our ancestors were clearly tired. Tired of the illness and the sight of the soft, round protrusions where this illness dwelled and breathed.

'Cure us of life! Cure us of this life!'

The female breasts were no longer breasts: radical mastectomy of the breasts and their surrounding lymph nodes, genetic modification of the chest wall, a restructuring of the cells of the chest glands, a meddling with DNA composition. This was followed by things that could not even be whispered about. A medical cure or a medical holocaust. It did not matter. The soft, round protrusions with the secret to life were wiped out of existence by the procedures or the trauma. It is not clear how long this took or what happened immediately after. No record of this exists in documented form. What my great-grandfather or his great-grandfather knew was possibly transmitted by word of mouth.

I suspect that, when the outline of a breast appeared on a woman's chest every decade or so, the death penalty followed. I do not know why the death penalty was given. I suspect it was the longstanding fear of that which held the secret to life. Only death was a befitting cure. In any case, it seems the world soon forgot why it was giving the death penalty, but still gave it. Sometimes, those with soft, round protrusions committed suicide before the death penalty was ever considered. The world had become so acquainted with flat-chested female forms, that anything with a soft, round structure was strange and terrifying.

Today, it is this irrational fear that sees me sitting in a three-by-four prison cell, awaiting my death sentence. I am here in place of my patient, whose death penalty would have been imminent, had I not facilitated her escape. I cannot tell you how, for even prison cells have ears. I know that news of her presence and condition travelled across the hospital. Not by my

ABIR HAMDAR

negligence, but by an act of betrayal. It is not important which of my assistants, medical students or colleagues found out and betrayed me. Suffice it to say, a collective 'restlessness' spread. I prefer to call it an awakening. Whatever the phenomenon, it soon developed into a fully-fledged state of public panic. It is not only the people of Iraq who are now frightened. The world is in a state of terror. Breasts? What are breasts? Why do they grow? How do they grow? Are they contagious? Do men grow breasts? Will our women and daughters be afflicted with them?

'Cure us! Cure us!'

My patient was arrested. I stood at her trial, but did not defend her. What could I have said? I did not know much about female breasts myself. All I know is captured in an image my great-grandfather had saved in a grey box, in a grey file, which later came into the hands of my grandfather, then my father. As a child, I also heard whispers. Many whispers between the three generations of medical experts, and strange people who visited late at night. But, is all this sufficient to make sense in an international medical tribunal? I will not live to find out. The authorities discovered that I helped my patient escape from prison and have put me in her place. They have also issued the death penalty. This was not met with any opposition, even from those I have worked with closely for many years. I do not mind the prison, the death sentence or the abandonment by one and all. I realise how frightening it all sounds to everyone. Female breasts? What breasts?

I now know what breasts are, what they look like and how they look on a woman's chest. I have seen them up close and personal, scrutinised them and touched them. I have felt their power and their appeal. If anything, I am possibly the only eye-witness who can even begin to attest to their presence in history. And I tell you, I am willing to die for them in the same way that you would be willing to die for them, if you ever set eyes on them. The question is: Will you ever? Will my patient be cured of her illness? Will she be cured of life itself?

THE WORLD TO COME

1913: THE WORLD TO COME IS MADE OF LOVE

Jeannette Delamoir

The posters for my stage performances are everywhere. On every thick, splintery electricity pole; on walls outside shops; on tall corrugated iron fences. Everybody knows who I am. Everybody knows I see the future.

The posters show a photograph of me. Loops of pearls garland my neck and arms. I look down, concentrating on a crystal ball. Well, it's glass, really, not crystal. The photographer, a very clever man, applied some sort of trick process in his darkroom, adding bolts of lightning to the ball, which somehow looks full of a thick, swirling gas. The energy crackles across the gas, the brittle glass barely containing the flashes.

At first, the image unsettled me. My downcast eyes look perilously close to the crackling, flickering lightning. The glass ball looks as if it might explode and fling glass shrapnel into my face. Or into the face of anyone looking at the poster. But now I understand the image. I have to understand the image. And I understand that something that began as mere ballyhoo is ghastly truth.

My husband, Richard, is a magician. We perform together and travel with the Great Mystical Company. We present our show everywhere. In theatres and schools of art and halls. Capital cities, tiny settlements, up north, out west. Travelling by steamer and train, and sometimes there's no other way but by horse and cart.

I'm not complaining, but it's hard work. The advance man is crucial. Weeks before the company reaches each new town, he pays local boys to paste the posters all over the place.

By the time we arrive, everybody wants to talk to me. The schoolchildren, the mothers with prams, the factory girls, the businessmen, even the young loafers with no direction; all with their lives shining ahead of them, so unknown, so full of potential. Everyone wants to know about the world to come. Well, their little bit of it, anyway.

We perform publicly at night; I consult privately during the day. All I need to do is hire a room and place a tiny classified advertisement in the newspaper. Then we make sure we amaze and puzzle the packed theatres with our act. And wait.

By the time the first customer visits, rose oil is warming in the burner. I pull the curtains closed and light a candle. Its glow gilds the plush of a Kashmiri rug I've draped over the table and burnishes the carved wood of the Indian folding chairs. The crystal ball gleams on the table. It's decorative rather than functional, but the posters on every bus stop and vacant-lot fence have promised there will be a crystal ball. So there it is.

You might think I'm cynical about the people I see and what they ask me. You might think the darkness hides some kind of devious practice. But it's nothing like that. I darken the room because my clients feel safer that way. As they enter, momentarily blind while their eyes adjust, I speak softly and gently. I encourage, I soothe. Often I reach through shadows cast by the wobbling candle flame and clasp a client's hands. Sweaty. Or shaking. Or freezing.

They don't seem disappointed that there is no flashing lightning inside the crystal ball. They register its presence, but the purpose of their visit overwhelms them. I know they walk up the path mentally rehearsing what they want to say to me. And, in the close, heavy, rose-scented darkness, their painful, tremulous questions tumble out. They blurt the words that most wrench their hearts. They stammer their greatest vulnerabilities.

> Does he love me or does he love another?
>
> Will I ever marry?
>
> Will she return?
>
> Have I made a terrible mistake?

It's not easy for people to reveal their most cherished and secret desires, especially if someone – even a total stranger like me – can see their face blushing or blanching, contorting with

                    JEANNETTE DELAMOIR

despair, fear, shame. Their well-controlled, everyday masks dissolve. Something has to fall away before they can put into words what it is that they most want to know.

Will we have a child?

Will I find my brother who is missing?

Where is my little girl? Did she drown or did someone take her?

Our father went shearing and has never come back. Where is he?

It's about love, it's all about love. Oh, yes, it's true that sometimes people ask about lost objects. Money or watches or rings. But, you know, the lost objects are not just possessions. If I ask the customer another question, they will unfailingly tell me that the lost items link them to a loved one who is far away or has departed altogether. The ring is all that remains of a marriage. The watch was a gift from a family member now deceased. There is no limit to the pain people feel. When these objects disappear, the tangible proof of their intangible connection is gone, and they are bereaved all over again.

And yes, sometimes there are trivial questions, but usually people ask these during my stage performances. Which horse will run first in the Melbourne Cup? Which local politician will win the upcoming election? These are just tricks asked in public so any mistake will also be public. Usually yelled out by young rowdies and, usually, after several fast pints of beer during intermission. Yet these same, brash, young men sidle into the private readings, hats pulled down over their eyes, and ask questions in halting voices, rubbing tears away with trembling hands, exactly like everyone else.

On stage, I wear a dress made from yards and yards of sequinned sari fabric. I am blindfolded and I sit on a chair. The house lights are turned right up, the theatre bright, my sequins flash.

Richard, distinguished in his dark suit and top hat, hands out paper and pencils and invites members of the audience to write down the questions they want to ask. They fold up their paper so the questions can't be seen, and they place the paper in their pockets or handbags. Then I give the answers. Without hearing the questions. Without seeing the faces of those who asked.

Of course, there's a trick to it. It's taken years of practice for my husband and me to perfect our act, and it's mainly based on knowing the questions that people always ask over and over. I give them a local twist, freshening them up by making them topical. Always mention the success of a citizen's new business venture. Always 'refuse' to answer one question. I say: 'A young lady has asked a question about a very delicate matter and the answer will compromise her modesty and her good standing. If she comes to see me tomorrow, I will answer her in private.' My voice projects to the back of the theatre, strong but warm, inviting trust, building confidence in what I say. Through the blindfold, I sense the audience – astounded, intrigued, puzzling about how it's done.

But it's not all an act. Behind the blindfold, I focus hard on giving a performance, making it entertaining, picking up the prearranged code in my husband's patter. I listen for the sharp gasps or muffled shrieks when someone thinks I have answered his question, her question.

On stage, I cannot afford to lose myself as I do during the readings in the darkened room, fragrant with rose oil. In that dark privacy, I listen to each customer. My chest tightens. My heart squeezes. I say a few words and ask a few questions to reassure each customer that, at a deep level, I recognise him or her, even though we have only just met. But of course, any professional fortune teller can do that. When people are desperate they grasp the slightest hint, magnifying it to their own advantage. But it's not a trick, not really. I tell you, it leads the customers further into the reading and that is where they want to go.

They talk, words tumbling out. Disappointments, affronts, crushing rejections. Regrets. Resentment. Longing. Lust.

A mist gathers, white and rose-scented. My fingers and toes grow numb. A soft breeze passes over the nape of my neck, a gentle stroke that raises the hairs on my arms. I can't tell any longer what is mist and what is me. I can't tell any longer which voices are questioning and which are answering, which voice is mine and which is the customer's – and which voices are coming from somewhere else, somewhere on the other side.

I just know that I am borne on sighs and yearning. Sometimes there are sobs, sometimes quiet weeping. Anxieties collect in

     JEANNETTE DELAMOIR

pools that run downhill and fill the hollows and indentations, forming puddles that seep into the soil and poison it. Like a swarm of insects, worries cluster around tender new shoots, sucking sap out of buds and new leaves. The whole of creation vibrates to the cicada-shrill of fear. It's all energy, different kinds of energy. Lightning flashes barely contained within the fragile human body.

Is my dead child in a safe place now?

Has the baby I gave away grown up in a loving family?

Does my mother feel pain any longer?

Was the death an accident or something else?

The spirits whisper. They rush in, eager to talk, to connect, to answer questions, to ask questions themselves. Everything else has dissolved except for the jolt, the charge, the love that motivates them. They want to contact their loved ones, to let them know they are still here. They love, they forgive, they remember.

The spirits reach out to me, through me, although I am only a clumsy and inefficient connection in a circuit. Their pleas and sighs are so quiet, so soft, created from fragility, human weakness, yet insistent. Persistent. Across the boundaries of life and death, the ties endure. Through loss and illness and anger. Against all logic.

In the future, when we die, we will be like them, those sighing spirits. The howling winds of the Universe will wither the buds, desiccate the insects, disperse the poisoned soil. Strip away our soft flesh. Lethal white flashes of lightning will sear and crack our bones. In a poisonous green gas, everything crumbles and blows away like dust. The only thing that remains is love: the essential core, the driving force, flowing in whispers, seeking currents, dispersing into a mist of charged particles that cluster together like a fuzz of iron filings around a magnet.

Of course, I don't tell everyone everything I see. I see ... I see these young rowdies putting on their khaki uniforms and their brave faces. I see explosions, shrapnel, barbed wire, grotesque technologies of death, aircraft delivering pain and fear and dismemberment. I see suspicion, betrayal, tall corrugated iron fences around internment camps full of innocent people – yes, here, in Australia. And so many mothers weeping, so many fathers stumbling outside with a telegram gripped in a clenched fist, so many men with their faces destroyed and their bodies shattered. The schoolchildren, the mothers with prams, the factory girls, the businessmen, even the young loafers with no direction – how can I tell them about the force of shrapnel and how it will pierce their lives? How can I put into words how the shock waves will be felt through this generation and the next?

Yet, I still believe the future is an ocean of love. A world of love. An infinite, electrified universe of love – murmuring, pleading.

> Are you there?
> Has your pain gone?
> Do you love me?
> Can you forgive me?
> Do you feel how very, very much I love you?
> Do you know how much you are missed, every single day?
> Can you give me a sign that you are there? Any sign, the smallest sign, the slightest, tiniest, most subtle sign, please, just one sign?

The mist lifts. My fingers and toes tingle. I talk about love. The customer, face tear-streaked, thanks me, grasps my hands and thanks me again. And hurries out.

I pinch out the candle, open the curtains and take up my mending as a breeze sweeps the rose fragrance out the window. Last night, I tore the skirt of my costume. I sew, and I wait.

          JEANNETTE DELAMOIR

THE OUTER TERRITORIES

Tim Richards

Advancing through Customs, Kyle Hampson was greeted by a chunky redhead who looked like she'd just returned to work from a three-week bender.

'Reason for coming to Gorolya?'

'I'm here to teach Australian Studies at Paul Hogan High.'

'Ah, to improve the calibre of our young people... Any knives or offensive weapons?'

'No.'

'You might regret that... Are you carrying any sexually explicit or religious materials, Kyle?'

'No.'

'Proscribed drugs or alcohol?'

'No.'

'Mate, I'll pay top dollar... It'd be between us.'

'Sorry.'

'Yeah. Sure you are.'

Sarcasm and resentment were traits the travel guides warned about. The bureaucrats who governed the Australian Outer Territories had few jokes and recycled the ones they had on a regular basis. Hence, the question was not whether Gorolya, with five per cent less oxygen than Earth, had an atmosphere suitable to sustain human life, but whether it had more than its inhabitants deserved. If you didn't laugh at their jokes, they'd keep telling them until you did.

Had this mob – The Raj, as they called themselves – been given another fifty years, they would have totally fucked the place. When the Federal Ministry of Housing acquired Gorolya from the Outer Territories Commission in 2067, the boutique-sized planet was described as a 'secret delight'. Plenty of water, fresh air, and fruit trees, though not much in the way of minerals or arable soils. Five decades on, Gorolya was a cultureless, low-income, high-unemployment planet for welfare types. Even with the grandchildren of the pioneers hitting school-leaving age, the construction of the planet's first university had been on hold for twelve years.

The real concern was that no-one seemed worried about it.

Paul Hogan High was the newest of eight secondary schools in Irwin, the capital of Kidman Province. Graduates with the best grades could hope for a job in the bingo halls or to apprentice as park rangers, but most kids left school at fifteen intending to work in the fishing or fruit trades, or the huge canning factories. Less than a third who left with those hopes found their desired employment. Some found work in retail or small businesses, others were picked out by pimps, most just lolled about between dole payments.

You might imagine that the kids who stayed at school beyond leaving age would have been the more motivated students, the ones who prized learning or had higher ambitions, but the few employment opportunities available to them involved IT support or low-rung clerical work with The Raj. All senior officers were imported from Australia and they had no intention of relinquishing their influence and status.

*

'Jesus, Kyle, this says you volunteered to teach here,' Principal Di Jenson, a fifty-something who moved like an injured sumo wrestler, noted with undisguised horror. 'You'd be the first.'

'I like a challenge,' Hampson told her.

'Bullshit! You're on the run from something. Kyle, don't take this personally, but I'm having your history double-checked. The mums and dads might not trust a teacher who chose to come here.'

'Would they care?'

'Fuck, no. But complaining gives them something to do. There's no porn here. No cameras, so we can't even make our own. All the tele comes from those mincers over on Jackman... Don't tell me there's not a secret deal between the OTC and the mob running the bingo.'

'What are the kids like?'

'Mate... You teach Australian Studies.'

'They'll eat me for breakfast?'

'It's just a matter of grilled or fried.

  TIM RICHARDS

Since married teachers couldn't be forced to work in the Outer Territories the conscripts were all single, most of them fresh from college. These youngsters lived in a secure complex next to the school grounds. In Australia, stories abounded about teachers who'd returned from the Outer Territories with a taste for salty fish, moonshine and group sex. The odds on a chalkie choosing to live among the locals were less than nil, so Hampson's desire to live in Irwin's 'Theatre District' – a joke that never wore thin with Gorolyans – left both colleagues and locals flummoxed.

'This says you're a teacher,' a Housing Commission official noted with surprise.

'That's right.'

'Wouldn't you rather be getting your end in at the school condo? It's meant to be anything-goes up there ... discipline, waterworks. The lot.'

'I doubt it,' Hampson told him. 'But I'm looking for something quiet. A place that will give me the chance to see how people live here.'

The agent muttered a crude blasphemy before recomposing to tell Hampson that he looked like a decent bloke and he'd see what could be done. Most likely, he'd be forced to tell landlords that their applicant had a rare form of the clap. They'd understand those imperatives much better than someone actually choosing to fraternise with the locals.

'Mate, the danger is they'll smell a missionary. God-botherers get shot on sight up here.'

'No hymns in the shower then,' Hampson promised.

Though the thirty-hour days were often used to explain the listless stupidity of native Gorolyans, Hampson, who adapted within a week, was more inclined to attribute their slowness to inherited values, limited education and the potent illegal cider brewed from the Pig Apple – a juicy, pink-fleshed fruit that grew in abundance along the foothills of Mount Ponting. To Hampson, it tasted like fish urine, but a half-glass at recess was enough to send a sober kid silly.

'Never threaten to call their parents,' Kelly Ryan, a button-nosed twenty-five year old with six months left on her bond told Hampson. 'They'll puke themselves laughing. Best thing is to threaten to have their football club membership revoked.'

'Teachers can do that?'

'Mate, it's practically martial law here. Sporting threats are one thing they pay heed to. That, and cancelling the subsidies on their clap-creams... Caught anything yet?'

'Not yet,' Hampson told her.

'There's a thing up here, it sounds like a Greek dip – Fracillus. It makes your eyes weep green pus. All your eyes. If you want my advice, Kyle, never fuck someone who wants the light out... Blue Bite's way worse, but the OTC will send you home if you get that, so it's worth the risk.'

Hampson took a mental note of that, but lost Kelly's sympathy when he too readily turned down an offer to make a fourth in that evening's foursome. The very worst excuse he could have made was to claim that he needed time to write lesson plans, but that was the truth of it.

The set curriculum featured a four-week learning block called 'Australian home baking', where students were to be taught the rudiments of making lamingtons, banana bread, pavlova and raspberry tarts, but the outline failed to advise where one would obtain ingredients like coconut, banana or passionfruit. The canned substitutes found in local supermarkets were nearly toxic and the synthetic substance passed off as whipped cream was so inedible that Hampson made the mistake of complaining about it early in his first class.

'Who needs you to tell us that life here is pox? All teachers do is whinge about how shit things are.'

'I'm not talking about local culture, just the stuff pretending to be whipped cream.'

'Cows would wreck the soil and the soil's crap already,' Penny explained. 'If we were to fuck it up even more, we'd all be fucked.'

'But there's no use teaching Australian cake-craft if we can't use the ingredients Australians use.'

'Why should we give a rats about Australia?' a tall, pock-faced boy named Jacko asked. 'We're Gorolyans. My parents were born here and this is where we live. Australia was never happier than the day it told our grandparents to fuck off. Now

     TIM RICHARDS

Australians won't let us think of this place as home. Fuck 'em. This is where I was born and, unless I'm made to fight some fuckwit Australian war, this is where I'll die.'

Of course, Hampson could have said that these were odd complaints coming from someone enrolled in an optional Year Eleven subject called Australian Studies – usually he made his students endorse some form of good faith contract – but instead he asked this group to outline what a subject called Gorolyan Studies might look like. 'What's different about life here?'

'The Swamp Monkeys,' Toni ventured and Hampson repeated this as he began to make a list on the whiteboard.

'The Spazzo Bats and Dumpling Birds,' Oz said.

'The flora and fauna here are unique, that's true,' Hampson told them. 'As different from Australia as Australia's animal and plant life are from the rest of the world's... How many of you have eaten Dumpling Bird?'

Only two students put up their hands and not even they could describe the taste. Salty. Joe's grandpa said it reminded him of anchovies on blue cheese. Aside from local fruits like the custard berry and the grape-like udder berries, most kids admitted a preference for pre-packaged frozen foods transported from Australia. Hampson wasn't keen to appraise them of the scandals that had embroiled those industries 'back home'.

'What else is so different... ? All the music I hear is Australian, the books are written by Australians and, while the television might not be made in Australia, it's made by Australians and just as bad as the Australian-made stuff you'd see in Australia. You're governed by Australians who have a duty to apply laws framed in Australia.'

'The grog laws are different. In Australia, it's legal to drink real alcohol, not this piss we're forced to drink,' Adam suggested.

'The main differences are freedom and democracy,' Sandy told Hampson. 'None of us are free. Not even to go back. They make it so expensive, it's impossible. Yet Australians want us to miss Australia and to think that life anywhere else is third-rate.'

'The only way you can get back to Australia is if you're a football star,' Erin complained. 'So what good is that to a girl, unless you're smart enough to get knocked up by a boy who might get recruited? Even then, he's just as likely to dump you.'

Hampson would have liked her to expand on that, but with the whole class chirping with ideas, he didn't want to halt the flow.

On Gorolya there were no waves worth surfing, but the mountains were spectacular and pollution was minimal. Many students thought that the almost total absence of religion and churches was a good thing, though some had heard rumours about underground churches in The Raj quarter, and considered religious groups to be a long-term threat to the planet. Here, there was no flu, no guns, no hunting – at least, no hunting in the sense that Australians understood the term. Boys often did unspeakable things to the native species. One squat boy named Jex complained that there was no-one for ordinary Gorolyans to pick on, not unless you counted the Swamp Monkeys.

Unprepared for the rush this discussion elicited, Hampson would later conclude that no-one had ever invited these kids to speak in this way about their homeland. It was as if he'd opened a cage door. No teacher who valued the desire to explore new terrains of thought would have forced them to re-focus on the set components of the Australian Studies curriculum. Instead, he set them a one-page homework assignment: If you could change one thing about life on Gorolya, what would it be? Even as the bell went to end the class, the students were bubbling with thoughts and priorities.

As he rode the light rail back to his apartment that evening, the proud teacher began to view his work in a new light. Hampson had imagined the need to smuggle learning into his classroom the way that pet owners hide medicine in the mince, but there was a real energy here that he could work with provided he found the right way to channel it. These kids were a long way from the hopeless, mentally enervated types he'd been given to expect. They seemed keen to cast off their shame.

*

Having lugged his briefcase and bag of groceries up three flights of stairs, Hampson was surprised to find a stocky, but not unattractive, brunette standing at his front door.

As soon as he produced a free hand, the woman introduced

     TIM RICHARDS

herself as his landlady, Nerilee Lynch. The agent had previously described her as a hard-bitten prison guard, but Nerilee didn't seem to fit that mould, moving gracefully as she invited herself in. She was soon uncorking a bottle of rough-as-guts cider.

While leaning forward to allow Hampson to look down the front of her blouse, Nerilee described herself as a second-generation immigrant – although she couldn't say when her parents had left Australia. As far as she was concerned, Gorolya was a dump and deserved to be treated as such. Sooner or later, Australia would expatriate all its worst criminals and then the incarceration industry would take off.

Just one glass of her cider was enough to send Hampson's head spinning. He would have liked to shepherd Nerilee out so he could make dinner, but she obviously needed someone to talk to, and for the next two hours while he drank three more glasses and gradually lost his capacity to absorb meanings, Nerilee spoke of gangs and rapes and tortured Swamp Monkeys. She only cheered when saying how fortunate she'd been to win a job as a prison guard. These jobs almost always went to members of The Raj. For all the grief of having to deal with scum five days a week, she did see the occasional fringe benefit – most notably access to black market goods that senior Corrections officials smuggled in from neighbouring planets. The last thing Hampson would recall from that evening was his landlady standing at the door telling him what a joy it had been to spend time with a gentleman. If he ever wanted anything, anything at all, she was right beneath him.

While one great thing about the thirty-hour day was having more time to sleep off a bender, Hampson was still queasy when fronting his Australian Studies class the next morning. However, the moment they were asked to produce their homework assignments, the students flung open their folders and, when Hampson asked who wanted to read their essay first, their hands punched holes through the third-rate air.

None of the dozen students granted the chance to speak of things that would improve Gorolyan life openly disparaged the planet and Hampson was touched by their affection for a place that seemed to have so little going for it.

Several were excited by the fact that just one-quarter of the planet had been fully explored and they hungered for a chance to take part in detailed surveys of land and sea. Unlike the Australian geologists who had been so quick to write the planet off, they were sure there was value still to be discovered.

No fewer than five essays rated dogs as the addition that would most improve Gorolya. Even little Sandy Vorst, who cited justice as the great change whose time had come, concluded her piece by asserting that there was nothing wrong with her planet that home rule and dogs couldn't fix.

Everyone in Hampson's class had been told stories by their parents and grandparents about the playfulness and unstinting loyalty of dogs. They knew the names of these long-deceased pets better than they knew the rural cities of Australia.

Though he always tried to keep personal biography out of the classroom, Hampson was moved to tell some anecdotes about his favourite collie-kelpie cross, Mickey: how the dog used to bark with glee as he crashed through waves at the beach, how he always liked to round up smaller dogs as if they were sheep, how he could repeatedly volley a balloon to keep it from touching the ground, how his ears would prick like antennae whenever Hampson spoke and how Mick's gentle snoring by his bed at night was the most comforting sound he had known.

Hampson wouldn't tell them that Mickey's violent death at the hands of anti-dog environmentalists had informed his need to escape to a place where there were no canines to break hearts. Nor would he tell them that he'd actually taught some of these same anti-dog agitators in his previous appointment at an exclusive private school. Rather, he chose to ask what these dogs might represent in the minds of kids who had never felt a dog's wet tongue.

'They're loyal and they never judge you,' Jacko told him. 'Just being with you is enough.'

Hampson promised to tell more dog stories as the year went on, but the students' response to the first assignment had given him some ideas how he might shape the year's work. The course he had in mind was one he'd never dare propose to the politically disengaged teenagers back home. While this class would look at Australia, its true focus would be Gorolya and its future. To begin with, they might examine how the separate Australian colonies arrived at a Federated nationhood and contrast this with how so many other colonies around the world

　　　　　　　　TIM RICHARDS

had achieved self-government. Would violence, instability and increased poverty necessarily result from severing ties with the colonial master?

'How could we afford to operate our own space transport system?' Gary asked.

'Maybe you wouldn't have to… Maybe there'd be new alliances and trade-offs and accommodations. But those are questions we'll be looking at,' Hampson told them, before admitting that these were matters that he'd barely considered himself. He'd be learning with the class, informed by them quite as much as guiding their studies.

'Gorolyan Studies,' Erin suggested.

'Yeah. Why not?'

*

As soon as the school day finished, Hampson sent a video link message to his mother in Melbourne. Things were better than he could have hoped for. There was a genuine prospect of doing good work. If she could send the videos she'd taken of Mickey playing in the surf and running down the steep hills at his brother's farm, he'd put them to good use.

He was so deeply locked into thoughts of his mother and whether she might plausibly choose to retire to a down-market planet like Gorolya that, when arriving home to find his front door wide open, it didn't cross Hampson's mind that the burglars might still be in his residence. After calling 'hoy!' he was surprised to be met by Nerilee who emerged from the kitchen wearing a plastic apron.

'I had the day off and I owed you a meal after staying so long last night.'

Following her into the kitchen, Hampson found a pan of sauce bubbling on the stove and could hardly fail to notice the two bottles of moonshine Nerilee had deposited on the bench. From recent experience this would have been enough to knee-cap a team of footballers, but once she'd pulled a cork he didn't beg her to ignore his glass. Hampson liked her. Nerilee had a coarse sense of humour, a rough no-bullshit manner and the generous shape he always preferred. He wasn't sure that he wanted to sleep with her, but he'd have a hard time turning her down if that's what she wanted.

As they ate, she regaled him with tales of the hardest hard-arses in prison and the psychotic child-killers who would never be released. She then listened intently as he spoke of the triumph he'd had with his Year Eleven kids.

'Gorolyan Studies! Who'd have thought there was anything here worth exploring?' she joked.

Though the cider didn't rattle Hampson like it had the previous evening, it soon impeded his capacity to put ideas into words and it wasn't long before the teacher and prison officer were adding naked friction to the carpet in the living room. When Hampson came too quickly, Nerilee looked ready to vent her displeasure, but then she did a thing with her middle finger – a skill her work no doubt gave her the chance to perfect – that soon had her lover ready for more vigorous fucking.

Sometime after that fuck and still more grog, they found their way to his bed and Hampson's last happy memories were of Nerilee kissing the hollow between his pectoral muscles.

When he came around, two darkly dressed men were standing above him and Nerilee was nowhere to be seen. Hampson might have begun to ask what they'd done with her, but the smaller man slapped him hard with an open hand to the thigh and, moments later, all was oblivion.

*

There would be no telling how much time passed between that needle-wielding slap and his waking to find himself still naked, but strapped to a chair with wires attached to his head, fingers and anus. As far as Hampson could establish, he was alone in a white room facing a white screen that most likely enabled one-way observation.

Some minutes passed before a male voice emanating from a speaker in the floor told Hampson that the evidence gathered against him was overwhelming. His only sensible policy would be to tell the whole truth. Should he be suspected of lying, the consequences would be excruciating.

'I've done nothing wrong. You have no reason to arrest me,' Hampson told the screen.

'Who is your contact in the GLO?'

'I have no idea what the GLO is,' Hampson answered and

                                    TIM RICHARDS

immediately felt an unspeakable pain shoot through his anus and prostate.

'You're not dealing with fools, Kyle... Who do you know within the movement?'

'No-one. I don't know what you are talking about.'

If anything, the second shot of pain was harsher. Even as it subsided, Hampson must have felt as if the teeth were tumbling from his gums.

Moments later, a video image of Nerilee appeared on the screen in front of him. When asked who she was, Hampson identified her as his landlady. The unseen man then asked Nerilee to formally identify Hampson and to repeat what Hampson had said about his class.

'He'd asked them to shape their own course and told me that the students had expressed interest in looking at various independence movements. He'd laughed when one suggested that the subject be renamed Gorolyan Studies.'

Invited to confirm the truth of this, Hampson did so. But when he attempted to qualify that answer, he received a prolonged shot of electricity to the nether regions. By the time he recovered, Nerilee's face had been replaced on screen by blurry images of himself standing before his Year Eleven class.

Having been shown footage of Sandy Vorst insinuating that no Gorolyans were free and that 'they' had made it impossible for Gorolyans to 'go back'; Hampson was asked who he understood 'they' to be.

'I don't know... I imagined that she meant the Outer Territories Commission or the Australian Government.'

'Why didn't you correct her?'

'How could I when I wasn't sure what she said was wrong?'

'If you didn't know whether it was right, why didn't you ask her to explain herself?'

'It was a classroom discussion. A free exchange of ideas.'

'Yes. That's what you wanted it to be. A free exchange of ideas.'

Although Hampson by now understood the pointlessness of being confronted with further evidence, that his fate – whatever that might be – had already been determined, he was compelled to view other moments that had taken place in his classroom: him being informed that there were 'secret churches', that young

Gorolyans caught and tortured Swamp Monkeys, his view that Gorolyans might need to make trade-offs and accommodations in order to achieve independence, and his suggestions that 'Gorolyan culture' was in some way distinct from Australian culture and was worthy of being treated as such.

After each scene was shown, Hampson had little choice but to concede that these events had happened in his classroom and that he'd taken no measures to prevent them taking place. The male voice he must have come to think of as his prosecutor or judge – possibly both – then said something Hampson asked to be repeated, a phrase that included the word 'treason'.

'If I'm to be charged with treason, surely I have the right to legal representation,' Hampson blurted at the screen.

'No-one's charging you with treason, Kyle,' the voice told him. 'But, three of your students have pleaded guilty to treason and they've already accepted five-year prison sentences... You've been found guilty of state terrorism. Your one hope of receiving mercy from this court is to name those who recruited you.'

'I am not a terrorist. I belong to no group. I am a free speaker. Free speech is my birthright as an Australian citizen.'

In the long silence that followed, Hampson must have speculated about what might happen next: whether the offences he'd been found guilty of brought a long prison sentence or worse, and he might have questioned whether he'd see his mother again or if she'd ever learn what became of him. And then he would have heard a loud slapping noise, like a hand slamming a wooden table, and if he never guessed what was coming next, he was much better off.

*

Almost fifty-three years later, a short, elegantly dressed, white-haired woman will stand before a huge cheering crowd in Assange Avenue having just been elected first President of the new Gorolyan Republic. After graciously acknowledging Veripu Tays, leader of the peoples not long before disparaged as Swamp Monkeys, now known as the Mooroolyan Nation, President Sandy Vorst will speak with great eloquence about the sacrifices made in her planet's long struggle to bring forth this day, recalling the many heroes of Gorolyan independence

     TIM RICHARDS

who had fallen without seeing their freedom-loving cause brought to fruition.

On this day, she will particularly want to remember a man hitherto neglected by history, a man whose thoughts and courage had been crucial in the formation of her own revolutionary consciousness. Though he had taught her for just two classes shortly before paying the ultimate price for his belief in Gorolyan culture, she would never forget Carl, nor would her people. In tribute to this great mentor, the province's capital, Irwin, would henceforth be known as Hampton.

PREFACE TO A SELECTED HISTORY OF THE TWENTY-FIRST CENTURY

Lucy Greenwood

A document claiming to have been sent from the future mysteriously appeared throughout the Great Southern and South-West regions of Western Australia ten days ago – in the offices of local newspapers and libraries, and community groups such as the Greenham Historical Society. Its appearance has instantly generated hot controversy, with many claiming it is a hoax.

Simply entitled, 'Preface', it appears to be the first part of a much larger body of work called, A Selected History of the Twenty-first Century, *which has either been lost in transmission or not yet written – depending on your point of view. Some believe that if councils record in their minutes that 'Preface' was received, minus the body of work, the rest will arrive shortly. Gill Smith, a councillor from Balbarrup Shire, is promoting this idea. She is meeting strong opposition on the grounds that this is illogical. The opposition is refusing to record any mention of the document. We, a group of concerned citizens,* say *this is illogical if they truly believe the document is a hoax. We think that vested interests are seeking to suppress the History out of fear of its impact.*

We have obtained a copy of 'Preface', which is attached to this email and published on our new website: www.preface. org.au. Please be patient with any problems on our website, as we have created it in a hurry. We believe this document is important. Please read 'Preface' and send our link out to your networks.

Also, please contact your local Shire Council and insist that they record receipt of 'Preface', as we hope this will result in the appearance of the rest of the document.

PREFACE

This work I have transmitted to you is part of the challenge I have undertaken for my Initiation to become a third-level Keeper. We have four levels of Keeper with increasing responsibility at each level.

In my world, we live in small communities and the Keepers look after our social structure, and much more. Our roles include: co-ordination of practical tasks, record-keeping, research in our fields and spiritual guidance. We do not decide policy. That is made at the grassroots level by the people in our small communities. Even our children participate in making decisions, if they wish to be included. At wider levels, such as regional areas and planetary consultation, elected representatives inform the world about the functioning of their community, which links the communities together and provides advice concerning appropriate uniformity for standards that need to be upheld.

In this way, we interact globally, while living locally.

My name is Loris Windsong. I am a woman in my prime, near the end of childbearing years, but have never borne a child. In my world, only those people who feel especially called give birth to new ones. Yet, all adults are parents, uncles, aunts and mentors to the children of our village. Every year, each Keeper of the Peoples tallies the birth rate and asks accordingly for more or less children.

I am a scientist, teacher, historian, musician, storyteller and second-level Keeper of the Mysteries. You must think me very busy, but in truth, my world is a lot more relaxed than yours. This chronicle, my Initiation work, is mainly a history of social conditions during the time of my mother's childhood and youth.

My mother was born in 2025. There was much hardship in those times as humanity adjusted to living without easy access to the enormously rich, but finite, source of energy: petroleum. Extreme weather conditions, caused by an increase in greenhouse gases, were at their worst in those years.

But there were many advances as well. That time saw a rapid lifestyle change with a major shift from living in towns and cities, to creating local, rural villages and urban neighbourhoods. These local communities eventually became self-reliant in governance and in much of their requirements, such as food,

     LUCY GREENWOOD

energy sources and building materials. Although, there was, of course, a lot of trade and interaction between neighbouring communities. The emphasis on using local resources, including all of our waste, greatly reduced the demand for energy and the creation of greenhouse gases, which helped to clean up the environment. In chapter two of the History, I write in detail about this radical change in living conditions.

During that time, there was an enormous burst of innovation in transport with the emergence of wind-powered shipping (not sailboats, but, of course, we use those too), solar-powered aircraft and a refinement in waste processing to produce energy for powering land transport and farm machinery, such as tractors.

Hydrogen is an excellent, but highly flammable, fuel. In your time, hydrogen gas was usually derived from electrolysis of water – a process that is very expensive in use of energy and cost of safe storage. During my mother's childhood, they perfected the conversion of solid and liquid wastes into methane gas and the cool-separation of hydrogen gas from the methane – reclaiming valuable carbon along the way. This created hydrogen gas on demand and it no longer required expensive storage. These processes could be carried out in small, local communities, where the waste was produced and where the newly available energy was needed.

I address the transport revolution in Chapter Three of my book. This chapter also reveals that nuclear power became a non-issue, even before the 2020s, because it was not financially viable. Building nuclear facilities required huge investments of time and money and, as more safeguards were set in place at the demand of an increasingly active 'people's power', support for the nuclear option was swept away in a tsunami of renewable energy innovation and development.

I include in this chronicle the personal story of my mother, Flame Robinson, partly to help release the ghosts in my family history. I believe that personal stories give heart to a written history and help us see the real people who lived in other times. Flame's mother, Paris, became mentally ill not long after giving birth to her only child. Eventually, when Flame was six years old, Paris took her own life. Flame moved with her father to one of the new communities, which provided her with great nurturing and support in her time of need. My mother believed that if her parents had lived in an intentional community – rather than a city – at the time that Paris began to develop her mental illness, her mother would have survived and perhaps even been healed. Chapter One of my book comprises Flame Robinson's story.

Chapter Four of the History details some of the developments in communications technology that has allowed us to live globally, while rarely moving far from our local regions. Our elected village and regional representatives are able to virtually attend distant conferences in ways that are similar, but of course not identical, to actual attendance. If they wish to go sightseeing, they can also do that virtually with a strong feeling of being truly there. Although they will not have the same experience as someone who actually visits and is fully present in a place, we believe their experience is as satisfying as the way people travelled in your time.

People who live distantly are able to develop strong friend-ships through communications media and can even make love virtually, if they wish. Of course, we realise and honour the fact that couples often form strong bonds. If two people develop a deep relationship apart, they are free to live together, but do so with the understanding that at least one of them will rarely visit their family and home community. That is the reality of our world at this time.

We do recognise the benefits of cultural enrichment, of communing with nature in environments very different from our own, and the intellectual broadening provided by travel. However, we no longer have the option of being able to waste non-renewable resources through constant travel. Distant journeys are occasionally available for each individual and for particular reasons. There is new technology that has been discovered, but not yet developed, that could allow greater amounts of travel in future. There is also the possibility that spiritual means of moving between regions will one day replace physical journeying. It is still not possible in my time, but I feel we are getting closer to it.

Overall, this work looks at social trends and the evolution of consciousness in the twenty-first century. Concentrating on the period 2020–2040, it finds roots in history and reveals some

     LUCY GREENWOOD

of the long-term developments since then, including the 'Great Mid-Century Peace' and the rise of the 'Underworld Warriors'.

During the 2040s and 2050s, life on planet Earth became very settled, quiet and comparatively gentle. During that period, many people deluded themselves into thinking we had reached the time of a thousand years of peace, as promised in mythology. The arts flourished in those years, especially music, poetry and dance. My childhood was very rich in those things. It was also a highly spiritual time, with widespread sections of the world's population practising the myriad forms of meditation or prayer. There were not a lot of practical changes, but the oceans of the world were given profound and true protection, with a series of agreements between regional areas signed in the 2040s. The oceans had been in trouble for a long time. They had been filled with vast amounts of poison, including fossil oil, acidification, radiation and massed fragments of plastic. They were also depleted by decades of overfishing.

By universal agreement, we began to heal the oceans by leaving them alone. Using them as roads was greatly reduced, as trade became more localised and the continuing advances in communications technology allowed virtual travel. Occasionally, when we did undertake real travel, mostly for interaction with other cultures, we preferred to do so using small solar-powered aircraft.

By then, education on how to grow fish and shellfish in onshore farms had progressed rapidly, without destroying the environment in the way that shrimp farmers tended to do in your time.

In Chapter Seven of my book, I chronicle in detail a story that does not belong to my chosen historical period, but which I felt must be told. During the 2060s, a dangerous monster appeared, having grown in secret due to our complacency. This monster was a grab for power by individuals who had joined together in a planetary movement they called, 'Underworld Warriors'. When the Warriors surfaced, they took the world by surprise. The struggle to prevent their violent takeover lasted seven years, causing much damage and bloodshed – although nothing like the World Wars that occurred in the twentieth century.

There were many lessons learnt about the nature of leadership and the hunger for power, with formal research later conducted and safeguards put in place. A beneficial result of that terrible time – which I remember well, as I was approaching adulthood when it began – was the development of a complete system of non-violent disarming of brutal authoritarian individuals and groups.

The historical data used in my chronicle have been extracted from many archives, including personal writings from your local area (please see Appendix One for the list of historical references). I also collected much of the information from my mother before her recent death. Some of the data you would call my imagination, but in my time, we call it 'Knowing'.

I send this History to you as a warning and an inspiration, not so you will do other than what you are about to do, but so you may be enabled to do what you were always going to do. You can only be who you are, but who you are includes change.

Even so, there is much information I have withheld for many reasons. It is not in your interest, nor ours, that you should know every story.

The time in which I write is a period of consolidation. We all work to repair the damage created by those before us, to disseminate, through time, what we have learnt and to continue to raise the vibration of this precious planet.

Here is the work that will lead to my third Initiation. I trust and hope it will be of interest and use to you, my ancestors.

—Loris Windsong, planet Earth, 2093.

CARETAKERS

John Fulton

This morning when Mr McGuire arrives to take them to the hospice, as he does every morning, Jane wants somehow to fix her mother's face. It is chapped, pale, unmade and her lower lip is cracked and bleeding. She hasn't worn make-up in weeks and has let her hair grow wild. No matter how much Jane combs it, it sticks up in odd places making Mary appear both old-womanish and boyish. At nineteen, Jane shouldn't be taking care of her mother. But once again, she needs to remind Mary to wear a winter coat in what is yet another unusually cold February day of ice and snow in Denver.

'You'll freeze to death,' Jane says, wishing right away that she hadn't let that word slip, a word her family has carefully avoided since Jane's father was diagnosed with cancer last year. Mary hardly seems to notice it as Jane helps her work each arm into a parka and zips it up to Mary's chin.

'Thank you, sweetheart.'

'Let me put some cream on your face,' Jane says, but Mary is already headed out the door, waddling down the icy walk in her white Reeboks and fat parka to get to her husband's bedside.

Jane is relieved to see Mr McGuire, to sit again in his Mercedes sedan, the warm air blowing and the lull of Mozart turned down low on the stereo. A week ago, when it became clear that Jane's father was in his last days, Mr McGuire offered to drive Jane and her mother to and from the hospice and Jane meant to say no. She meant to insist on driving herself. If only for the company, he said at the time. In truth, Jane wanted the company, perhaps even wanted his company, and so she accepted. Her father's closest friend, Mr McGuire is slim for a man of fifty and there is something comforting in the fact that he has worn his hair short and parted on the right side, that he has dressed in the same clothes – dark suits on workdays and khakis with pastel sweaters on weekends – ever since Jane can remember. Recently, Jane has been uncomfortably aware of looking forward to these short trips in his car, to sitting next to this family friend, this man whom she practically grew up with, whose daughter, Lizzie, was her best friend for years, this man who glances now in the rearview mirror, his soft blue eyes falling on her and asks, 'Everyone buckled up?', before pulling out of the driveway. For some reason, the fact that he has always cared intensely for his wife, Bobbie, who is bound to a wheelchair with severe MS, makes Jane feel protected, as safe as Mrs McGuire herself must feel. For years, he has taken her everywhere in her wheelchair – to parties, concerts, dinners, restaurants – without showing the slightest sign of annoyance or impatience. And now he treats Jane and her mother with the same quiet goodwill, the same gentle determination to help. At the hospice, he parks and opens the car doors to let Mary and Jane out, then follows them to the entrance and again opens doors for them. He'll return around five for Jane, he assures her.

At noon, downstairs in the cafeteria that smells perpetually of lukewarm mashed potatoes, Jane lifts a spoon of chicken noodle soup to Mary's mouth and pleads with her to eat.

'I can't,' Mary says, as she stares off into nothing. 'I'm not ready for this to happen to your father. I'm not.'

Jane wants to beat the bowl of soup with the spoon until hot chicken broth splashes all over. 'Eat!' she wants to yell. Other families of the dying sit around them and they are eating. Why can't Jane's mother do the same? Looking at Mary's chapped lips, her dazed eyes, Jane is ashamed of the fact that she can hardly wait for tonight when Mary will stay at her father's bedside and Mr McGuire will drive Jane home. Now that Jane's father will die any day, Mary insists on spending every last moment with him and sometimes remains at the hospice until after midnight.

When Jane leaves her father's room later that afternoon, she finds Mr McGuire in the main room reading *People* magazine.

'I sometimes can't resist the trashy stuff,' he says, smiling and gesturing at his reading material.

'Mom's staying late again,' she tells him.

'Would she like me to come back for her?'

'She'll get a cab.'

'I'd be happy to come get her.'

          JOHN FULTON

'She'll be fine,' Jane insists, feeling the slightest bit jealous of his concern for her mother.

Once again, it's snowing and Mr McGuire drives skilfully, cautiously, having lived through years of Colorado winters. He pulls on to the icy road and passes two abandoned cars on the roadside, their hazards blinking. He invites Jane to eat with him at a restaurant. Bobbie has the bridge group over tonight.

'All ladies,' he says, smiling. And he can only imagine how quiet it must be for Jane at home alone.

But once they've seated themselves and the food has come, Jane cries. Her tears come all at once, without warning, and she's blowing her nose and wiping her tears with paper napkins like a child.

'I'm bothering you,' she says.

'Not at all.' He hands her more napkins.

Jane can't eat any of the soup she ordered and Mr McGuire seems to feel obliged to chat cheerfully about his daughter, Lizzie, who would love to hear from Jane, he assures her.

'Sure,' Jane says, though she would hardly know what to say to Lizzie, who loves her first year at Smith College and has a serious boyfriend named Buzz. Buzz is a classical harpist, a strict vegetarian and a cross-country runner. They plan to hike the Continental Divide Trail for two months this summer, Mr McGuire tells her. Jane can only smile and act happy for Lizzie.

More than a year ago, Jane and Lizzie applied to all the same schools together, but her father's disease became terminal and Jane decided to stay home. She had a boyfriend then too, Craig Nelson, who drove her around in his 1972 Oldsmobile: a huge brown cruiser that he called the Hog. In the Hog, he, Jane and Lizzie smoked pot for the first time, sipped *Southern Comfort* and gorged on *Ho Hos* and bags of *Chips Ahoy* in their drug-induced sugar low. Later, after Jane had gone on the pill, she'd lost her virginity in what was a slightly brutal backseat initiation, though she and Craig gained expertise. He kept poetry books in the glove box, along with a pair of pliers and a hammer. Once, after they'd had sex on a grey afternoon with the rain thumping against the Hog's top and streaking down the windows as they lay beneath sleeping bags in the backseat, he'd read her an E. E. Cummings poem about rain and little hands – the only details she can remember now – that seemed unimaginably beautiful to her at the time. Craig hasn't called in months, which is fine with Jane. When she learnt the news about her father, he didn't know what to say. 'Colon cancer,' she explained, feeling unexpectedly embarrassed now that she had said it out loud to someone her own age. It was so bodily, so private. She told him about what the doctor called an apple-core lesion: a tumour in her father's intestine that showed up on the x-ray like the jagged edges of a gnawed apple. Not good news. News that suggested his cancer might be inoperable. Craig just shook his head, looked awkward and boyish, and said something like, 'Jesus, Jane, that's terrible.'

'Tell Lizzie I apologise for not calling,' Jane says. 'I'm sort of out-of-it right now.'

'I think she understands,' Mr McGuire says.

Jane puts her spoon down and gives up on the soup. 'Maybe when he's dead,' she says. 'I'll go away to college.'

She can hardly believe the frustration and cruelty in her voice, though she can't stop now.

'I wish he'd just do it. I wish it were finally over and done. It would be better if they just gave him a shot and he'd sleep until it happened.' Then she looks up at Mr McGuire, who is nodding and listening to her every word.

'Do you think about it happening to Mrs McGuire?' she asks. 'Do you think about her dying?'

He looks down at his coffee. 'We do. Bobbie and I talk about it together. We talk about it with Lizzie too. We don't want it to catch us by surprise. We'd like to be ready.'

'I'm ready,' Jane says. 'I'm ready for it to happen.'

Mr McGuire nods at her calmly. And maybe it's to break through his calm, his sensitivity and understanding that she says, 'Do you ever feel hateful?' He gives her a confused look. 'I'm not a good caretaker. I treat my mother horribly. I don't know why. But you always seem so good, so perfect with Mrs McGuire. You're always helping her. You're always taking her places. You never seem to mind anything. I'd get angry. I *do* get angry.'

Mr McGuire takes his glasses off and rubs his eyes. 'I wouldn't call what you feel hateful,' he says.

Jane laughs. 'I'm the one who feels it. It is hateful.'

He shakes his head, as if he really does know better than her.

'I'd call it exhaustion, fatigue. And if it helps you to know, I do get tired. I love my wife, even though I sometimes dream about getting in my car and driving away, going somewhere for a long time. For a vacation. For a break.'

'Okay,' Jane says. 'Let's go somewhere. Let's get in the car right now and go wherever. For a break. For a vacation.'

He looks at her and smiles, and for a moment there seems to be something between them – a joy and recklessness that would make her suggestion possible. And then he shakes his head, puts his glasses back on and the moment is gone.

'I think we're both very tired,' he says.

After Mr McGuire walks Jane to her door and drives away, she already misses him and can hardly bear the quietness of her home. She takes three of her mother's sleeping pills – a safe dose without which, lately, she can hardly sleep – then walks through the dark house turning lights on – in the kitchen and hallways, in the bathrooms, even the one down the hall that she never uses – and hopes that this brightness will let her forget the winter outside, the hard black gleam of the windows around her, though it never does. As she falls asleep on the couch in the lighted living room, she thinks of something Mr McGuire did years ago at the Williamsons' Christmas party. Bald-headed Mr Williamson had been teasing Jane and Lizzie with a sprig of mistletoe. Christmas music was playing. Outside a light snow fell. Someone shrieked when Mrs McGuire fainted and tumbled out of her chair in the living room. Jane remembers vividly the sight of Mr McGuire, dressed in his khakis and a peach-coloured cardigan, sprinting through the kitchen and across the living room, hurdling a couch, shedding coins from his pants' pockets and losing a penny loafer on the carpet, to reach her. He moved with more speed and passion and physical force than Jane expected from any middle-aged man. And when he held his wife and saw her recovering in his arms, he said his wife's name with a rawness of feeling that startled Jane.

Jane wakes in the dark of early morning to find that her mother has come home and fallen asleep on the carpet next to the couch. Her white tennis shoes still on, she sleeps with an Afghan blanket pulled up to her chin and her hands tucked beneath her cheek for a pillow.

'Mom,' Jane says. When she doesn't move, Jane shakes her awake. 'You need to get in bed.'

Mary murmurs in her sleep and Jane does something she immediately regrets. She jabs her mother in the side with a fist. 'What?' Mary looks around in a near panic and Jane again urges her mother to get in bed. 'I'd rather not be alone right now,' Mary says.

But Jane would rather not sleep so near her mother. Jane drags herself from the couch, helps her mother up and walks her down the hall to her bedroom. Mary sits on the edge of the queen-sized bed while Jane kneels down and begins untying her tennis shoes.

A traditional man, strong, quiet and decisive, John, Jane's father, paid all the bills, balanced the accounts, managed all financial matters and finally – perhaps to spare Jane and Mary the task – arranged his funeral. He researched mortuaries, price-shopped, wrote out the cheques, chose a death notice, an urn. He knew he would be cremated even before he was diagnosed with cancer. Though he never said why, Jane could have easily guessed: cremation was cheaper, more economical and one way of avoiding the slow mess of decomposition. John hated messes.

Jane hardly knew what had to be done to die. But as the weeks and months passed and he became sicker, he made dozens of lists and put them beneath magnets on the refrigerator. While John had always been a list maker, he had never before used the refrigerator for his business. He had a large office in the house with two desks and filing cabinets where he kept all his papers in meticulous order. So when he began to post the lists in the kitchen – with items, such as 'finish taxes for the year', 'show Mary how to read social security statement', 'call man about life insurance collection', 'send cheque to Mr Katz at Morton Mortuary', 'change oil and rotate tyres on cars', 'fix hinges on downstairs closet', 'replace back porch screen', 'talk to contractor about roof' – Jane and Mary both knew he was putting on display for them the manner in which he would organise and manage his own death.

It was an errand, a task like others and, as he had been a project manager at a large company for the last twenty-five years, he knew how to get projects done, how to organise and finance them.

And he wasn't going to let anybody help him or tell him what to do. While Jane and her mother both wanted him to die at home, John hated the idea and refused to discuss it. He didn't want his wife and daughter to suffer through every stage, to hear his every last breath, his every last cry. 'I won't do that to my family,' he'd said. Jane's mother didn't understand it, but months later, as her father became sicker, Jane did. The words 'home' and 'death' didn't belong together. Once, Jane had gone into her father's bathroom to empty the garbage – a chore she'd done for years – and found fresh blood on the tiles and toilet seat. The water in the toilet bowl was a viscous red. She wanted to scream. But she knew that he bled when he used the bathroom and that he was sometimes too tired to clean up after himself. And so she wiped flecks of her father's blood from the enamel edges of the toilet bowl with handfuls of tissue, which she flushed down the toilet. She kept flushing – three, four, five times – even though the water was clear.

Jane and her mother have devised a system to ensure that they are at his side when it happens. They each carry cell phones to which only the hospice and the McGuires' have the number. Any time, any place, Jane and her mother can be called and told that he is dying.

On Saturday afternoon, Jane sits at his bedside keeping watch while her mother rushes home in a cab to shower and change her clothes; both tasks Jane had to urge Mary to do. It is late and, from the windows of her father's room, Jane can see the grey twilight bearing down on what has been a chalky, sunless day. She is trying to read *Jane Eyre* – a book college students should read – but its story and language invade Jane with the cold, colourless damp of England and its stony orphanages. Her father stirs in his bed and she secretly hopes that he does not wake, that she does not have to hear his struggle to breathe as he tries once again to talk to her. But his eyes are open and he is smiling.

'Hi, Daddy,' she says. 'How are you feeling?'

'Hi there,' he says, surprising her with the easy tone of his voice.

At times, the pain and grogginess lift and he seems almost cured, though this never lasts long.

'You don't have to be here,' he says. 'I wanted to tell you that. Have I told you yet?'

'Yes,' Jane says.

He has problems remembering now because of the drugs and the physical exhaustion, but he has already told her three or four times that she should not worry about being with him when it happens. It could happen quickly, after all, and he doesn't want her to feel bad if she isn't at his side. But, she would feel bad. She would feel terrible. She doesn't tell him this. She only says, 'I want to be here.'

'But if you're not, if you can't... ' He turns away then, his jaw muscles clenching and his body arching. She can hardly imagine the current of pain that could do this to the man she always saw as twice her size, the giant who took her hand as a little girl whenever they crossed the street. She pictures the tumours – black, offensive growths – that burrow in his intestines, that *involve*, as the doctors say, the nerves and send him into fits of agony that may soon cause a massive haemorrhage and kill him swiftly, though he may just as likely die slowly.

'Daddy,' she says. 'Why don't you use the button?'

At his side is, what they call in this terrible place, a self-delivery pain relief system. The device is brightly coloured, the brand name, *POLAMAR*, highlighted in yellow. He can press the blue button and receive a dose of drugs strong enough to knock him out. But he won't. He wants to stay awake and talk.

'There,' he whispers, relaxing now. 'I feel better.' His face shines with perspiration and his breathing is labored. 'What do you want to know?' he nonetheless asks her and Jane feels herself recoil. 'Ask me something.'

He has urged her to pry into his life for weeks now. He wants them to know each other better, though Jane wants to remember the quiet, strong father that John has been ever since she can remember – the man who was always so hard to know, who spent most of his time in his office, who made lists, who checked the oil in Jane's VW Jetta and took it in for an oil change whenever it needed one.

'Okay,' Jane says, preparing to ask what is, for once, a real question, a question that may go too far. 'You love Mom,' she

   JOHN FULTON

says and her father nods. 'But did you ever think about anyone else? Did you ever act on thoughts like that?'

He closes his eyes and, at first, Jane thinks pain might again overcome him. But then she sees that he is considering his answer. 'Once,' he says.

'Oh.' Jane is stunned. She thinks of her mother – not a contemporary woman, not a woman of her liberated era – who has taught first grade for years and has relied on her father too much, not least of all financially. She even hates to pay the bills, though she has taken them over in the last month. Jane can only imagine how terrified Mary must have felt at the thought of another woman.

'It happened before you,' her father tells her. 'Your mother forgave me. She took me back in. She was more than gracious.'

'I don't want to know the details,' Jane says.

'Okay. No details.'

'But Mom was better,' she continues. 'She was the best, wasn't she?'

Her father smiles. 'Of course. Didn't we get you out of it?'

He begins to laugh before the pain comes again. His face freezes into a grimace and Jane turns away while he struggles. After it passes, he wants to talk again. 'What else would you like to know?'

'Maybe that's enough for now,' she says. 'Why don't you press your button?'

'I think I might,' he says. Jane kisses his cheek – a brief goodnight kiss – and he turns over, presses his button and, within minutes, to Jane's relief, he falls asleep.

It's early morning when Jane hears, just beyond her deep sleep, the whir of the death phone, the cell phone that is only to be used in cases of emergency.

'Jane.' It's Mrs McGuire. 'Your mother just called us. It's time, they think. For your father. David's on his way over.'

I need to be there now, Jane thinks. But sleep pulls her down again – it has only been an hour since she took a few of her mother's sleeping pills – and she does not wake until Mr McGuire lets himself in the front door with a spare key.

Jane is sprawled out on the living room couch in only a t-shirt and underwear. Mr McGuire is careful to look away.

'We're going to have to hurry,' he says.

When they arrive, Jane is relieved to see Mary sitting beside her father and to see that he is still breathing. Jane sits and begins to wait. An hour passes and his heart is still beating. Two and then three hours go by and the grey of daylight begins to swell into dirty white clarity. 'Die,' she wants to say out loud. When a nurse escorts Mr McGuire's crippled wife – she sits bent over in her wheelchair – into the room and Mr McGuire goes to her, puts his hand on her shoulder, Jane feels that her space, *their* space, has been invaded. Why should she come now, at the end? Jane leaves the room, but is haunted by the thought that her father might expire in the few seconds of her absence and so she rushes back in. It's late afternoon before the doctor finally arrives, examines Jane's father and softly announces that he seems stable for now. He will probably not go any time soon. Not in the next few hours, in any case.

When Jane rushes out of the room, Mr McGuire follows her. She kicks the wall, leans into it with her forehead and clenches her eyes shut.

'Jane.' Mr McGuire's voice is gentle.

'Take me somewhere, please.'

The apprehension and caution she hears in his voice surprises her. 'Bobbie is here, Jane. I need to take her home first.'

'And then you will come back?' she asks.

'Yes.'

In less than an hour, Jane leaves her mother and meets Mr McGuire out in the hallway. He seems determined and – though the word is strange and old-fashioned to Jane – brave. 'What shall we do? Where shall we go?' he asks. He wants to make her feel better and knowing this is relief in itself. Fresh snowflakes melt over the black shoulders of his overcoat. Outside, a thick snow falls and Jane and Mr McGuire decide to walk in it. The cold air and the darkness surprise Jane. How many hours have passed since this morning? Only a few cars drive over the hushed, snow-covered roads and no-one else is out walking. Jane looks up into the falling white, a bright flurry in the glow of a street lamp, and breathes deeply.

They stop at a small café in a neighbourhood near the hospice that is strange and new to Jane, and Mr McGuire orders soup and a half-bottle of wine, from which he pours Jane a small glass. The waitress, a blond girl about Jane's age, believes – or so Jane imagines – that she and Mr McGuire are a couple. 'I'm only nineteen,' Jane whispers mischievously as she takes a sip of the wine and Mr McGuire smiles at her. They talk about the snow, how quiet and beautiful it makes things, how bright the darkness can become after a storm, how nice it is to walk in. For once, she has an appetite and her soup, the hot vegetables and pieces of potato, taste better than food has tasted in months.

'Why are you doing this?' Jane asks.

'Doing what?'

'Being so nice. You don't have to be here,' she says. 'So why are you here?'

'I'm your father's closest friend. Your father asked me to look after you. You're like a daughter to me.'

Jane feels her face fall. She has no right to feel rejected. 'Not because of me.'

'Of course because of you.'

'I'm too young to be interesting to you.'

'You're like my own daughter,' he says again. 'I can only imagine how Lizzie would suffer if she had to go through this.'

Jane reaches across the table, takes Mr McGuire's hand and touches it in a way that cannot be mistaken or confused for what it is not.

Mr McGuire takes his hand away and glances behind them, as if someone might be watching. 'Jane,' he says with reproach in his voice.

Jane shouldn't say it, but she's suddenly angry. 'Isn't it sometimes lonely with Mrs McGuire? Aren't there certain things that she can't do?'

He shakes his head.

'Aren't there?' she says again and he gives her a deeply disappointed look, as if to tell her how obviously and shamefully wrong she is. 'This is terrible,' she says. 'I'm terrible.'

'No, you're not terrible,' Mr McGuire says.

But they can't talk now. They walk back to the hospice in a silence that is not broken until Jane speaks again on the drive home. 'My father told me he had an affair once.' Mr McGuire nods. 'You know about it?'

'We've been friends since before high school,' Mr McGuire says. 'The young woman was—'

'I don't want to know the details,' Jane says.

'Everyone is allowed at least one mistake,' Mr McGuire says.

In the next instant, Jane does not at all like the stiff moralist who sits beside her making his pronouncements. She would not risk hurting anyone to have him.

'Maybe it wasn't a mistake. Maybe he loved her. Maybe he needed to do it,' Jane says.

Mr McGuire sighs. 'I understand him. I've made my mistakes too.'

'You made a mistake?' Jane feels relieved. She feels her dislike for him seep away.

He says nothing and is careful to keep his eyes on the road.

When they reach Jane's house, they sit in his car without talking. The snow has stopped falling, the moon is out and Jane can see the long, inky shadows of trees and street lamps spreading over the new snow. This time when she takes his hand, he doesn't let go, though he does say quickly, almost as if he's suddenly afraid, 'You'd better go in.'

'Is it bad if I try to forget about him, about everything?' she asks.

'I don't know,' Mr McGuire says. He looks at her now and then looks away, out his window, where the glass fogs up with his breath. He is struggling, she sees, trying to make a decision. 'I don't want... ' he starts to say and Jane hears an uncertainty, an honesty in his voice that startles her. 'I don't want you to pity me, Jane. I don't want you to think that I resent anyone. I know people think that I'm good to Bobbie, that I do everything for her, that I don't get anything back. I know they feel sorry for me.'

'That's not what I think,' Jane says.

'I want to be with my wife,' he says. And though his voice is stronger now, more solid, Jane can feel his hand trembling.

They remain silent for what feels like a long time. 'David.' She says his name for the first time, but it doesn't sound right. It lacks the sturdy formality she's always associated with him. Nonetheless, she embraces him now and he pulls back, flinches so that she feels like an aggressor in the moment that she kisses him. Jane wishes she did not have to do everything: to reach down and press the knob that moves the seat back, to pull her underwear down and off and to hike her long skirt up above

                    JOHN FULTON

her thighs. She kisses him and finally he relents and begins to kiss her back. They hold each other for a time, breathing, saying nothing, then begin again. But something isn't right. She wants to be propelled by desire rather than what feels now like determination as Mr McGuire sits stiffly beside her. When she sits on his lap, Mr McGuire raises his hands slightly above his head as if she were robbing him at gunpoint. When she reaches for his buckle, he pushes her aside and says, 'No, no.' It's over for now, Jane knows. But they have come this far and that's more than she expected. That's at least something.

Mr McGuire sits up, holding out a piece of her clothing to her. 'I'm sorry,' he says. Jane hears the shame in his voice and she won't take whatever he's holding out to her. Finally, he puts his hand down.

'You don't have to be sorry,' she says.

He shakes his head. 'You're a child. You're my daughter's friend.'

His voice is almost whiny. She always believed he was stronger than he seems now. 'I'm almost twenty years old. And I'm not Lizzie's friend. Lizzie is off doing whatever she wants. To hell with Lizzie.'

'It's my fault,' he says. 'Your father is dying and—'

'Don't say that!' Jane yells. 'Please shut up now.'

He's shaking his head and Jane can see that he regrets everything. 'I have to go. You'd better get dressed. You'd better get inside. I'm sorry.'

Jane just wishes he would stop apologising and what she calls him next seems true and just brutal enough. 'Coward,' she says.

He looks over at her in the dark car now. 'Out,' he says.

In that moment, she experiences a rush of anger that makes her arms and chest and face feel light, consumed, and she thinks she might hit him, hit him as hard as she possibly can. Instead, she steps into the cold with only her skirt and bra on. Her bare skin burns against the freezing air. She feels a sheet of ice through her thin socks and slips, almost tumbling over the concrete.

'For God's sake,' Mr McGuire yells from the open window of his car. 'Put your clothes on, Jane.'

Jane stands in a yellow circle of lamplight, tiny crystals of ice falling on her shoulders and in her hair. She hopes that the neighbours see her, that they see Mr McGuire as he stands out of the car now holding her shoes, her blouse and underwear out to her. 'Please, Jane. Please.' He's no longer yelling at her. He's begging, pleading with her. In the end, he places these items on the ground and pulls out of the driveway, his car revving, speeding down the street, fishtailing for a dangerous moment before it turns the corner and disappears.

After that night, Mr McGuire becomes even more polite and dutiful towards Jane and her mother. He arrives at Jane's front door one evening with bags of groceries to stock shelves that have been empty for days.

'Bobbie suggested it,' he says as he and Jane put the groceries away. 'She's always been good at thinking about the home front.' His careful mention of his wife relieves Jane and him. They do not need to discuss what happened between them and what will not, it seems, happen again.

It snows nearly every day and Mr McGuire shows up in the mornings and afternoons to clear the walks and driveway and lay down salt. Jane cannot help thinking that in some way a part of this man belongs to her now. Afterwards, he knocks at the door to ask Jane if she needs anything and she says no, despite her loneliness. He invites her to dinner with him and Mrs McGuire. 'We'd be happy to have you,' he says.

When she arrives, Mr McGuire is wearing an apron that says in large letters 'Grill Master'. He is always the cook, since Mrs McGuire's wheelchair renders her useless in the kitchen. But she sets the table – placing plates, flat wear and napkins in her lap to transport them to the dining room. Her hands are shaky and she is not shy about asking Jane to put the drinking glasses on the table for her. 'I break those half the time,' she admits, to which her own green plastic cup is testimony. In the kitchen, Mrs McGuire looks on, admiringly, lovingly, as Mr McGuire grills marinated chicken breasts. 'David's a great cook.' Mr McGuire smiles, glances at his wife and winks. But he won't meet Jane's eye, won't so much as look at her until they are at the table when, in the middle of a conversation about Lizzie and her decision to be a chemistry major, Mrs McGuire suffers a minor seizure. Her arms shake. Her fork and knife fall to the floor, along with her cup of water.

          JOHN FULTON

'She'll be fine soon,' Mr McGuire says, backing his wife's chair away from the table.

Jane has seen these seizures before and understands that they pass in minutes. She tries to look away from Mrs McGuire's stunned face, her warm, dark eyes that are trapped there. Mr McGuire is on his hands and knees mopping up the water with a cloth when Jane approaches and offers to help. 'I've got it,' he says.

'Let me do something,' she says.

She bends down, beginning to pat the carpet dry with her napkin, but this time he says with quiet fury, 'Don't you touch anything.'

Jane stands up and slowly backs away. Mrs McGuire is already recovering, asking quietly for David who puts his hand on her shoulder. 'I'm right here,' he says.

'Where's my napkin, sweetheart?' she asks and Mr McGuire reaches under the table for it and places it in her lap.

Later, when he parks in Jane's driveway, Mr McGuire apologises. He shakes his head, looks down, then across the street at the quiet houses there. 'I get frustrated sometimes. Just sometimes. I wish Bobbie were better. I wish she could stand up, walk across the kitchen, get her own damn glass of water. I wish... ' But he sounds angry now and he stops himself from saying more.

'I guess I should go,' Jane says. Outside the car, a dust of snow blows over the yards and streets.

'Jane,' he says. And before she can open her door, he takes her hand and holds on so tightly that it almost hurts. He's looking at her now and she can see something in his face – fear, desperation – that she doesn't want to be close to.

'I've got to go,' she says. And when he still doesn't let go, she wrenches her hand free.

That night, Jane sits down to type out requests for college applications. She planned to write colleges only after her father died, but she no longer knows when that will come and cannot bear to put off her future another minute. So she writes to the schools – Swarthmore, Yale, Bowdoin, Dartmouth, Cornell, Rutgers – all of them out East, all of them as far away from home as possible. Two days later, Mrs McGuire, who is with her mother at the hospice, calls to tell her that her father may die and once again Mr McGuire pulls into the driveway. Her hurry to get on with life, she tells herself, has nothing to do with the event that may happen in the coming hours. Nothing at all.

It takes only ten minutes after she enters his room for her father to die. A nurse quietly announces it. Jane's mother puts his hand beneath the blankets and, now that her father is merely a body, Jane wants to leave the room. First, she holds her mother, who cries openly and cannot stop – *will never stop*, Jane thinks – though she herself feels only relief when she should feel sadness.

For the last time, Mr McGuire drives both of them home from the hospice. Parked safely in Jane's driveway, he opens the car door for Jane and helps her walk her mother to the door, to her bedroom, where he leaves Jane to undress her and put her to bed. Jane sits beside her for an hour or more before Mary opens her eyes.

'I thought you might like to know something,' she says. Jane nods. 'I'm a mess right now. But I'm going to get better. I'm going to get back on my feet again. I won't need you forever. I promise.'

Jane feels her throat catch. Until now, she has had no idea that Mary ever sensed her fear, her anger. 'I don't mind,' Jane says.

'Of course you mind,' Mary says, smiling through her tears. 'You're nineteen. You want to be off doing other things. You deserve to be off doing other things. You don't have to sit here now. I'm fine on my own. I might try to sleep.' Mary turns away from her and pulls the covers closer.

Mr McGuire is at the kitchen table when Jane comes out of her mother's room. 'Bobbie suggested that I stay for a while... just to make sure.'

'I don't want... ' Jane begins to say, but cannot finish her simple, cruel thought: *I don't want you.*

Fortunately, Mr McGuire doesn't need to hear it. 'I know,' he says. He looks at her and smiles reassuringly and, in that moment, he becomes safe and fatherly again.

Jane sits down and, because she has to tell someone, she says, 'I don't feel sad, not as sad as I should feel. I'm mostly just relieved.'

'You'll feel sad later,' he assures her.

     JOHN FULTON

Jane looks at Mr McGuire now and notices that his hair is uncombed. He is unshaven and is not wearing a tie, as he almost always does. Deep purple rings his eyes. Jane sees his exhaustion and can imagine how much he has suffered as a result of her. He has feared that everything – his wife, his reputation, the love of his daughter, the trust of his neighbours – might crumble at his feet. He has spent, Jane imagines, hours alone, terrified, sleepless. He has hated himself. He has perhaps even hated his wife. He has hated Jane as much, more even, than he has desired her.

'I'm sorry,' Jane says. 'I'm sorry for everything.'

He doesn't say, as she half wishes he would, that she shouldn't apologise, that nothing is her fault. He nods. He says, 'Me too.'

And then she asks him the question she has wanted to ask for a long time. 'If you did drive away from Mrs McGuire and everything, like you said you sometimes dream of, where would you go?'

Mr McGuire removes his glasses and takes a long time to think. He takes out a handkerchief and wipes his eyes because he is crying now. Very gently, without any mess.

'I try not to dream about that anymore,' he says. 'And if I do, I never get far before I worry sick about Bobbie in her bed alone. I want to know that she's safe.'

Jane nods and for a moment she thinks of Mr McGuire again at the Christmas party hurdling the couch in the living room to rescue his fallen wife, coins spilling from his pocket. She feels again what she felt then: amazed that he could run like that, that any of the middle-aged men at that party, sipping drinks and conversing about work, about football, about stocks and bonds and whatever else, could run like that, could hold their wives as he did, could care so fiercely about anyone. Looking at Mr McGuire's face now, seemingly raw and naked without his glasses, Jane feels it just as he promised her she would. It falls on her – it crushes her all at once from the inside – the grief, the excruciating knowledge that her father is gone.

Dirk Strasser

What year is it? His mind shunted onto the default question. *What year is it?* He shook his head – or least fired the nerve impulses which would have, under normal circumstances, resulted in him shaking his head. *I don't know. I don't know what year it is. That's a bad sign.*

He tried opening his eyes, but only managed to let in a tiny sliver of light.

How come I'm not trying to remember what my name is? That's more important, isn't it? Okay, what's my name? Yet it was as if his mind was negotiating a frictionless surface and he slid back to the first question again: What year is it? He had no choice but to give in to it and churn away at the question, trying to force the answer into his consciousness. *If I can work out the year, the rest will follow.*

Suddenly something sparked in his brain and images and understanding flooded in. *Ah, it worked.* The nano-trojan he had implanted had been activated just as he had planned, triggered by the impulse question about the year he had also implanted.

So, the bastards had brain-wiped him! Well, he had outsmarted them. Making a cache of his memories and concealing the trojan in his own brain, ready to be triggered by his memory loss – that was a master stroke. But how did they manage to get him? The trojan was a last resort. He was always so careful. *Ah,* Serge could feel the memory repopulating his neurons...

Serge felt the sensation of wind on his face as he led Danton through the crumbling skyscrapers and neo-gothic buildings that guarded the barren asphalt streets of the Old Town. What had struck him like a biting gust of pain the first time he had felt it now seemed to have morphed into a half-pleasant caress.

'That's what they call cold,' said Serge. 'We don't really get to feel it anymore.'

Serge stared straight ahead. He had been in this crumbling urban pocket many times before and, now that he had decided to trust someone and spill the beans to his friend, he was fired with a determined sense of purpose.

Skirting around a pile of rubble, they entered a wide street interspersed by a tangled forest of trees, some of which lined the sides like a parody of a boulevard, while others broke through the decaying asphalt.

'Just be patient, Dan, okay?' said Serge, wearing his poker face.

'Something's up, buddy. You don't like my company this much. I'm just not that funny.'

'True, in fact you're not funny at all, but I *do* want to show you something.'

A sharp gust swirled a pile of leaves into the air in front of them. 'I don't know why you want our babbles switched off,' said Danton. 'Mine has a pretty good tracker function.'

Serge motioned for Danton to follow him through the archway of one of the neo-gothic buildings. The vaulted ceiling inside was crowned by a large circular gap that let in the weak rays of sunlight from the open sky.

'They used to have an interesting idea about aircon, didn't they?' said Danton, staring at the billowing clouds.

'This way.' Serge's voice was the same as when he was raising in poker.

He led Danton through to a back room and onto a flight of stairs.

'You look like you're out of puff, Dan,' said Serge, stopping after climbing three flights.

Danton sucked several gulps of air deep into his lungs and put his hand on his friend's shoulder, the way he often did. 'You're ... not ... wrong.'

'While you're catching your breath, can we try something?'

'Okay, then, let's get this mystery out in the open.'

'When did John Howard die?'

Danton's breathing started to ease. 'Who?'

'He became Australian prime minister, in the latter part of last century.'

   DIRK STRASSER

'Sorry, but I'm not up on my Australian presidents. I know the important ones, but the rest are a bit of a blur.'

'*Prime ministers.* They were called prime ministers then.'

'Whatever. Anyway, I can just look it up – what's your point?'

'Well, look it up.'

He took his babble out of his pocket and switched it on. '*Hey, Danny boyo, what can I do you for today?*' said the cheerful voice that Danton had customised to sound like Ches Wilford, one of the nova-hot comics on the circuit.

'When did John Howard die?'

'*There's a lotta Johnny Howards, Danny boyo. You'll have to give me more than that.*'

'I want the one who was presi ... er ... prime minister of Australia.'

'*Boy, what happened to who won the Brownlow in 2068? Or what's the record number of cans downed on a Mars voyage by a national cricket team? You're getting a bit cerebral in your old age, aren't you? Do you want me to define cerebral for you?*'

'No, smart-arse. Just give me the answer or I'll switch your personality back to default.'

'*Okay, okay. No need for the insults. I may just be a piece of nano-technology, but I got feelings too, you know – well ... digitised equivalents of feelings anyway. Right, John Howard, prime minister of Australia died on ... mmm ... sorry, Danny boyo, someone's giving you a bum steer. There was no Australian prime minister by that name.*'

Danton frowned. 'Hey, Serge, are you sure they weren't called presidents then?'

'Try it,' said Serge, his face expressionless.

'Right,' said Danton to his babble. 'Let's see if he was a president.'

'*Nuh, sorry Danny boy. They were still called prime ministers late last century. You musta got the name wrong.*'

Danton looked up at Serge. 'I don't think—'

Serge interrupted him. 'John Winston Howard. Try that. He was Australian prime minister at the same time as George W. Bush was president of the US and Tony Blair was prime minister of Britain.'

'I've at least heard of the other two. I just don't see—'

'Try it.'

'Okay, Serge.' He bent his head slightly towards his babble. 'Try John Winston Howard.'

'There's a few of those, Danny, but none had any prominence in any significant area. Definitely no prime ministers or presidents or world leaders of any kind by that name.'

Danton glanced up at Serge again. 'It looks like you're wrong.'

Serge raised his eyebrows. 'Am I?' He nodded his head in the direction of Danton's babble. 'Can you switch it off?'

Danton opened his mouth for a moment, but then simply followed the instruction.

'What's going on, Serge? *Why* are we here?'

Serge's voice took on a deeper tone. 'This is bigger than Ben Hur, Dan.'

'Bigger than who?'

'See, you have no idea who Ben Hur was or that I was referring to a twentieth-century film.'

'Why do I have to? I could just look it—'

'Yes, I know. You could just look it up on your babble. That's the whole point: Why does anyone need to *know* anything anymore? All the facts are at our fingertips.'

'Yeah,' said Danton. 'It's great, isn't it?'

'Dan, it's not so great. Listen to what I'm about to tell you and then see if you still think it's so great.'

'Shoot.'

Serge took a deep breath. 'John Winston Howard was definitely prime minister of Australia, but every database and digital record in the universe now says he never existed.'

'What?'

'I said just listen, Dan.' Danton nodded. 'Do you know how I know he existed? I know because I'm the one who erased him from every database and digital record in the universe.'

'You're nuts, Serge. I know you're a clever bastard, but you're also nuts.'

'It's really nothing but an almighty global search and replace algorithm. I've been working on it for years, but looking back, now that I've done it, the principle is really quite simple. It's just a self-replicating virus.'

'I don't believe it. You're having a lend of me, aren't you?'

'No, Dan.' He glanced at his watch. 'Just do as I say. Switch

   DIRK STRASSER

on your babble and ask the same question about John Howard again.'

Danton grimaced, but did as Serge said.

Ches Wilford's unrelentingly upbeat voice came back at him. *'John Winston Howard is his full name, Danny me boyo. He had quite a long spell as prime minister of Australia. He died on 3 July 2023. Anything else you wanna know?'*

Danton switched off his babble and ran his fingers through his hair before looking up at Serge who was studying him.

'What's going on, Serge?' he asked.

'It's a bit like finding out the Earth moves around the Sun, when all your life you could have sworn the Sun moves around the Earth, isn't it?'

'No, it's a bit like finding out your best mate is having it off with your missus.'

'You were always better at analogies than me, Dan.'

'So, what gives here?'

Serge seemed to relax, as if he had just let go of a giant weight. 'Like I said, I made the change. I erased all references to John Howard from the universal digital system and I had set a timer to ensure he was reinstated just before I got you to ask the question again.'

'So, the record was gone? From everywhere?'

'Yes, there was absolutely no evidence that John Howard was ever prime minister of Australia.'

'So I could have searched for his name anywhere and gotten a big, fat zero?'

'Yes.'

'Why?'

'I picked an obscure Australian prime minister because I thought that no-one would notice if he was off the records for a short time.'

'But, why do it at all?'

'I wanted to prove it could be done.'

'You're even more nuts than I thought you were. It sounds to me like a pretty dangerous joke.'

'It's dangerous, but it's no joke, Dan. Do you see me laughing?' His lips were thin and straight and he wasn't smiling. 'Don't you see the point of it? Do you really think I'm the only person in the world who can work out how to do it? I know my way around ether programming, but there would be at least one person in any large organisation who would have the expertise and creativity to do what I've done.'

'That's a scary thought.'

'What's scarier, is that others have probably already done it. How would I know I was the first?'

'But, it would be all over the e-casts. The journos would be onto it as quick as a laser.'

'Would they? How could anyone know something had been changed if *every* record showed exactly the same thing?'

'They... they would remember it differently... '

'Memories for facts aren't what they used to be, Dan.' He nodded in the direction of Danton's sleeping babble. 'Those things make your mind lazy. You don't need to recall names, places and facts if you carry an infallible, all-encompassing memory with you all the time.'

'But I know what I had to eat this morning, Serge. That's a fact, isn't it?'

'The things *you* remember aren't what's important. No-one cares about your disgusting eating habits. It's the other stuff. It's easy to change the record of something so far in the past that it's out of living memory. But it works for more recent things too. People don't trust their memories of events. Hell, memory is unreliable anyway. That's why we record things in the first place.'

'So you reckon others have been changing history?'

Serge nodded. 'Anyone who needs to spin anything. Corporations. The government. They wouldn't be able to resist. How many people does that include?'

'But... but... '

'Yeah, Dan, you may as well say but, but. We can't trust anything we haven't directly experienced – and even that stuff needs a pretty powerful memory and more than a touch of arrogance for you to believe something when every record tells you something else.'

'Are you arrogant enough, Serge?'

'I don't need to be.'

Serge gestured for Danton to follow him through a doorway into a large room barely lit by pale sunlight slanting through the gaps in the boarded windows.

     DIRK STRASSER

'Do you know what this building used to be called?'

Danton strained as his eyes adjusted to the low light. 'Come on, Serge. I think you can guess historical buildings are not my strong point.'

'It's called a library.'

'A what?'

'A library – and don't bother looking it up on your babble. It won't be there.'

'Okay, then I give up. What's a li-bary?'

'It's pronounced *library*, Dan, and it's a place that houses a collection of books.'

Danton watched Serge move towards a shelf. 'You're not helping me here, Serge. So, what are books?'

Serge picked something from the shelf and handed it to Danton. 'This is a book. See, it's made of paper, which is a bit like plastic, and it's fastened on one side.'

'Mmm... a collection of plastic – nice.'

'It's what's in it that's important. This is a special type of book called an encyclopaedia, sort of an ancient Wikipedia. This particular one is for words beginning with the letter 'H'. You can look up John Howard, if you want to.'

'You're a bit fixated with this guy, aren't you?'

Serge flicked through the pages until he came to the small John Howard entry and then handed the book to his friend. 'See, it's captured on the page.'

Danton stared at it. 'I see what you're saying. This is proof, isn't it? Proof.'

'Damn right, it's proof, Dan. The 'B' volume is here too, and you can look up the word 'book'. That's something else you won't find referenced anywhere on your babble.'

'You've uncovered something awesome here, Serge. How many of these books are here?'

'Hundreds, including a full set of encyclopaedias, history books, dictionaries. Do you see, we can now prove everything. We can fight the spinners.'

'And you've been reading these?'

'Yes, I've started crosschecking against the digital records. That's what I do when I come to the Old Town, but there's so much. I can't do it on my own. I had to tell someone. I'm bursting with all this inside my head.'

'Geez, Serge, I'm... glad you decided to share it with me.' Danton put the book back on the shelf. He was breathing slowly and deliberately, as if every intake of air was a conscious decision.

Serge felt Danton put his hand on Serge's shoulder in his familiar way.

'I know... this is a big ask, Dan. A huge ask. But hopefully with the two of us... '

'Yeah, the two of us,' said Danton, his breathing even more controlled.

Serge felt a sudden jab of pain in his neck and immediately felt a growing weakness in his limbs. 'What the hell?'

'Sorry, Serge. I'm just doing my job. It may be a bit crappy, but someone's gotta do it.'

Serge slowly slumped to the floor as he stared at Danton holding a hypo in his hand.

'Don't look at me like that, Serge. You're going to make me feel bad. You'll be good as gold again tomorrow. I didn't want to have to fight you. It's better this way.'

'What's better?'

'We've been monitoring you for years, Serge. Even from before the two of us met. Stop bloody looking at me like that! I reckon you're a good guy – this isn't personal. We knew you were getting close to the algorithm on how to change the records. We just weren't sure about what you were doing in the Old Town. And it looks like you've done better than any of the others who cracked it. You worked out how to make the global changes *and* you discovered these books here. You should be proud of that.'

Serge moved his fingers slightly, but they froze in position. 'You're one of them, aren't you? You're one of the ... spinners?'

'I'm afraid so, Serge. The world spins.'

'You lying bastard!'

'Come on, I've been a good mate to you. We've had some fun times.'

'You shit!'

'Don't worry, it'll be all back to normal again tomorrow. You'll feel fine after we do a bit of brain-wiping. Poker as usual at your place on Friday? I'm going to have to keep hanging around because you may rediscover the algorithm again some time. I'll still be your mate.'

 DIRK STRASSER

'You're no mate of mine.'

'Come on, Serge, see it from my point of view. Don't be so selfish. I'm going to have to carry you down those stairs now. You're not exactly at your fighting weight, are you?'

Serge's chin slumped to his chest. 'What about the truth?'

'You know the problem with these paper books? They burn pretty easily. If you like, I'll let you watch.'

Danton put his hand on Serge's shoulder again, but there was no sensation.

The memory seemed to stutter. *Was there something wrong with the trojan? Had he made some error in the code?* Serge tried to open his eyes and managed to let through some more light, but nothing came into focus. *No, I couldn't have made an error. That must have been how they got me. I just lost consciousness, and they took me to be brain-wiped. And yet ... something is nagging at me.* The memory re-formed...

Danton put his hand on Serge's shoulder again. This time Serge grabbed it suddenly and wrenched it behind his back so violently that he heard something snap.

'Shit!' yelled Danton, just before Serge crunched his face into the library floor.

Serge pulled out his own hypo and jabbed it into Danton's neck. He released his grip, saying, 'And I know you're not smart enough to have taken an antidote as a precaution.'

'So you had me pegged, Serge.' Danton tried to get up, but couldn't.

Serge shook his head. 'I'm not sure if I did. I had a niggling doubt about you, but you were so convincing. So bloody convincing. You were a mate all these years. I just didn't want to believe you were one of the spinners. I felt guilty for even thinking it. It was tearing at me. I had to finally prove it one way or the other – that's why I brought you here.'

'It looks like you're even smarter than we thought you were.'

'You know what, Dan? I can see you're so cut up about it; I'm going to show you what made me start to doubt you. Maybe I'll leave the shitty feeling in your head after I brain-wipe you.'

Serge started searching along one of the other library shelves.

'*You're* going to brain-wipe *me*?'

'You bet, Danny bloody boy. You think I can work out how to wipe history, but not your sorry little brain? And before I do, I'm going to download every stinking spinner name and detail from it.'

Serge grabbed a small book. 'Do you know what this is? It's a novel called *1984*. It used to be famous. When I've finished my work, it's going to be famous again.'

'Come on, Serge, buddy. Give me an antidote. I can't move here.'

'You're kidding, aren't you? I know you don't care about this little book here, but I'm going to tell you anyway. The guy in this book, Winston – yeah, as in John Howard's name – they get him in the end. Like you were trying to get me. He gets betrayed by someone he trusted. Get it?'

Danton's eyelids started to close.

'And you know what's funny? This *1984* book here – it's only fiction. It's made-up words on paper. *It's not true.* And look what it's done! This book is what gave me the niggling doubt about you. And now ... and now it's going to rescue the truth, mate.'

Danton's head slumped to the floor.

So how did they get me? Serge thought, as the memory stuttered again. *I'm lying here with a brain-wipe triggering the trojan, so there's no doubt the spinners still managed to get me, even though I turned the tables on Dan. But how?* His thoughts layered into complex folds. *I know the year. It's 2084. I know my ... wait ... do I know my name?* A cold wind gusted through to his nerve endings and he opened his eyes wide.

To his horror, he saw Serge's face staring at him, smiling grimly.

But I'm Serge...

'Have you worked out what happened yet, Dan?' asked Serge.

Danton ... I'm Danton?

'I was simply going to brain-wipe you, you know, Dan, so you wouldn't remember what happened in the Old Town.' Serge came closer to the bed where Danton was lying, still paralysed from the neck down. 'But I didn't think that was enough,

     DIRK STRASSER

somehow. You would still be the same lying shit. You needed to know what it was like to be betrayed by a friend. And the best way I could do it was to show you what it felt like from my point of view. I let you see my memory as your own, you bastard. Did you like seeing yourself?'

Danton trembled. 'I'm sorry, I—'

'Don't say it, Dan. I don't want hear any apologies. After what I've just done to your head, they don't mean anything. You did what you did and nothing else matters now.'

'Please, Serge. Let me make it up to you. I can help you bring down the spinners. We can do it together.'

'You know, I really wanted your help. I wanted to trust you.' Serge showed Danton the hypo in his hand. 'I just can't risk the trust a second time.'

Danton had regained just enough sensation to feel the jab in his neck.

     THE WORLD TO COME

THE WHALE GOD

Jeanette Zissell

Cherry Tree:
The cherry tree is dead. I thought it was before, but today I am certain.

It never grew any cherries and the flowers have fallen away. They fell like snow as the ash came down from the sky. Now they're mixed in with the layers of that dust, scattered all over the ground.

The petals are buried in dust, out on the great hill where the cherry tree has died.

The flowers have gone. Today I dug through the layers of dust and ash and the other powdery things that fall from above, and I could still find some rotting leftover flowers. They smell sickly-sweet, like cough drops stuck to the bottom of a handbag I found in the closet. A heavy smell – a not-right smell – like the one that comes out of the barn where the cows all died.

Most things died when the Whale God filled the sky. He came with a great corona of light that illuminated his great shadow. The deep rumbling whale-cry of his voice filled the air and echoed out over the cow field. That was a long time ago. I don't know how long ago. It was when there were still flowers on the cherry tree.

When it happened, I ran out onto the grass, past my tyre swing under the old oak tree. Everyone else fell down. But I wanted to see. The great shadow came over the ground – over my face. The Whale God moved slowly through the great ocean of the sky. The earth trembled and the air grew cool. The ash began to fall.

Now it falls every day. Every day, I try to be good. I sweep the front step so the dust goes away. But the next morning, there's six more inches drifted up all over in piles, like snow.

But it's not really snow. It's too light for sledding. It's something like the cobwebs and dust that gather into little balls under bedposts and behind dressers. It floats like dandelion seeds when the wind kicks up.

I ripped the lacy silk off the hem of an old nightgown and I tie that around my face when I go outside. It's smooth over my skin and it's pretty. It helps me breathe so I can go outside and play on my swing. I tie it in a bow in back and I twirl around on my tyre swing. The long, silk ends make circles as I go.

I suppose I shouldn't go outside so much. But it's so dark. I can't see well from inside. I have to draw the chairs towards the windows.

The dust fills the sky and the sun comes through old and orange.

He's a tired sun. He wants to rest, I think. I think he sings to us, like a lullaby:

> *Go to sleep, little ones.*
> *Sink into the ocean.*
> *Sink deep and sleep under the shadow of our father.*

Not-Person:

I like to have tea parties under the cherry tree. The problem I continue to have is that no-one will come to join me.

The last person I saw was the Whale God when he came. I think he is a person, but he is a very big person. He is so big, he couldn't notice little me. He has no hands to hold teacups.

And there was one other person. But I don't think *he* was a person. Not really. He was something else.

I saw him once when I was spinning around on my swing. I heard him coming because he was laughing so hard. It sounded strange. It was high-pitched, like a cartoon voice. It was thin – flat. The dust everywhere must have made it sound like that. The cartoon-voice man – the not-person – came running out from behind the barn, laughing.

He was wearing a very nice business suit. He had no hair and he was very white, and he was carrying a fire poker out in front of him in both hands. He thought his fire poker was very funny, and he screamed and screamed at it with his cartoon laugh.

I planted my feet on the ground right away, to stop the swing. The dust kicked up around my green wellies, floating everywhere. It tickled my legs. I held my breath. I didn't want him to see me. The whole effect of him coming out like that, you see, was very unsettling.

It's always so dark now that I thought he might not see me. I thought I would disappear right into the dust if I stayed very still. He ran out in front of me. Then I was certain he'd see. I didn't know for sure what would happen if he did. But really, I felt like just being seen by him would be the worst thing that *could* happen.

He ran by and the dust swirled around him as he went. I felt it brush my cheek.

I got a very good look at him. He wasn't a person. His suit had pinstripes – but he didn't have any ears. So he couldn't hear me, and he was too consumed with running and laughing and his fire poker to care what I did.

He ran away and I never saw him again.

Considering him, mostly I don't mind that no-one comes.

Tea Party:

So I need to have my tea parties alone. The only guests I entertain are the books from the big bookshelf in the great room. I wasn't allowed to go in there much, before. But now, I have to look after the house. I need to keep things nice. Keep the dust out. Keep watch for screaming men. So I think it's alright if I go in there and choose a book with a pretty, old binding every day – just like it's alright to wear the pretty dresses from the old steamer trunk. I'm the lady of the house and I need to be dressed to receive, should the opportunity arise.

Lately, it's been too dark to read inside. So I set up my tea things out on the great hill, by the cherry tree. It takes a great deal of preparation to see to the party just right.

To begin, I take out Grandma's tea set and I hold it up to the picture window. A warm, orange glow sifts through the curtains at midday. I pull the curtain back and I look at the cups, at the pretty roses and songbirds and bluebells painted on them. I look at how the orange light makes them glow, because they're so thin the light moves through them.

Is it called bone china because it's made from bones?

I look at the shadow child on the window glass, holding a cup and staring back at me. She won't come out to play because she only lives in windows and pools of water.

Then I put the set away. There's no tea at this party. I can't easily take tea out there, in the dust-fall. Besides, when the Whale God came, all the mechanical things died altogether. Not a single one of them works. All our tea has gone cold.

And flames don't light. Not with Granddaddy's lighter, not with matches, not even with tinder and sticks rubbed together. An ember or two will spark and glow, and then they disappear in a tiny, little sigh of smoke.

The sparks are pulled down in the undertow of the Whale God. They are quenched in the depths of his sea.

So I carefully put away the tea set, cup by cup, in the china cabinet. I lock the doors with their pretty brass key. There's a bright blue ribbon tied to it. I hang the key on the hook on the wall. Then I go into the great room.

I squint and squint to read the titles, if I'm able. I've gotten quite good at reading. And I hope one of the books will tell me about the Whale God and his distant ocean. But so far, they haven't.

I'm not worried. The books are amiable friends and I will keep their friendship for as long as the light holds out and I can see to read them.

At last, I take my book and I get out my green wellies. It's cool and dry outside, but I don't like the feeling of the dust working its way between my toes. I tie my pretty silk strip around my face. I wear netted gloves and I take Grandma's parasol. I walk under its canopy of ivory lace. The light flows through it as best it can and it keeps the dust away.

I take the little, red stool from the kitchen. I walk with it under one arm and the book in another. I climb the great hill.

I need to be careful to pick the best spot – the brightest spot where I will be able to see. If there are pictures in the book I want to see the colours, if I can. It's getting hard to do that unless it's noon precisely. It's getting so dark.

Day after day, it's getting darker.

I put down my stool and sit on it. I open the parasol. I wipe away the dust from the cover.

I sit on the hill by the tree and shield the pages from the fall of ash. I try to read slowly, in case I run out of words. And then I wouldn't have any friends left.

　　　　JEANETTE ZISSELL

Friend:

I have made many book-friends on the great hill.

Today I read about Jane Eyre's Lowood school. She made friends with Helen Burns because Helen was reading a book. I can imagine her walking up to me and asking me what book I was reading, like she did with Helen.

And then I could say, 'Why Jane, my dear Jane, I'm reading all about you! Won't you sit down and look on with me?' And we'd be best friends and she would be able to read to me on the hill and share my party.

House:

Things are changing.

I've finished my time with Jane Eyre and her story is over. She's resting, now, on my bookshelf, the bookmark ribbon spilling out from the closed pages. Her spine is covered in a heavy shadow.

The house is getting very dark.

A tree branch fell in the wind yesterday and it cracked a big glass window in one of the upper bedrooms. I had to shut up the whole top level of the house. It was raining dust everywhere, clouding up like smoke and getting in everything.

I didn't mind too much. Even before I finished with Jane, I was afraid of the attic – and that's only just above the upper bedrooms.

I'm glad Jane's so happy with her one-armed man, but I'm sad she's left me. Her story made me think there might be something up there – and now she's gone and left me, to be happy somewhere else.

She'd protect me, here – she'd know what to do.

She should have never grown up.

There might be not-people up there – like the one from the barn – rolling around and gnawing on the walls. I can hear them at night, I think, gnawing away.

Sometimes I worry they'll gnaw the house down and I'll have nowhere to go. I prefer to sleep in my great book room now. I took my favourites and built a wall of them and I sleep inside, hiding in the shadows there. I'll eat my canned preserves in the evening, sticky-sweet, and then I'll clean up carefully and cuddle into the shadows in my corner.

I've been going out every morning with my tea-books, but recently it's getting rather dark and I'm worried about how much longer I'll be able to see.

Dream:
Last night, I dreamt of the Whale God. Of his distant cries. I woke and the sound seemed to linger and echo through the dark room. And then away, away – it faded away.

And I still remember my dream. I was on a school outing in the time before, at a big steel-and-glass science museum in the far-off city. We were stiff from hours and hours on a rumbling bus. The teacher in the red dress and primly-heeled shoes walked across the floor towards us. Her heels made a pleasant, crisp rappity-rap on the granite floor of the vestibule.

She made us all hold hands in a line as we entered the great room of the museum. Above was a skylight, shot through with metal trusses like a spider web.

Hanging from them was a giant whale.

It was fibreglass, or some sort of plastic, and it took up the entire room, four storeys high above our heads. The bright light poured out around it and its shadow drifted over our faces.

I could imagine it moving through the sea, a dark silhouette, impossibly large. It would move silently through the water. It would create no waves. Only its whale-cry would echo out from its movement.

It would sail over the little creatures below it, deep below in the dark of the deep water. The small things would squint up at it and be overwhelmed by its vastness. So accustomed were they to the murk of the bottom. It overshadowed them and their smallness.

And standing on the museum floor, in the dream, I wondered: _What might lie above the great whale? Is there a big glass skylight somewhere and we're all in the cool, quiet shadows of the museum?_

Catch the Purple:
It's time to go away. I can barely see to write on the paper and

     JEANETTE ZISSELL

the dust-fall has come on thick and heavy. It's covering the paper and blurring my ink.

All on one side of the sky, the horizon is black. The other side is purple, the colour of a bruise. I've made a mistake – I've waited here too long.

I need to chase the purple and hope it's not too late. I've waited so long. It's so hard to leave home.

So I've packed a bag with my special books – my very favourites. I've shut up the house. I don't want to go back in. The attic is getting so loud I can't sleep anymore. Even though I've blocked up the staircase, I'm afraid that things will chew through and spill out at any moment.

I hate to leave my friends behind. I've put a tablecloth over the remains of my book pile in the corner. I hope it hides them well enough. It'll keep the dust away when it reaches the great room, at last.

Still, I don't want to think of them sitting there. Silent – waiting. Vulnerable.

And I have to go into the barn today.

I have to go where the smell was. I have to pass through the dark hole – the great, big, half-open door.

I need to go into the barn to get my bicycle. I can't hope to catch the purple, to chase the light beyond the grazing pastures, if I can't move faster than my feet can carry me.

If I don't catch the purple, I am afraid I'll never be able to read again.

I need the bicycle. The red bicycle leaning on the wall where I left it before the Whale God came.

I need what's inside the barn.

As soon as I'm done writing, I'll shut my book up and slip it in my coat pocket. I'll button the flap to make sure it won't fall out.

The bicycle is in the barn where the cows were, once. It's in the barn with the too-sweet, not-right smell. It's behind that big mouth of a door that gapes at me as I sit here on my swing, spinning back and forth.

It wants me to go in. It wants me to pass through.

The not-person sprung out from behind the barn. But I need to go in the barn.

If I go in there, then I can ride away. I can get away and chase the final ripples of movement of the Whale God.

I need my friends with me. I'll hold Jane in my hand and we'll go in together. We'll grab the bicycle fast and run.

I hope it's still light enough in the yard so I'll be able to tell which way is out.

PROGRESS

John G. Shulman

Martin reflected that this barren landscape was where man himself had first emerged. It was no Garden of Eden. From his vantage point on a scrubby hilltop, Martin gazed across the Kalahari Desert. *How ironic,* he thought, *that now the fate of the species rested in so few hands.* He glanced down at his own hands. Capable, strong, well-trained. How could he have known twenty years ago, when he had undergone his training as a Navy Seal, that so much would rest on his capabilities. It was one thing to slip into a village at night and deliver impromptu justice; it was another altogether to save all of humankind. *If anyone had to be chosen,* he supposed, *why not him?*

Martin glimpsed a sudden movement on the landscape. His right hand reached instinctively for his knife. His left hand shaded his eyes against the sun sinking on the western horizon. It was a ball of fire unlike any Martin had ever seen at home in the US, but one he had seen every damn night in hell. That would be in war, wherever it was, always in some godforsaken place that a politician told the public was crucial to the national interest. Of course, that place changed over the decades, but in a sense, it was always the same.

Martin refocused on the desert landscape below him. He looked for movement. He glanced at the sky. The damned vultures continued to circle. He shaded his eyes and scanned the desert. Then he saw the movement again. It was a springbok, a young buck by the look of it. For some strange reason, an image of Martha flashed before Martin. He blinked. He saw her smile, her teeth, her breasts. He shook his head. That was a past life. He would never see his wife again. She was gone. They were all gone.

*

Gita smoothed the reflective foil cover of her solar power charger. She had made the charger herself from the only materials she could scavenge. At least the desert provided an ideal power source: unimpeded access to the sun. She looked at her bare arm. The sun blazing on her arm reminded her of her childhood in a village near Madras. That seemed so long ago now. She had left before Madras became Chennai. And now it was nothing but a pile of cinders. She tried not to think of that. She thought instead about her colleagues.

Who would pair with whom? She had done the math. Based on the matrilineal DNA evidence, a mere six people had crossed an ice bridge from Asia into what was now (or until a week ago) known as Alaska. Those six individuals had mated among themselves and populated the Americas before the Europeans arrived and wiped out millions of the descendants of those original six pioneers. Despite the desert heat, Gita shivered at the thought. How eerie the parallel! Again, the technologically advanced, morally impoverished European had brought catastrophe to humanity, this time including himself in the carnage.

Again, Gita considered her options from among the chosen few, the survivors by design. Martin was out, based if nothing else on his direct link to the military machine responsible for this holocaust. That left Wei or Joao. Not a close call. Ever since Zhou Enlai had deceived Nehru, what self-respecting Indian would trust a Chinese man, especially a man who dressed as poorly as Wei? On sabbatical from her post at MIT, Gita had visited Tawang in Arunachal Pradesh. What a place! She wondered what it would look like now, without living residents. As the deceased monks would surely have predicted, the Chinese triumph over India had been a mere illusion. But then life itself is an illusion. Gita had caught Wei checking her out last night. But Nehru's descendant would have the last laugh. From a one child policy, she would take China to a no child policy. Gita smiled to herself. Her rejection of Wei had nothing to do with politics or nationality, since neither politics nor nationality existed any longer. It was his age, pure and simple. Wei was older and, if truth be told, uglier than Joao. Gita decided it was Joao with whom she would form the beast with two backs.

*

Joao hiked through the gully looking for plants. As he walked, he could not get the image of Stefanie out of his mind, no matter how much he tried. Joao understood the stakes. He could be the father of mankind – not figuratively, but for real. All the same, he realised he was at a profound disadvantage. He could not fight Martin. And he doubted he could out-think Wei. But Wei seemed to have a thing for Gita, anyway. So that ruled him out of the Stefanie sweepstakes. And Joao had the advantage of romance language over that monosyllabic mercenary, Martin. How close were Portuguese and Spanish? As close as lovers on a moonlit evening, Joao mused.

He stumbled, shattering his reverie. Joao looked down and saw a scrawny, thorny plant. A small bush, really. Joao knelt close to the ground, examining the plant. As a trained botanist and successful businessman, Joao had always seen opportunity where others had not. Profits had followed, but that was not what motivated Joao. It was the thrill of discovery. Here, it was not the plant but the possibility of protein that motivated Joao. Protein meant survival. It also meant access to Stefanie and procreation. The father of all humanity, he mused again. It aroused the poet in him.

Joao found a bare spot at the base of the plant and tugged. The hardy plant held firm. Joao jerked it back and forth, trying to free it from the sandy soil. Though dry and thin, the plant's root held it in place. It resisted his efforts to prise it from the ground. He kicked it with his boot. Still the thorny plant would not give. Drawing upon the football skills from his youth, Joao kicked the plant repeatedly from different angles. Sweat poured from his forehead into his eyes. He wiped his eyes with gritty hands and kept kicking the root even as his eyes stung and he had to squeeze them shut. Finally, the root gave and Joao beamed through stinging eyes as he pulled the roots from the ground and ran his fingers over plump, glistening larvae: protein.

*

Stefanie did not have the heart to tell the others how unlikely they all were to survive. In her career working for the UN to safeguard the rights of tribal peoples around the globe, Stefanie had seen firsthand how hard it was to eke a living out of harsh environments. And the Kalahari was undoubtedly one of the harshest. The best they could hope for was to pool their talents. If they did not co-operate, they were finished.

Convincing three men to co-operate would be the hardest part. But if anyone could do it, she could. Even as a teenager in Barcelona, Stefanie had never had a problem attracting men – and putting them in their place when necessary. She had stayed single by choice, though that was no longer an option. The question in her mind was how she could maintain control. She did not like the way Martin and Joao were sizing her up. It looked like typical male competition – admittedly more restrained than the maniacal mating dance of the Kalahari ostrich. But in a post-chivalrous era, an era that screamed for co-operation, Stefanie found even the subtle moves of her suitors unseemly. If Martin and Joao failed to co-operate, the group would not survive. And if these last five humans did not survive, all the copulation in the world would not save the species. They were, after all, the only humans left on the planet.

As she gathered and catalogued the group's few remaining belongings, Stefanie typed an inventory into her tablet computer. She marvelled at Gita's ingenious solar power charging device that kept the group technically (and literally) in the computer age. But that link felt so tenuous. At best, Stefanie's computer would be the last computer operated by humanity for many generations. Stefanie wiped away a tear. *How could it have come to this*? she pondered. She had long debated with her colleagues in development work, whether capitalism's focus on individual capabilities or a communal approach to development made more sense. Back then, those debates had seemed almost trivial as advanced societies blindly pursued policies of competition and destruction. How ironic that now, after global calamity, Stefanie's innate desire to bring people together would prove to be humanity's last hope.

*

Wei had no idea how he was supposed to find water. It was a fool's errand. At least it was marginally better than the hunting assignments, for which Martin and Joao had volunteered. *Fool's errands for foolish young men*, Wei scoffed. Young men were hot-headed and competitive. They would destroy the

　　　　JOHN G. SHULMAN

group, Wei had quickly concluded. Two fecund females and one extremely feral male was all it took. And that, of course, was exactly what they had.

Wei sat down. What was the point of expending more energy in a futile search for water? He thought about what he had learnt of human nature over the years. He was a politician. Well, he *had been* a politician. Before the event. Some politicians were technocrats, others autocrats. Wei was neither. He was a student – a student of human nature. He knew people, usually better than they knew themselves. And he had long ago learnt that, in a crisis, people's true natures always came through. In a crisis, the only things that held people together were family, social bonds and culture. Without these, even the most civilised humans deteriorated rapidly. They became feral.

He thought about his fellow survivors. Each had strengths, but each had weaknesses that overwhelmed the strengths. Take the American. The man had been born feral into a feral society. The land of the free, they called themselves, as they incarcerated more people than any other society. A feral man born into a feral society and trained in the feral art of killing. With such a man among them, had they any hope of survival? Wei's political instincts never failed him. He knew the answer and it was not pretty. The best he could hope was to find amusements in the brief remaining interval before death.

Wei stood and stretched his legs. Then he saw the damnedest thing. Not by nature a superstitious man, Wei could not avoid the thought that this was some sort of sign, perhaps even a miracle. Most important, Wei now knew that they were not alone.

*

'We're alone,' Stefanie whispered, though why she did was beyond her since she and Gita were indeed alone in the vast expanse of the desert.

Gita tried to ignore the young Spaniard.

'We should be clear, Gita, about our terms,' Stefanie persisted.

'Stefanie, dear, I think it's a bit soon to be talking about making babies.'

'But I've done the math,' Stefanie insisted.

'I'm sure you have,' the MIT professor interrupted. 'And I

know as well as you that we must persuade Martin, Joao and Wei how this is to be done. I just don't think this is the time ... '

'I didn't mean to be hasty,' Stefanie apologised. 'It's just that I think the men are already thinking about it.' Stefanie hesitated, trying to think of a way to broach the subject without offending the sensibilities of the prudish Indian woman. 'I just think that, as women, we should assert control over our bodies and our reproductive rights.' She regretted the words as soon as they were out. She sounded too much the human rights lawyer.

'Do tell,' Gita responded coldly.

Missing the cue, Stefanie launched into her proposal. 'Look,' she began. 'We should decide which one each of us wants first. That way, there's less danger of inbreeding.'

'You don't say.'

Encouraged, Stefanie continued: 'And I would be willing to let you select your mate first.' She paused again, aware that she was about to stride into dangerous territory. 'Of course, since we must consider, to some extent, the wishes of the men, they may act as a natural constraint on your choices.'

'Really.'

'I'm glad you understand.' Stefanie smiled.

'You mean, I should not be destroyed if Wei turns down my proposal?'

'You like Wei? I knew it!'

At this most auspicious moment, Wei entered the camp leading a monkey with a rope tied around its neck. 'At your service.' Wei bowed to the women.

'Where did you get it?' Stefanie asked, running over to Wei and the monkey. The monkey, barely ambulatory, appeared to be in grave distress.

'To be honest, it found me.' Wei shrugged.

Gita knelt next to the monkey. 'He's thirsty.'

Wei nodded. 'Aren't we all?'

'Then you didn't find water?' Stefanie frowned.

Wei looked at the ground. 'I'm afraid we're in the desert.'

'I must give this monkey a little of our water,' Gita proposed. 'Or it won't survive. It looks quite dehydrated.'

As Gita led the monkey on the rope to the group's water canister, Stefanie raised her eyebrows at Wei and followed Gita with her eyes. Wei grinned and nodded.

 JOHN G. SHULMAN

'I couldn't help overhearing your conversation,' he called to Gita, catching up with the professor and the monkey.

Gita pretended not to have heard, as she bent down to pour water into the parched simian's mouth.

Wei bent down next to Gita and the monkey. 'You've made the right decision,' he whispered. 'I'm a good lover.'

Gita glanced sharply at Wei. 'Don't count your chickens before they hatch.' She sniffed and turned away.

'I don't mean to interrupt,' Stefanie ventured, interrupting.

'Please.' Wei smiled. 'You are never interrupting.'

'It's so peaceful,' Stefanie agreed. 'With just the three of us, I mean.'

Wei pondered his next move. This was getting interesting. 'I do not mean to make light of our situation,' he observed, 'but this may be the most peaceful moment in human history.'

'That would be making light of our situation,' Gita countered.

'One older man and two attractive ladies is perhaps as peaceful a grouping as we could possibly configure. Especially for a species that has been as unfortunately violent as our own.'

'You're not that old.' Stefanie smiled.

'Oh yes he is,' Joao interrupted, having wandered back into camp.

Like teenagers caught in a compromising position, Stefanie, Gita and Wei spun to face the unexpected intruder and plead their innocence.

'Really, it's not what you think... '

'Don't jump to conclusions... '

'We were just talking... '

'It's okay.' Joao laughed. 'We're all adults. Family planning is not a luxury at this point. It's a necessity.'

The other three relaxed.

'We have been giving it some thought,' Gita conceded.

'As a government official in my previous life,' Wei suggested, 'I have uniquely relevant experience with family planning policy.'

Stefanie frowned. 'As a human rights official, so do I.'

'Touché,' Joao whispered.

Wei frowned. 'It seems humanity's peace was short-lived.' With that, he turned and walked away from the others.

Joao shrugged at the women and, for the first time, spotted

the monkey with the rope around its neck. The monkey appeared to be foraging in the dwindling supplies.

'Where did you find that?'

Stefanie glanced in the direction of Wei, who was now some distance from the camp.

'I'll go talk to him,' Gita offered and left Joao and Stefanie alone.

Stefanie smiled conspiratorially at Joao, who did not discourage her.

Gita found Wei sitting on a large rock with his back to the camp. 'May I join you?'

Wei nodded, but did not turn to face her.

'We're all struggling,' Gita began. 'Each in our own way... '

Wei shook his head. 'I should have told you before.'

'Told me what?'

Wei appraised Gita. 'I didn't want to say anything in front of Stefanie.' He paused. 'She's so young and naïve. I'm afraid it would break her ... '

'What?' Gita prodded.

'I know you're a mathematician,' Wei began. Then he lapsed again into silence.

'What is it, Wei?'

'You must have calculated that if we five survivors manage our ... let's call it, *how we choose to combine our DNA...*' Again, Wei seemed unable to go on.

'You can call it sex.' Gita smiled. 'Look, I've done the math. We can make this work.'

Wei shook his head sadly, as if the fate of all humanity rested on his next words, which of course, it did. 'I have bad news... '

Gita was growing frustrated. As a teenager in India, she had been sheltered from the melodrama of dating. Her introduction to sex as a graduate student at MIT had been as a purely recreational activity to blow off steam. Gita felt uniquely ill-equipped to handle a lovelorn, middle-aged Chinese man who was both unsympathetic and (again it occurred to her) *unattractive.* 'It's okay,' she whispered. 'You'll get your turn.'

'It's not about me.' Wei frowned. 'It's Joao.'

'What?'

'He's impotent.'

'I'm sorry?' Gita shook her head. 'I didn't get that.'

JOHN G. SHULMAN

'He cannot make love,' Wei pronounced. 'He told me last night. We are doomed.'

Gita stood in shocked silence. This was unimaginably bad news. It changed everything.

*

Joao pulled two fat squirming larvae from his pocket.

Stefanie jumped back, revolted at the implication of decay and death.

'Protein,' Joao explained. 'We can share them.'

Regaining her composure, Stefanie shook her head. 'Just two? That's all you have?'

'I have more. Take this.' Joao handed Stefanie one of the larvae. The translucent slug squirmed in her palm.

Joao placed his larva on his tongue and bit down. The slug popped. It was bitter, chewy and unpleasant.

Stefanie pretended to eat her larva, but slipped it into her pocket instead. 'We have to share them with the others,' she said, when Joao had finished chewing.

'They're too small,' Joao protested. 'There's only enough for you and me.'

'We must share everything,' Stefanie insisted.

'Everything?'

'Everything.'

Joao's tongue felt numb. 'I think these worms are an aphrodisiac.'

Wei and Gita reappeared.

'An aphrodisiac?' Wei grinned.

'Well?' Stefanie waited for a response from Gita, who ignored her.

'What are you eating?' Wei demanded of Joao. The Brazilian's tongue seemed to have betrayed him, as it involuntarily twitched inside his mouth and a white juice leaked from his lips.

Joao pulled three more larvae from his pocket. He offered a small one to Wei, who gratefully accepted.

Gita recoiled. 'Thank you, but no. I'm vegetarian.'

Stefanie placed a hand on Gita's arm to reassure her. 'Gita, dear, I understand your feelings. Under other circumstances, I would also stick to my principles. I rarely eat red meat. But we cannot think only of ourselves. If we do not find ways to overcome our selfish prejudices and superstitions, our species will end.'

'Thank you for your advice, dear,' Gita responded. 'And thank you for offering your culinary treasure, Joao.'

'If you don't want my insects, there's always Wei's monkey,' Joao suggested as he chewed on another bitter slug.

'Joao!' Stefanie admonished and retreated to comfort the simian, who was still rummaging through their stuff. 'I do not mean to cause distress,' Stefanie called to the others as she pulled the monkey by the string around its neck. 'But our species has all too often fallen into racism, religious bigotry, tribalism. We cannot afford to continue on that path. It will lead to the downfall of our species.'

'Bravo!' Wei clapped. 'Religion has no place in modern society. And racism is no longer possible for us. By the time we finish mixing, there will be no races.'

'As if there ever were... ' the Brazilian enjoined.

'I am vegetarian,' Gita stated. 'I will not eat a living thing.'

'Well said.' Wei applauded again. 'Very Gandhian.' He held his slug aloft, then slurped it down. 'It's a bit bitter,' he observed.

'That's because it's poisonous, you fool,' a voice boomed from the edge of camp.

Wei tried in vain to regurgitate the larva.

'Martin!' Stefanie greeted the American, abandoning the monkey.

'A born diplomat,' Joao said under his breath, telling himself that Martin would be the last to distinguish friendly protein from foe. All the same, Joao did feel sick.

'Oh my god!' Stephanie continued. 'What is that?'

Martin smiled. He dumped the carcass in the middle of the camp. 'A springbok. I fielddressed it. Start a fire. We're having meat tonight.'

Gita gagged.

*

As the smell of roasting meat wafted across the camp and the twilight deepened, Joao pulled Wei aside. 'Where did you get the monkey?'

'I found it wandering in the desert.'

     JOHN G. SHULMAN

'But the rope,' Joao pressed. 'You didn't have any rope when you left this morning.'

'I found it too.'

'Where?'

'On the monkey.'

'The monkey was carrying a rope and said, 'Here, please place this around my neck?''

'It was already around the monkey's neck.'

Joao stared hard at the Chinese man. 'Wei, we cannot afford to keep secrets from each other.'

'I told you the truth.' Wei shrugged and left to rejoin the others.

'Wei, dear,' Stefanie said, when he reappeared, putting her arm around his waist. She caught Martin watching her, felt the heat of his gaze. Pulling the Chinese man closer, she continued: 'Where did you learn to speak such elegant English?'

Wei also felt Martin's eyes burning into him. He tried to loosen the foolish Spanish woman's embrace. She would get them both killed. 'In Iowa, young lady. I went to college there. Land of pigs and straight talk. I never lost my fondness for both; though under present circumstances, it seems I'll have to settle for desert antelope and straight talk.'

'I may change my mind.' Martin glowered. 'You went to school in Iowa. So you know it's my prerogative whether I share my kill.'

'Oh, Martin, stop,' Stefanie chided. 'You know we must share if we are to survive.'

'I'm not in the sharing mood,' Martin spat.

'Neither am I,' Gita agreed.

'That's not very Gandhian,' Wei rejoined.

'This is survival.' Martin turned on Wei. 'Spare me your Confucian doublespeak. You think I don't know what you've been up to while I was away?'

'Really, Martin. Let's take a deep breath,' Joao suggested. He did not feel well. He slumped to the ground.

Stefanie slid easily from Wei to Martin. She touched the American's arm with her fingertips. She could feel the tension. She winked and he relaxed.

Wei took the opportunity to slip away. Gita followed him quietly. The two sat together in silence, basking in the twilight far from the camp. After a long time, Gita whispered: 'I've reconsidered your offer.'

Wei put his arm around the Indian woman. She leant her body into his. Wei realised the time had come to harvest a ripe fruit.

*

'Where is my water jug?' Martin roared. 'And where is that damn monkey?' The Navy Seal raced around the perimeter of the camp, but it was clear that both monkey and water had disappeared. 'You better start praying,' he warned the others. 'Without water, we're on a short clock.'

Still breathing heavily from the exertion of trying to find the monkey and water, Martin slumped next to his sleeping bag. He rummaged for his flask inside the bag. When he located the flask, he realised there was enough whiskey for one last night. After that, no whiskey and no water. Martin drained the flask and savoured the last pleasure of civilisation. He was in no mood to share.

A sense of impending doom settled in the camp as each of humanity's last survivors – the best and the brightest – lay down for what could be their last night. The desert did not negotiate. Either you had water or you died.

*

Joao awoke with a start. He heard heavy grunting in the dark. He slid over to Wei, who was snoring. 'Wake up, Wei,' Joao whispered and prodded the sleeping Chinese politician.

Wei opened his eyes and started, but Joao restrained him. 'Listen,' the Brazilian whispered again.

The two men lay together in silence, listening. A muffled scream jolted them upright. Gita stirred as well. The first scream was followed by more, somewhere nearby. Joao had heard hyenas before, but never so close. He peered through the moonlight to make sure everyone was safe, but he could not locate Stefanie. He looked for Martin, who was probably the only one who could defend them from hyenas, but Martin was not in camp either. When the next scream rang out, he realised there were no hyenas.

'Do something!' Gita pleaded with Joao and Wei as the screams continued, but they were frozen in place.

     JOHN G. SHULMAN

*

When Stefanie limped back into the camp, Joao and Wei could not meet her eyes.

Gita rose and embraced Stefanie, who collapsed in her arms. Gita glared at Joao and Wei as she comforted Stefanie. Gita stumbled with Stefanie to the last of the group's water. The water was in a small plastic bottle that would long outlive human civilisation. Gita used the last of the water to clean Stefanie and preserve the young woman's dignity. The men could go thirsty for all she cared. And if they died, and the species died out, perhaps that was for the best.

A few minutes later, Martin stumbled back into camp. He was drunk and singing to himself. Joao and Wei watched the American sway over his bedding and collapse. When he was sure the wretched military man had passed out and they were safe, Joao lay in a foetal position. His stomach contracted violently. All of the tension released in one motion. His bowels released and his stomach heaved. When he finished, he felt empty, weak and lost. His bowels released again and his stomach heaved. There was nothing left, but the worms. But the worms would not leave him.

*

When the women awoke, they maintained their protective embrace. Stefanie felt parched and raw. Then she remembered what had happened. She sobbed. Gita held her. The sun was already searing.

After Stefanie had calmed down, Gita rose and went to look for the men. She found Joao lying on the ground, holding his stomach and moaning. Wei was sleeping. Martin was nowhere to be found.

Gita wandered out from the camp. She did not know what she would find, but felt compelled to look. It did not take long. Four vultures remained, though there seemed to be little to hold them. Less than fifty metres from the camp, she saw the large skeleton. His hunting knife was there next to the bones. The meat had been picked clean.

*

Gita staggered back to camp. She could not get the image out of her mind. As she approached, Joao retched, but nothing came out of his mouth. Wei stirred. Gita spotted blood on his shirt sleeve. She squatted next to Wei and Joao. 'You shouldn't have done it,' she said.

Neither of them responded. Gita waited. Joao retched again. Nothing came out.

Gita walked away. Stefanie waved to her. Gita kept walking. She disappeared.

*

Wei got up and stretched. He felt surprisingly alive. Then his stomach cramped. He glanced at Joao. The Brazilian did not look good. Larvae squirmed out of his pocket and onto the parched ground. Wei strolled over to Stefanie. She looked good. Wei's stomach cramped again, this time stronger. 'I'll fetch Gita,' he said.

Wei looked pale. Joao had grown listless. Stefanie nodded.

As he walked, Wei felt an irresistible urge to heave. He doubled over, then fell to the ground on his hands and knees. His stomach convulsed over and over again, until everything came out from both ends. He had soiled himself. He could feel slimy chunks of springbok gristle in his pants. There was no water to clean himself and no clean clothes. Wei pushed himself to his feet. He steadied himself and continued after Gita.

*

Gita smelled the stench before she saw him. She closed her eyes and meditated, knowing she had the seed of a baby inside her. She stayed as still as she could – her back ramrod straight, her legs crossed, the tips of her fingers on each hand touching those remarkable, opposable thumbs. What Brahma and evolution had given, Shiva and technology had taken away. The longer she sat and meditated, the less she felt. She no longer felt the sun burning her arms. She did not feel thirst. She did not hear Wei.

*

Wei felt dizzy. His tongue swelled in his mouth. His throat constricted. His stomach convulsed again, but there was nothing left to expel. He could not get Gita's attention and he

    JOHN G. SHULMAN

dared not touch her. He had fouled himself. He could not bring himself to foul her.

He turned and lurched back toward camp. It wasn't until Stefanie reached him that he realised he would not make it back to camp. Stefanie eased him to the ground and sat with his head in her lap. She shaded his face from the sun. He did not sweat. There was nothing left to be sucked out by the sun. Wei's breathing became laboured, then weaker. Stefanie waited until Wei stopped breathing.

*

N!amce squatted on his haunches and watched Stefanie from a nearby outcrop. She was an unattractive female, pale and soft. She would die soon. The vultures, hyenas and insects would make quick work of her corpse. As the last human passed into history, the San Bushman did not reflect further. He had another monkey to find to lead him to water.

OF LIFE BELOW

Leah Swann

Karol wakes from dozing on the train with an unpleasant tightness around her neck. Her hands reach up to massage the skin. Outside, scenery flashes by: golden fields, church spires, window boxes brimming with red geraniums. The sky is pale blue – the same colour she was thinking of before she opened her eyes. She wipes her brow with her cuff and peels her ponytail away from her damp neck.

Like night sweats, she thinks. *Only they're day sweats.*

She'd told her friend Bel about them before she left.

'It started when Jarvis and I split up. I see things: a colour, a picture on a wall. It's like having a memory of something that hasn't happened to me.'

'Maybe you're picking up on something psychically.'

'Yeah, right. I doubt it.'

Bel's dark eyes were round and gullible.

'No, think about it,' she persisted. 'Maybe you're picking up on something that's *actually happened* somewhere. The trauma of your break-up is *opening* something in you.'

At Colmar, Karol disembarks and drags her suitcase across La Place Rapp. She stops for coffee and pancakes by the carousel and watches the children playing. The pancake is deliciously thin and coated with an orange glaze. An old man manages to strum a banjo, smoke a pipe and drink his coffee nearby. Karol listens wistfully to the children calling, their adorable French voices filling the sunlit square. Nothing clings to them as they run freely from slide to ladder to swing.

I can still have children. I'm only twenty-three, for godsake, Karol thinks.

But they won't be Jarvis's children and it's painful to imagine any other kind. She drains the last of her coffee and tosses the cardboard cup into a bin. She drags her case across the grassy square, crossing the busy road into the old town of cobblestoned streets and half-timbered houses with shutters painted red, blue and green. Tourists to her left and right. She pauses to let the excitement ripple up through her chest. She is here at last. Europe. It isn't the holiday they'd planned together, but she's here in spite of Jarvis and she's glad. She pauses to study the little map in her palm.

At the Hotel Saint Martin, she lets herself into Room 29 and opens the windows to look out at the Grand Rue. To her left is a handsome building that juts out hexagonally. Hot pink flowers sprout from window boxes in bright contrast to weathered stone and wood. Karol's gaze sweeps over the street, taking in the wrought-iron balconies, the lanterns and oaken beams. She sighs with pleasure. Nothing ugly to be seen. No loud billboards, no jarring modern buildings.

She takes a shower to wash off the travel; the jet is strong and hot. She slips on a sundress that is light without being suggestive. She doesn't want attention. In her mind she plans her visits. The Musée d'Unterlinden. Le Mont Sainte-Odile. She's looking forward to seeing the statue of Saint Odile holding open a book with eyes staring out of its pages. The brochure promises visitors that on the mountain's summit, where *mystic sensibility rubs shoulders with cosmic emotion*, you can forget the worries *of life below*. There's nothing she'd like more.

The evening is as soft as a dove's wing when Karol sets off for La Collégiale Saint-Martin. The soft atmosphere is comforting after the minor shock of arrivals, departures and connections. The sights and sounds of the walk are so charming, she longs to share them with someone. When she sees a stork landing in its massive, wheaty nest on the cathedral roof, she says, '*Look*', as though Jarvis is beside her.

Inside the dark cathedral, Karol glides over the stone floors towards a little chapel filled with gold mosaics and is disappointed to find that it's already time to leave. The cathedral closes at six o'clock. She hears an unexpected strain of music. It's an odd choice, but so beautiful that Karol puts her hand over her heart, whispers 'oh!' and turns to see a man, neither young nor old, playing *Rustle of Spring* on a harmonica.

    LEAH SWANN

Back at the Hotel Saint Martin, she catches sight of a computer in the foyer. She knows she shouldn't, but she sits and writes an email to Jarvis.

> Hey, J. Arrived safely in Colmar. Had dinner by the canal. They call it 'Little Venice' and even have gondoliers. The houses hang over the water. There was one house painted eggshell blue and every window was covered with red geraniums. I wondered what sort of a life you could live there. I couldn't help wishing you were here to see it all. Love, K.

She presses send before she can change her mind. She won't be seeing him for months, anyway. What harm can it do?

During the night, Karol is awoken by horrendous clattering. Her breath comes in sharp gasps. She sees the thread of images again; a set of moments fluttering on a string, like bunting. Large hands pulling a cloth around someone's throat. An oak beam. A funny little drawing. The whistle of indrawn breath over the murderer's teeth as he draws the cloth tighter and tighter.

'Oh, God!'

Karol sits up in bed and tries to shake it off. She's sweating all over again. The clattering goes on and on, metallic and thunderous. *What on earth can that sound be?* She climbs out of bed. Through the window she sees two men dragging massive steel bins over the cobblestones below. Bin night in Colmar.

Karol meets another guest in the dining room the following morning. Breakfast is included in the room price and she's making the most of it with muesli, yoghurt, boiled eggs, a mug of café au lait and a pain aux raisins, which she's planning to wrap in a serviette and stuff into her handbag to eat at the museum later. The guest stops by her table to admire her hair.

'It is so pale and shiny,' he says in a German accent. 'Is it natural?'

He sits down at her table and introduces himself as Steffan. He's fortyish, tanned and growing a layer of fat over his powerful body.

'Pardon me,' he says. 'But I cannot help noticing you are alone, like me.'

Steffan circles his mobile number on a business card and gives it to her.

'I am getting a car tomorrow. We could see the sights. Not in a romantic way. You are young and pretty, yes. But I have not put *my sights* on you. Please, do not misunderstand me. But why catch a bus?'

'We'll see,' replies Karol, tucking his card into her wallet.

Dear Jarvis,
This morning I went to Musée d'Unterlinden and saw the Isenheim Altarpiece, which takes your breath away. There was a panel that shows St Antoine meeting St Paul in the desert. Every day, the raven brings a roll for St Paul. But on this day, the raven has a premonition of St Antoine's visit and brings two rolls.

There's a guy I've just met who wants me to go with him to see castles and things. I don't really want to, but then I suppose travel is about being open to people, isn't it? I don't know. I sort of can't bear to talk to someone else. That's strange, isn't it? I don't know why I keep writing to you; I hope you don't mind. I noticed you haven't written back. But that's okay. It kind of makes it easier to write, because if you wrote back, I might start wondering about what you mean by this or that word and it wouldn't be good, would it? To open everything up again? Love, K.

After a day of sightseeing, Karol spots a shoeless Steffan in the foyer rubbing his bare feet into the carpet. For some reason, she finds this odious. She nods politely and escapes through the courtyard, climbing the spiral staircase instead of catching the lift.

 LEAH SWANN

She looks through the windows. Each oblong of glass is like a postcard framing a scene from the guests' lives: a baby waving her chubby wrists, a couple sitting on a couch or a man folding his clothes into neat squares in his case. She spies on him for a moment, savouring his privacy.

Someone downstairs had told her that the hotel was a thirteenth-century building. People had married, made love, murdered, given birth, wept, laughed, eaten dry bread, spied on each other, died of the plague or just died, raised families, drunk wine, eaten eggs and poached pheasant, read books by candlelight, remembered, forgotten, despaired, prayed, changed and stayed the same in these walls for centuries.

In the car, Steffan talks endlessly about his failure as a businessman, due to not knowing how to speak French. They're driving to Le Mont Sainte-Odile. Steffan has made an effort with his appearance, wearing a clean shirt and a green silk neck scarf – the kind of thing that Jarvis would despise.

'But now I can speak French fluently! Now, finally, I will succeed!'

Karol nods and smiles and clenches the map in her hands with regret. She looks out onto the freeway.

'When we get there, I suggest we split up for a little while,' she says. 'I want to walk the Stations of the Cross.'

'Oh, but I too want to walk it!'

Karol says nothing.

'But of course, I understand,' says Steffan. 'For you, it is a religious thing?'

After they get back, Karol falls asleep in her room. She dreams of a pair of marble-white hands opening a white book. On each page there's a kind of fleshy pouch, which shudders and opens, revealing eyes. Someone says, 'It's the book of your life.'

Karol rolls onto her side. *What on earth did that mean?* She must remember to never sleep late in the afternoon. It's so disagreeable to wake up. She looks at the picture hanging on the yellow-washed walls: a little cartoon of a peasant woman pulling a cart with a child waving the French flag. The drawing is unpleasantly familiar. Her skin pimples into gooseflesh as she recognises it from her day sweats. She licks her lips. All the moisture seems to have left her mouth.

Could Bel be right? Could she be seeing something that really happened?

There's a knock on the door and Karol utters a tiny squeal. She smooths her hair before answering the door. It's Steffan in a clean shirt and too much aftershave.

'Ah, hello. I am about to go out for dinner and I am wondering if you would like to come?'

'No, thank you.'

'Can I come in?'

'No. I need to rest.'

'Perhaps later?'

'How did you know I was in this room?'

Steffan waves his hand vaguely.

'I am sorry I have disturbed you,' he says, bowing his head. 'I thought we were friends. There is no harm in it, but I see I have offended you.'

'No, not offended. Just surprised.'

'Well, perhaps I will see you tomorrow,' he says, bowing his head again and hurrying towards the lift.

> Dear Jarvis,
> Went to Le Mont-Sainte Odile today. Odile was an abbess who was born blind. Her sight was restored when she was baptised. It was back in the eighth century, so who knows if it's true. But I liked the story. There were paintings of her and a statue where she holds open a book. On each page of the book, an eye stares out. I thought it was a Bible. Turns out it was a book of monastic rule.

Karol pauses, her fingers hovering over the keyboard. Why did she mention that? She's probably fooling herself to think he's even the slightest bit interested. She glances over her shoulder and is reassured by the burly presence of the concierge. Should she write this next bit?

LEAH SWANN

Steffan came up to my room tonight. I asked the concierge if he had given Steffan my room number and he said he had not, which means at some point Steffan probably followed me. Which is creepy. I don't know why. He just wanted to have dinner with me, as friends. He's obviously lonely. I don't know.

I think I'll go back to the Musée d'Unterlinden tomorrow. I want to look at the paintings and drawings of Martin Schongauer again. How amazing is art? Someone can make something that has the power to evoke joy or sadness in you, as you look at it nearly five hundred years later.

As I write this, it seems like an obvious thing to say, but I've never thought about it before. What amazing things we are; how we can take art in, hold it and remember it. We're sort of like lightboxes with all our histories, knowledge and our childhood impressions and emotions, with their sharp, hot or cold prickles. How we catch all these things and make connections. All this plays through us every day – from a ghastly memory or the blip of a favourite computer game, to the sea sparkling on a summer's day or *Rustle of Spring* on a harmonica in a cathedral...

Karol stops abruptly, critical of what she's just written. What the hell is a human lightbox, anyway?

There's a pressure working away in her temples. She closes her eyes, seeing the cloth and hair on a pillow, hearing that horrid indrawn breath. These things aren't memories. They belong to someone else.

She needs air. She presses send. Without bothering to sign off, she picks up her bag and walks to La Place Rapp. She buys a coffee and sits on a park bench.

A tiny girl runs ahead of her parents, towards the carousel, calling back to them: 'Regardez là!' Her head is clustered with tiny, pale curls. She's running too fast, she trips and cries. Her beautiful mother flies to her, descends, embraces. The little head nuzzles into her mother's neck, full of tears. *One day, my own child might do that*, thinks Karol. But this thought, once so real, seems to have faded and its fading has a greyness to it, a painful nothingness, as though the possibility is being withdrawn or pulled out of her.

The girl chooses a red horse and rides the carousel, surrounded by other children and their lovable calls back and forth. The darlings! Karol again tries summoning the old daydream, but she can barely sustain it. Her own children shouting for joy: a boy with Jarvis's serious, heavy eyes; a girl with her own light hair and gift for happiness. Well, she *used* to have a gift for happiness. She must fight this depression. Split. That's a real word. Split up. She is split from something. A moan of regret swims up from somewhere deep inside. *Oh, Jarvis. Why?*

She has to get away from these children.

She buys a croque monsieur from a street vendor and strides away from the open space of La Place Rapp, losing herself in the maze of streets. She passes Quai de la Poissonnerie, where time hangs softly over the water, tangible and layered in the darkness. She leans into the flowers that line the bridge, sniffing lavender, salvias and marigolds.

Back at the hotel, she's lost her key. Did she leave it by the computer?

'Don't worry about it,' says the concierge, handing her the spare. 'They usually turn up.'

In the courtyard, she bumps into Steffan.

'Ah, hello. We did not meet up for a meal.'

'No.'

'Maybe tomorrow?'

She senses the sexual interest behind his courtesy and tries to imagine being with him, since he so clearly wants it. Maybe it would help her to move on, to heal, that kind of thing.

'Let's have breakfast together,' she says impulsively. 'Eight o'clock.'

'Yes,' he cries and catches her hand gratefully. 'Good night, fair princess.'

She snatches her hand away.

'Okay,' she says, trying to cover up her rudeness. 'See you then.'

LEAH SWANN

In the middle of the night, Karol wakes, coughing, white hot. Why did she flinch when Steffan touched her? He's a nice man. Well-meaning. Even a bit handsome.

She goes into the bathroom and splashes water on her face. She opens the bathroom window and leans out over the rooftops, catching a whiff of the old town breathing out through the mortar. She smells the soot of the centuries: the onions, dirt and stork shit threaded with something fishy. Smoke and cheese, potatoes baked to brown pellets, dust, sunlight, dried blood, fried sugar and geraniums. Strands of the delicious and putrid pulsing in the living rope of history.

Karol dresses, goes out to the lift and down to the foyer. It's dark. She feels her way to the computer and finds the switch.

> Dear Jarvis,
> It's good you're not answering. But I have to tell you this, dear, darling Jarvis. I still love you. I am haunted by your absence. It's like that poem by W.S. Merwin I heard at uni: Your absence has gone through me, like thread through a needle. Everything I do is stitched in its colour.
> I used to think about the children we would have one day. And now that we're split up, we won't have them. We've wiped something out of the future. I guess that sounds weird. Right now, I don't care. I love you. Is there any chance, any at all?
> I've got to tell you something. That guy, Steffan. I saw him tonight and told him we could have breakfast tomorrow. He grabbed my hand and I pulled it away. When I looked up, I saw on his face a strange look...

Karol hears a noise and presses send, her heart thumping. She turns and sees someone moving in the foyer. Is it the concierge? She knows whoever it is has seen her, because she is lit by the computer screen. She blinks and stares.

'Bonjour?' she says, stupidly, into the darkness.

'Ah, hello. You cannot sleep either?'

It's Steffan.

'Yes. I mean no.' Hearing the quaver in her own voice, she adds: 'You scared me.'

'So sorry. I didn't think anyone would be here. It's nearly morning. Shall we go out and find a café? There's a twenty-four-hour café near Musée Bartholdi.'

Karol gets to her feet. The computer screen blinks off and the room gets darker.

'Not yet,' she says. 'If you don't mind, I think I'll go back to bed. I'll see you at eight.'

She has to pass him to get to the courtyard and the lift. She can smell some kind of hunger emanating from him, vaguely reminiscent of smoked pork. She half expects him to grab her and try something, but he remains motionless as she hurries past, clenching and unclenching her fists.

Safely in her room, Karol paces up and down. She can't possibly go to breakfast with him. She has to get away. She has to check out of this hotel and get out of Colmar. She opens her drawers and suitcase and tosses in her clothes, not without a pang of regret when she thinks of the long hours she planned to spend in Saint Matthew's Church, sitting before Martin Schongauer's *Madonna of the Rose Bower*. But how will she pay her bill without Steffan knowing? She daren't go into the foyer with her bags. He might be lurking, rubbing his bare feet into the carpet. He might follow her to the station to see where she's going ... he might even get on the train.

Her bag packed, Karol lies on her bed paralysed by indecision, staring at that horrible cartoon on the wall. Eight o'clock comes and goes. She's being paranoid about Steffan. She could just go downstairs, be polite and simply endure that creepy-crawly feeling he gives her. Just fulfil her obligation, make an excuse and escape the hotel when she knows he's out. But she doesn't get up. At a quarter to nine, she hears a knock on the door.

She tiptoes to the door and sees Steffan smiling through the spy-hole.

'You are not at breakfast. Are you well, dear Karol?'

She doesn't answer. She creeps into the bathroom.

'Are you in there?'

She closes the bathroom door. There's no lock. She crosses to the open window, where the smell of old Colmar drifts towards her – the smell of lust and geraniums, the smell of the plague. She pushes it open as far as it will go. It's not far enough to let

LEAH SWANN

her body pass through, but she tries anyway. She pushes one leg through the slot, wriggling her body halfway through the opening, getting stuck.

'Oh, God,' she breathes out, unable to move. There's nowhere to run, anyway. Only impossibly steep tiled slopes. Nowhere to hide.

'Karol!'

Steffan's voice is insistent.

'Do you need a doctor?'

Still Karol doesn't answer. She painfully drags her leg back through the window and slides to the floor. She hears the key turn in the lock. Yes. Of course. *He* stole her key. Now it's serious. She feels herself shaking all over. She slips out of her body briefly and sees herself trembling on the floor, sees her own face with a sickly, greenish lustre to the skin. Then she's staring at the backs of her hands again. She's done this once before, as a child. She jumped off a roof and saw herself sprawling on the grass below before she was back inside herself, the grass soft beneath her.

Her pulse is racing. On all fours, she crawls to the toilet. Perspiration is running down her neck from her scalp and her bladder's opening. The backs of her hands are greenish too. She knows now; she knows what's coming. They weren't memories or psychic inklings of another's fate.

Steffan opens the bathroom door.

'Dear Karol, you are not well.'

She shakes her head, too frightened to speak. Her mind says: *scream now!* He comes to her side.

'Here, let me help you,' he says, lifting her up and leading her out of the bathroom towards the bed. 'Do you need to be sick?'

She shakes her head again and clears her throat.

'How ... how did you get my key?'

'I found it by the computer. I've put it on your bedside table for you,' he answers. 'Now, dear girl, sit down and I'll ring the concierge for a glass of sparkling water. The bubbles will settle your stomach.'

Karol stares at him, bewildered. Steffan picks up the phone and speaks rapidly into the receiver. She hears the word 'l'eau'. *Help is coming,* she thought. *When the concierge comes, I'll run out through the door, down the stairs and out into the street...*

She looks around for her purse. She'll need her purse.

'So,' says Steffan, smiling down at her. 'She won't be long.'

He's wearing a scarf again. Today, it's not silk, but cheap blue cotton.

'I'll be alright,' she manages to say. 'I'd like to be alone now.'

'I don't think so,' he replies. 'I think you need me.'

That comment, she thinks. *That comment is where it veers into weird territory.* She straightens up. What would Jarvis do? She imagines her unborn son, her happy daughter – she would have called her Eleanor...

'Please leave now, Steffan.'

'Not yet. I am not finished.'

Karol stands up and says calmly: 'If you don't leave now, I'll scream.'

Steffan pulls something out of his pocket – a sock? a hanky? – and rushes at her, driving the cloth into her mouth. She falls backwards. Her body writhes. Thoughts tumble confusedly through her mind. This can't be happening. This happens to other people, in the news, in movies, in nightmares.

Steffan is kneeling on her shoulders, grinning down at her. She tries to spit out the sock by moving her head violently from side to side. Steffan's loosening his necktie. He slides it slowly from his neck, so it trails over his shirt. Karol feels a hot wave of nausea rising up through her throat. She gags. She turns her head away from him, so she can't see his horrible grin, and finds herself staring at that picture on the wall, the little child waving a flag. She feels the cloth sliding around her throat and drawing tight. She claws at it hard, snorting for breath, her screaming muffled.

'Shut up,' says Steffan, pressing a hot hand over the sock in her mouth and shoving her head into the pillow. She blacks out. Then she's hovering above herself again, looking down at the contorted face on the bed and the body, thrashing madly only a second ago, now still.

*

When it's all over, Steffan gets up, removes the scarf and ties it around his own neck. He brushes himself down, straightens the bedclothes and leaves – pausing briefly to neaten his hair in the mirror by the door.

 LEAH SWANN

Karol looks down at herself. *Wake up*, she tells her body. How can she get back in it? She looks closer. She feels connected to it; only seconds from being able to stretch out those curled fingers and toes. Her body's life seems squeezed out entirely. It's just a husk.

Something is behind her, waiting. She can feel it, but she can't bear to look, not yet. There are things she's supposed to do, things she hasn't done.

Come on, you can do it. Breathe, she thinks, willing the chest to rise and let her surface through her body, gasping for air. Let me in. I'm not ready for this lack of sensation, this stillness creeping into timelessness.

She stares at the form on the bed, her fears and longings coalescing around a single, repeating thought: not yet. Not yet, not yet.

THE WORD FOR THE FUTURE

Eunice Ngongkum

In 1950

Weeks of gloom has made the once-bright woman distraught. Her mind works overtime. A wild sea in a raging storm. Unable to come to terms with why Andiliya, her husband, is stuck to a bed of sorrows like a leech to a healthy, bloody vein. The bamboo stool by his bed, on which she keeps watch, is privy to her confusion, fears and unease.

The fears are palpable. They have taken residence here and will not go. They are not fears of death, her mind insists. Death? No. Not the fear of death. Has she not wined and dined with death these past twenty years of life? Where are Iwih, Tem, Tsung and Lang, her beloved children? Prey, devoured by death. Plucked in the prime of life. Iwih and Lang, harvested even before their prime! Lang, barely two months ago. She has intimately known death. Her life has grown deep with the experience of loss. Death no longer frightens her. Her fear is of a different kind. The fear of the future. Yes, she is afraid of the future. No, not afraid of the future as such. Has Andili not assured her many times that the God they now worship would always be there for them? Always be there in trouble, in sickness, in health, in the present and the future? She believes him. She has always done so.

Her overawed mind is quiet for a while as she calmly contemplates the scene before her.

'I have always believed you, my husband,' she mutters. 'I have always believed you, father of my children. You know what is right and good for our family. You have always known.

'You saw a future in the God of a stranger and decided that all of us should worship and serve only Him. Even with fiery arrows of resistance from our people, Andili, you insisted we do.'

She pauses in recollection, then shudders involuntarily as the invisible arrows tear through her flesh anew. The pain is real. Fiery darts from the camp of the enemy, her own people, choking her to death with their venom. She gasps for air. After some moments, she resumes her argument.

'You stood to the challenge, my love. You are a strong man, son of Ketsom Ndzie. You are a true son of your father. Your standing enabled me and the children to stand. You have been the pillar of our belief these several years, owner of my laps.'

She pauses again, looking for signs of movement on the bed. There are none. Those in a coma always hear us, it is said. They hear and understand what we say, but simply lack the motion of speech. Her Andiliya must be listening. He must be hearing her. He has always done so.

'Yes, dear,' she continues. 'You have held us together in this new way, even though the stranger's God has not been fair to us.'

She shakes her head vigorously in affirmation, responding to Andiliya's silent rejection of her argument. 'Uhm, uhm, not at all. He has not been fair at all. You know it even though you won't admit it, *Tseli Lang*. Yes, my husband, where are the children, *enh*? Our four fine-looking children?'

She stops again. The pain of loss is clearly visible on her once beautiful face. The effort to embrace the bright side of life, as is the practice among her people, has yet to wipe it away. What, with Andiliya on that bed? She doggedly pursues her argument. The stranger's God must be shown for who He truly is.

'Iwih, Tem, Tsung and Lang snatched from us, for no reason. Of our six children, only Imbi and Bei remain.'

She recollects herself.

'You don't speak of God in such terms, woman. Hold yourself together before you utter abominations!' Andili's classic response.

'But it won't work today, Andili, because I need answers. I challenge the stranger's God to answer me. I refuse to hold back. I refuse to fear His wrath. Do I have to fear again? Has death not done its worst? It has. So, I refuse to be terrorised at this crucial hour when death holds life at bay. No, not when my future is lying there, already dead. I must bare my mind to do battle with death and make a stake for the future. God of the stranger, come to my aid in this hour of need.'

     EUNICE NGONGKUM

The woman peers again to see if the man has come around. The semi-darkness of the room clouds her vision. But he has not. She continues. '

'Andiliya Ketsom, my own, you told me the day we buried Lang, our fourth child, that the stranger's God had given us these children and now had begun taking them again. It was His prerogative.

'*Hai*,' I exclaimed. What was this, *enh*? Giving and then taking again? I asked you, in my pain then, why did He give if only to take back? Did He delight in inflicting pain on those who followed Him?

'You rebuked me, warning me it was not right to question the will of the stranger's God. He was sovereign in all His ways.

'Sovereignty? With you lying there dead, barely two months from burying Lang? Hmm, sovereignty.

'Anyway, I could understand then because, even with our people, the gods are sovereign in all their ways. So I kept silent, my love. I kept silent so as not to offend them. We continued serving Him, even with severe taunts from the entire village, openly mocking our newfound faith. Andili, you stuck to it like Muanah holding on to the reed by the Ntsem River to keep from being swept away by its current. Now see what this has done to you.

'You literally constrained us to do same, even though I had my own misgivings at times. I could not argue with you. I knew you enough to know it was not in your nature to break faith. You believed the God of the stranger could be trusted.

'And now here you are, my companion, stuck to that bed of sorrows, sick with a sickness that has defied all medical diagnosis – even the diagnosis of the stranger's doctors you so trusted. You refused the help of our own *Wungang*, the healer. You claimed he served the evil one, Andiliya. His knowledge of herbs and capacity to see into the future were all from the kingdom of darkness. And now, here you are. Sent home from hospital without any hope of recovery. Ah, father of my children, even the stranger's medicine has not brought you a cure.

'Tell me, what am I to do now that you lie there struck dumb by this unexplainable sickness? How do I carry on from here, *enh*? God of the stranger, come to my help, now, in my hour of need.'

The hapless woman's confusion is palpable. The walls of the house feel it and silently sympathise with her. If someone walked in, he or she too would feel it without being told. Why would they not? It is all over the place.

Her in-laws have been on her back these past weeks, as if she were the one stopping them from making decisions regarding the welfare of her husband, their son. Can you imagine? Accusing her as if she were the cause of their son's sickness. If their son dies without any word for the future, they say she would be to blame. Did she ask Andiliya to go after other people's gods, *enh*?

She sighs.

It was only customary respect for her in-laws that kept her from responding to them rudely. She fed her anger in silence after they went on ranting about how they would have consulted the traditional healer, *Wungang*, who would have made Andiliya talk or, at the very least, would have related what the dying man wanted to say to the living. As if she stopped them... oh, can you imagine?

She chuckles as it dawns on her. It is Andili's commitment to his God that is the problem. It fuels their frustration, driving them crazy like the heat of the desert on its victim. They have not gone to *Wungang*.

The woman smiles.

'Even on that bed, apparently helpless as you are, Andili, you speak. My beloved, in your presence you spoke and, now in your silence, you still speak. Your faith spreads out like a garden beside a river. It is evident to all. No-one dares challenge it. This is why my heart heaves in pain: you are not able, my bulwark, to stand up to them. But the stranger's God should see that you, at least, have kept faith and He should come to our rescue. Why isn't He coming to our aid?'

Her prayer is to Him.

'*Weiy*, God of the stranger, come to my aid in this moment of need. Please spare me this storm. Can't you see we have become the laughing stock of the village? Barely two months ago it was Lang, now it is Andiliya, your faithful servant. What can we do? We are helpless. Please come to our help, I pray. *Amin.*'

She remembers her mother's warning.

'My daughter,' Mama had said, 'embrace the way of your

　　　　EUNICE NGONGKUM

husband. It is right for you to do so, but never forget the ways of your people.'

Mama was right. Even if you forgot those ways, they always found a way back to you – confronting you in the valley of decision, daring you to challenge their reasoning.

That was where she found herself now. In the valley of decision. Looking for a word for the future, a word from the dying to sustain the living. That was the exigency of tradition. Among her people, those who died without a word for the living were evil – struck dumb by their wicked ways. Even in her newfound faith, she had somehow always looked forward to that crucial word from loved ones about to die. The word that would sustain the living. The word for the future. Interestingly, all her deceased children had each given a word.

Andili had never cherished her reminders. The words meant nothing. Words uttered in the heat of pain were delusions of the mind, seared by the soreness of pain. The dead were gone. They never spoke to the future. *'How could dying people perceive the future?'* he argued. No, they had no premium on the living. She tried to agree with him. It was the proper thing to do, but it just couldn't stand. The words her dying children spoke in that crucial moment, when death held sway over life, were a lifeline. They sustained the bereaved mother throughout the task of daily living. She cherished them. They were reminders of her dead. Treasure chests of memory to which she returned time and time again to vivify life.

A picture of Tem on his death bed comes into sharp focus. His face lights up briefly as he turns to look at her, his eyes radiant with an unearthly glow. The pain momentarily disappears from his features. Then the lad speaks:

'Mama, don't cry,' he says with a pale smile. 'Things will be fine. Help me to turn to this side, Mother. I want to sit up.'

She rushes to him. She tries to lift him up, but then he swoons on her tired shoulders. She shakes him, but it is all over. She lets out a shrill cry as the neighbours rush in.

'Did he give a word?' Matalina, her closest neighbour, instinctively enquires.

In that moment, she forgets that their bereaved family does not believe in tradition. In tears, she answers without hesitation.

'Yes, our son said all will be fine. That was the word.'

Jubilation, even in the hour of pain. There is a future and a hope.

'Andiliya Ketsom, my husband, you cannot be different from the others.' She is emphatic. 'You must have a word for the living. You have been a good man. So, I charge you, in the name of our love, speak up.'

She takes a long look at the unmoving man. She slowly stands up, then walks resolutely out of the room – the walls pregnant with her challenge to the dying.

*

The wait is longer than she imagined, but the woman will not give up. *Bangkembong* didn't when the moon, his friend, promised to come and take him to a better place. The legendary figure looked forward to his friend's coming. Waiting was long, but the rendezvous was kept and now *Bangkembong* lives happily with his friend in the skies.

'You can see them in harmony on moonlit nights. As surely as the moon came, so too will you speak, my husband. You have no choice but to speak. Tradition must be kept. The gods answer prayers.'

*

Sunday 5 November:

Zelah

Two months have passed. Nothing says this day will be special. I go about my chores as usual. I step out to steal a few minutes of respite from the drudgery. My daughter, Bei, is the watcher for a season. I am determined not to miss anything. When I have only walked a few metres to the small house, behind the main house, hurried footsteps follow me. I turn instinctively. It is Bei.

'What is it?' I ask in a muffled tone, all the anxiety and fear of the past weeks leaping from their hideouts into my voice. The urge that hitherto drove me to the small house vanishes instantly. I peer into my daughter's face, fearing the worst.

'Aha! Mama, you too.' Bei is smiling. 'Relax,' she says calmly. 'Papa has come around. He asks for you.'

   EUNICE NGONGKUM

'Come around? *Enh*, your father is up, Bei? Are you sure? You say he asked for me?'

I don't wait for answers, but push past my daughter. This is too good to be true. Two giant steps and I am in the room, by the bed. The scene is too beautiful to behold. Andiliya Ketsom, my husband, looks up from his long sleep, smiling a weak smile.

'God be praised, oh! God be praised! Andili, you are up, ha! Let me get you something to eat, my husband.'

I stand up, calculating what to prepare for a man who has been in a coma for months.

As I turn to go, a weak voice says: 'No, not food, but news. Sit down, wife. Listen to me first and then you can go for food. I have some urgent things to tell you.'

My buttocks find their faithful companion. I am all ears.

'My wife,' he begins, his face aglow with the same supernatural light I have witnessed before. The voice is faint. I need to bend my ear to hear him.

'I had a dream.' He stops as if he needs prompting, but it is only strength that he needs.

Bei has quietly entered the room and is silently observing us. I lovingly hold my husband's bony hand.

'A dream?' I urge him on. 'You had a dream, my dear, what was it all about?'

'Yes, a dream. I want you to know that our God is good. He never fails those who put their trust in Him. Zelah, my beloved, there is a future and a hope. For us who believe, a place of beauty and joy is reserved. A very clear dream, sweetheart. I am still seeing things as I talk to you now. In this dream, I went behind the house to ease myself. There was this new path that had just been cleared there. Who did it, I don't know. Intrigued, I decided to follow on to see where it led. Suddenly, a very large, beautiful fence came into view. Indescribable! Literally glittering, mother of my children. I hastened on to take a closer look. Behold, there was Lang, our own son, emerging from a sidewalk and moving on ahead of me with spritely steps.'

'Lang?' I ask, surprised. 'You saw Lang, our son, you say, Andili?'

I hope this is not a sickness of the head. *This would be an abomination*, my mind responds in fear. He reads my thoughts and shakes his head in denial.

'No, Zelah, my wife, there is nothing wrong with me. I am perfectly fine in my head, woman. Sickness hasn't touched there. I actually saw our son, hale and strong. You cannot imagine it, but it is as true as I see you now. He walked on before me. I didn't see where he came from, but there he was. I called him, but he didn't answer me. This was so unlike my son, Lang. I asked myself what the matter was. Why was he being disrespectful? Had I done anything to offend him? These questions needed answers.

'The boy walked quickly on and on approaching the beautiful gate. Someone opened it for him and he walked in. I hastened on and made to go in, but the guard stopped me. He said it was not yet my time to pass through that gate. I was shocked. Not time for me to go in? What did he mean? My son had gone in and how could I, his father, not go in? What time was he referring to, anyway? Were there specific times for people to enter there? I stood my ground. I would wait for eternity if it came to that. I had to see my son, to know what he was doing in there. The guard must have noticed my resolve. He looked at me with pity and then showed me a tree quite close to the gate.

'*Climb up that tree,*' he said to me. '*Behold the land that is fairer than gold. Take note of its beauty and then go back and tell the living that there is a land that is fairer than gold. Reserved for those who faithfully stand to the end.*'

'I did as I was told. Zelah, my beloved wife, I lack the words to paint the beauty of the place. Streets paved with gold. Beautiful houses of different shapes and sizes. Continuous light. It looked as if there was no night there. I lingered on, captivated by the sight. My every being longed to be there. To join Lang there. But as I tried to jump onto the wall, I found myself here. Back to this place. But, oh, my love. We must get there. We must hold on to our faith. Remember, wife, we are not of those who give up. Our God will not be happy if we do. Beautiful. What a land! My love, it is the most beautiful place ever seen by human eyes. It is the place to be.'

Andiliya gasps for breath as he closes his eyes, reliving the scene he has just described.

*

The day of the funeral is one of joy for me, even though I mourn. There is a future and a hope.

The song of the church members, borne out of my husband's vision, is particularly heartwarming:

> Andiliya has told us,
> what a good land.
> The land is beautiful,
> I've seen the nice land.
> By the great river,
> what a nice land.
> The land is beautiful,
> for us who believe
> in the God of the stranger.
>
> You can join us,
> in the land that is
> fairer than gold.
> Yes, you, too, can join us.
> To the nice land,
> a land that is beautiful.

THE WORLD TO COME

GAME

Tabish Khair

The C.5X was fully functional. He could see it on the plasma-sight. Not that he would need it, he had been told at the briefing. There was nothing that large out there anymore; radioactivity, pollution and resistant viruses had taken care of that. The C.5X was just for security: it was regulation carry. What they would employ to shoot 'game' would be the much lighter C.2A, a laser gun that was incapable of killing anything bigger than a large goat.

But then, it was claimed that nothing bigger than a large goat had been seen out there for decades. He could still hear Colonel Agent Joe's rasping voice from the final briefing: 'Expect the unexpected, but there won't be no tigers out there. Nothing bigger than a billy goat. Maybe some decrepit, mutant apes if you get lucky or unlucky, depending on your view. And, of course, the usual mutant beasts. Forget the movies: these beasts tend to be small, skeletal and slow. The worst that can happen to you is getting buggered by a randy ram. And that will only happen if you get out of your hunt suits first. But then, ladies and gentlemen, you would die slowly in any case.'

Colonel Agent? Who thought up such designations, he wondered. Probably the same people who thought up slogans like 'Home is Happiness'. That was the one on the screen behind them right now. They had just been watching a program on what to expect on the expedition and, of course, the program had to end with this slogan.

They continued to check their equipment as Colonel Agent Joe's improbably named assistant, Miss Maple, called out the names: 'C.2A (check), C.5X (check), insulated hunt suit (check), alarm node (check), mobile link... '

Miss Maple fitted the colonel designation much better than Joe, he thought. At six feet or so, she was far more muscular and tough-looking than her boss who, despite his tough voice, still looked like the travel agent he probably had been all his life, before he got this break. It was arguably the highest paying branch of tourism today, though of course, it was not called tourism; it was called 'life experience' and was a category 1-A government-controlled activity. You needed military security clearance that only one out of twenty-three could get, according to statistics. And then you had to pay a fee to the Life Commerce Department, which only one out of a hundred could afford. There were no official statistics on this though; they had stopped publishing statistics on such matters in the mid twenty-first century when governments legislated, after a few years of economic unrest, to discourage any kind of 'classism'. This was during the years when the 'Virus' struck many of those parts of the world – mostly in Asia, Africa and South America – that had already been in the throes of various kinds of violence, starting with pro-democracy civil wars in the early twenty-first century.

He looked at Sarla next to him. This had been largely her idea, though of course, he was paying for it. You needed to have an Ultra Plus credit ranking to even sign up for one of these 'Limbo Hunts', as they were called. He had it; she didn't. No university professor could even make it to an Ultra Minus Minus ranking these days. Sarla taught Cognitive Biometrics at the local university. Maybe that is why she was so keen on the expedition. Not that they would be allowed to bring anything back with them. Not that anything even half intelligent existed in the regions that school textbooks called the 'Limbo Lands'. Devastated areas, sometimes stretching for thousands of kilometres, surrounded the few civilised tracts protected by the vacuum walls and heavily armed soldiers. He had never understood the need for heavily armed soldiers.

Thanks to technology that evolved in the mid twenty-first century, vacuum walls could be created to completely isolate any tract of land. Nothing living could pass through them alive, unless it was intelligent enough and had the industrial means to devise complex penetration machines. And as the textbooks showed, nothing intelligent existed in the Limbo Lands that stretched over most of Asia, Africa and South America – except for sections in the east of Asia, the south of Africa and Brazil. Nothing but dwarf animals, most of them mutants. The Virus had killed off all the human beings and larger mammals. It

    TABISH KHAIR

would have erased all of humanity too, if the more advanced nations had not developed the vacuum walls in time. Even if they could have afforded it, it was too late to save the populations of the poorer countries. And he did not believe in the underground conspiracy theory that the technology for the vacuum walls had already been developed before the Virus struck, with some walls installed in areas where there was heavy illegal immigration from less affluent lands.

He was jolted out of his reverie. Sarla was nudging him. It was Miss Maple. She was pointing at him from the head of the room and asking something in her deceptively soft voice. He looked at Sarla, not having caught Miss Maple's question.

'It won't do, John. It won't do.' Miss Maple ticked him off. 'We have only one final week of training left. We cannot have people with us whose attention wavers. No, not even for a moment. You might have paid a fortune to join the Limbo Hunt, but we will not hesitate in returning the money, minus the expenses for the course, to anyone who we feel could jeopardise the expedition. It is too dangerous out there for people who are not on the ball every moment... '

Caught unaware, John blurted out the question that had been bothering him. And it appeared that it bothered no-one but him, for even Sarla had looked nonplussed when he tried to discuss it with her.

'Miss Maple,' he said, 'if there are no big animals out there and we are fully insulated against everything in these hunt suits of ours, even from snake or dog bites, then what is it that makes it so dangerous?'

There was a long moment of silence. John realised he had asked a question he should not have put into words. Sarla was biting her lower lip, looking upset and probably accusing John of trying to sabotage their trip on purpose. She had always taken his lack of interest for hostility. But John was not hostile towards the Limbo Hunt: he knew that ever since regulated tracts of the Limbo Lands were opened up for commercial use again – which basically meant these hunts, for nothing from those vast and desolate stretches could be brought into the civilised zones; no animal, vegetable or bacterium – it had become all the rage among the rich to go on these hunting expeditions. Whatever it was – the excitement of shooting skeletal goats and rabbits with four ears or that of going out dressed how spacemen in the twentieth century used to dress – the Limbo Hunt was the preferred activity of the rich these days. That is, if they could get top level security clearance.

Before Miss Maple could answer him, Colonel Agent Joe took over.

'Do I need to repeat to you, John, that there is a 7.5 per cent casualty risk on a Limbo Hunt. You do know that an entire expedition ... expired out there once ... everyone except the guides.'

John opened his mouth to answer. This was exactly his point: if there was no big animal out there, why was the casualty risk so high? What did these overly-equipped, highly trained, very competent tourists – the correct word was 'experiencers' – die of out there?

Colonel Agent Joe anticipated his retort. He held up a hand to stop John from saying anything further and continued: 'Do you have any idea, ladies and gentlemen of the hunt, how many things can go wrong out there? True, there are no animals big enough to kill you – no tigers, elephants, big apes or humans. True, your suits make you almost as invulnerable as the gods. But there are still mountains you can fall off, lakes you can drown in, quicksand that can suck you under. And remember, if we detect even a touch of residue – any leftover, living or dead, virus or vegetable – in the detoxification chamber on your return, you have actually signed a paper allowing us to isolate you for the next five years.'

John wanted to say, 'But that has never happened. You know it. All the deaths have taken place outside. No-one has ever had to be detained after the detoxification analysis. You, sir, are obfuscating issues.' But he did not say anything. He knew he would get in trouble with Sarla, and be kicked out of the expedition too. The governmental organisers insisted on total compliance. It was one of the virtues required for top level security clearance. And while John had no real wish to go on a Limbo Hunt, he knew that Sarla would never forgive him if he opted out. John knew that he could live without many things in life, but he could not live without Sarla.

     TABISH KHAIR

As the week passed, they practised the usual routines over and over again. By now, they could do what they were asked with their eyes shut. Each Limbo Hunt was preceded by a year of full-time training. Everything was practised, everything explained over and over again. The only thing they were not given full details about was the process by which they would be transported through the vacuum walls – that was classified information. All they knew – and they had to sign a sheaf of *actual* papers, not plasma files or reactive screens used in civilian life – was that they would be sedated and transported through the vacuum wall to Hunt Base One. As the walls were at least ten kilometres broad, this involved considerable periods of time and modes of transportation. And of this, they had no idea. From there on, they were to be under the guidance of Colonel Agent Joe, Miss Maple and their team of three anonymous military guides, who went by the denominations Alpha, Beta and Gamma. That would make a group of twenty: the rules stated that there couldn't be more than four experiencers per guide.

Sarla was dressed in an exquisite turquoise dress. Always a gym person, the last year of training had left her looking more toned and healthy than ever. This was their last evening alone together; tomorrow morning they would have to check in as a group at In-Station Seven, where they would be monitored one final time. No-one, from that moment onwards, would be solitary. From there they would be transported to Out-Station Four, where the process of sending them through the vacuum walls would commence. And a day later, they would awake in Hunt Base One, in the Limbo Lands. A night to recover and then the hunt would begin!

'Aren't you excited?' Sarla whispered to him, as a turbaned waiter came up to refill their glasses. This was a restaurant decked out in vintage colonial style and they had even found Indian-looking waiters to staff it. It must have been difficult; the percentage of coloured people in the civilised lands had dipped following the extinction of most coloured populations in the Limbo Lands, and decades of intermarrying elsewhere. Underground gossipmongers also claimed, with no evidence at all, that when the Virus had struck, and just before the infected Limbo Lands were sealed off with vacuum walls to protect the world, the immigrants in those days had been given the option of returning to their countries of origin – and surprisingly, many had taken advantage of the last rounds of free transport, despite official warnings that the Virus was deadly and incurable.

Was he excited? Not in the sense in which Sarla intended. He was curious. One part of him expected something out there; the other part expected something other than what the hunt promised. What was it? He did not know. He knew he could not explain it to Sarla.

Another turbaned waiter walked in balancing a basket of naan, a plate of tandoori chicken and a bowl of aloo gobi on a silver tray. He started serving them. John took advantage of the interruption to avoid answering Sarla.

'Hi guys!'

The interruption came from behind him. John turned around.

It was another couple from their group, Brian and Cameron. Brian was a leading businessman; Cameron was an actress and fitness model, whose presence in a restaurant less exclusive than this one would have loosened an avalanche of media interest.

Cameron and Brian came up to their table.

'Great minds think alike,' said Brian to John. 'We thought we should have a real dinner too, before we hit the wilderness.'

'Or the wilderness hits us.' Cameron giggled.

'Nothing will hit us, you know, Cam,' Brian retorted.

'There is nothing out there no bigger than a billy goat.' Cameron did a good imitation of Colonel Agent Joe.

'Join us for a drink later, will you?' Brian said as the couple drifted back to their table, confident in the attraction force of their celebrity status.

'You really want to join… ?' John asked Sarla when they were out of earshot.

But he knew the answer from the slightly glazed look in Sarla's eyes.

John woke up in Hunt Base One with a slight headache. As they had been told to expect, he had no memory of their passage through the vacuum wall. All he and the others – he discovered later – remembered, was the slight prick of the injection and a pleasant drowsiness. And now, seventeen hours later, they

 TABISH KHAIR

were on the other side in one of the Limbo Lands. He did not know which one. That was classified too. But he knew that only some swathes of land were used for such hunts; much of the rest remained too devastated, they had been told.

Sarla was already up. She looked impatient. John knew she was yearning to leave the protective bubble of the hunt base, where they could walk about without insulation hunt suits, and walk into the 'real' Limbo Lands. But they still had a group dinner to go to and a night to spend in this bubble. Next morning, after breakfast, they would enter the detoxification chambers and don their suits. It was only then that the hunt would begin.

Miss Maple was walking around the room checking pulses and patting people as they woke up. She was followed by one of the Alphas, Betas or Gammas. John knew he should remember them, but all three looked identical to him: tough, muscular men, with very little expression on their faces, each well over six feet tall. John knew they belonged to some elite military unit. All guides were crack soldiers, except Colonel Agent Joe who, despite his designation, was attached to the civilian wing of the military. *Even Miss Maple*, he thought. She came up to him, checked his pulse and whatever else by placing a small ticking device on his neck, then patted him on the shoulder and moved on. From the back, there was little to distinguish her from the Alpha, Beta or Gamma who trailed her, carrying and updating a plasma chart.

John could see that Sarla was disappointed. They had walked for hours now and it was almost evening. They would reach Hunt Base Two at any moment, where they would be duly detoxified and checked. They would have a grand dinner and sleep in the safety of the protective bubble teeming with soldiers like Alpha and Beta. They had seen no sign of life all day, except three false alarms raised by Cameron, who claimed to have seen a bird once and a mutant rat twice. Once, she had blasted at it with her C.2A and had been ticked off by Colonel Agent Joe and Miss Maple. They were not supposed to shoot unless they got permission by radio from one of the two.

Sarla had been expecting to see more life. But even the vegetation was sparse and mostly dead. John did not complain.

He had had a small, probably illicit, novel reader installed into the reinforced metal of his visor – it had cost him a fortune – and he sat there reading silently during the breaks they took every hour. The others sat quietly too. No-one really talked; they could only use their in-built radios to communicate, or use the n-pads installed into the gloves of their suits to send written information to each other. They could only communicate within the group. All devices, except those used by the guides, were programmed to do only that.

John was the only one who did not appear to mind this enforced silence. The others were always radioing back and forth, sending texts and images on their n-pads – mostly descriptions or photos of what they had seen, which was, John wanted to point out, exactly what everyone else also saw. A bleak landscape of brown stones, sandy earth, a few shrubs, an occasional blasted tree trunk left over from the decades when trees could still grow large enough – a landscape that belonged more on the moon than on earth. The sun was strong – forty-two degrees, his monitors told him, even in the evening – but of course, their suits were temperature-controlled.

The life alert sign came on in his visor and a small arrow pointed to the left. John looked. He did not see anything at first. Just a brown hillock with darker stones and a tuft of vegetation in one corner. Then, there was a movement within the shadow of a rock. It looked like a large rat, digging.

A number came on: it was Brian's number. Evidently, this animal had been spotted by Brian. He was entitled to take the first shot, unless he wanted to gift it to someone else. John could see Brian punching the n-pad on his gloves. A message flashed: Brian wanted Cameron to shoot.

The rat, or whatever it was, kept digging, oblivious of its death being plotted in silence.

Cameron raised her C.2A, put it on automatic focus and shot. She must have been shaking. The blast missed the beast by at least a foot. It looked surprised and raised its head. John could see it was a mutant of some sort. It had three long ears, like a rabbit's, and the body of a large rat. Then the rabbit-rat jumped and started running. It moved strangely, as if its back was broken: it propelled itself by the front feet, which were bigger and stronger than the rear ones, letting the back part almost

                    TABISH KHAIR

drag on the ground. Now the others were blasting at it too and John saw it being hit at least twice. It was blown a metre or so. It was not even twitching when it came to rest.

As the others went off to capture images and b-scans of the beast, and as radio arguments erupted over who had shot it first, John spotted movement behind another hillock. He looked at it. But nothing happened. He did not tell the others. It was perhaps just a shimmer of heat. And in any case, John had no wish to kill anything.

Miss Maple's voice came on. She was ordering the group back to the track. They had to reach the next base in half an hour.

The next afternoon, John saw it for the first time. They had, by now, shot five different animals, including some sort of fox. All of them recorded and abandoned. Then he saw it. It was an imprint in the sand, as if made by a small child. A barefoot child. He did not point it out to the others. But in the evening, one of the others spotted a similar footprint. The group buzzed with excitement. Miss Maple and Alpha or Beta inspected it and pronounced that it was the footprint of a rare mutant ape. The group was agog with plans. But the guides looked worried and, soon afterwards, they found a reason to curtail their expedition and hasten to the next base.

As they reached the base, they saw squads of soldiers setting out on their rovers – all of them like Alpha, Beta and Gamma.

What kind of expeditions do they go on? John wondered. He had discussed this with Sarla. She had given him the official answer: these bases were basically observation points and used for scientific experiments. 'In a phase of rationalisation', the Limbo Hunt was devised some years ago to reduce the expenses of running them. That, in any case, was what the system said and it appeared to satisfy intelligent people like Sarla.

That evening, during the lavish group dinner at the base, all five guides seemed a bit tense. And next morning, their departure was delayed because a thunderstorm was on its way. Around noon, with the ground still squelchy in parts, the sky overcast and the land misty, they finally left for what would be the second-last day of their hunt. By now, some of the members had received trophies, and the ones who had not were desperate to shoot something. Colonel Agent Joe kept warning them, both on radio and monitor, not to move beyond first level tracking distance of the guides, which meant a distance of ten metres maximum. Even at that distance, though, most of the other members in the group would be hidden in the fog.

Two hours after leaving the base camp, the area they were passing through had more vegetation than they had ever encountered before in the Limbo Lands. There were even some shoulder height trees and shrubs. The fog was denser too. That was why, for some seconds, John did not notice the silhouette under a bush. He thought it was one of the group members crouching. Then it struck him: it couldn't be. This was a woman without a hunt suit. She was wearing a rough and loose dress of sorts; her hair was tied with a piece of string. She was busy digging with a stone, grubbing by the roots of the bush. She was so intent on it that she failed to hear John approach.

He was only a metre or so away when she heard him. She spun around. Her mouth opened in a shriek. She must have been young, no older than eighteen: emaciated and wiry. As she scrambled to get away, she slipped and fell. John reached out instinctively to help her up. But she clawed his heavily gloved hand away and scrambled backwards on all fours, until her back was against the shrubbery.

At that moment, John sensed another presence behind him. It was Alpha or Beta or Gamma. He had his snub, black C.5X out and was aiming at the cowering woman, who was now speaking gibberish.

A part of John noticed the fact that the soldier had drawn his C.5X, which would fully pulverise a human being leaving only a handful of dust, and not the lighter C.2A. Another part of him lashed out at the soldier, knocking the blast from the C.5X away into the sky. The soldier pushed him back. They grappled, but were separated by a radio command. It was Miss Maple. She was behind them, half hidden in the fog.

'Stop it,' she hissed again on radio. 'What happened?'

'He was about to kill a human being!' John replied, still not understanding what had happened.

'It was just a fucking mutant ape,' replied the soldier, backing away from John, his voice calm and cold.

'No, it wasn't! It was a human being. Look!'

But there was no-one under the shrubbery. The woman must

have slipped away while John was tussling with Alpha or Beta.

'You are overwrought, John,' Miss Maple said, reasonably. The fog still hid the others from view. 'A mutant ape is what it must have been. One can hallucinate.'

'I saw her. I touched her. It was a human being! She spoke!' John insisted.

'No human beings exist here, John. You know that. They all died out decades ago.'

'I saw what I saw.'

'Are you sure?' asked Miss Maple, as softly as always.

John was still uttering his answer – 'Yes, I am damn sure!' – when he noticed that Miss Maple had her gun pointed at him. It was a C.5X. The plasma-sight blinked once, twice. That was the last thing John saw.

INTO THE STILLNESS CAME THE RAIN...

Crisetta MacLeod

At the deepest place in the deepest ocean, unfathomably, unimaginably deep, there is a minute crevice in the rock. The opening of the crevice is blocked by sand; below the sand the crevice continues far into the very crust of the earth. It reaches down into a hollow, a space in the primeval rock, so deep beneath the sea that it is subject to unthinkable pressure, so deep in the rock that it is warmer than the deep bed of the ocean. It is warmed infinitesimally by the molten heart of the world.

There is liquid in this space – is it water? There can never be light down here; there could never be photosynthesis. The soup consists of water, entombed fragments of vegetable matter long since dead, minute fragments of shell and exoskeletal remains and traces of minerals. Here, shut off from the biosphere above, there is no longer any interaction with the rest of earth since the plug of sand closing the crevice has sealed it since time immemorial. The turning of the earth and the pull of its gravity are all that can register here.

So what can it mean when a single cell forms and moves? Is it life? Is it sentient? Is it showing volition as it moves? What created it – unimaginable pressures, unforeseen amalgamation of substances, happenstance, God? One cell, one cell alone, is moving around in its tiny prison. Perhaps it is searching, perhaps it is playing, perhaps it is just drifting with no intention at all. Maybe that is all there will ever be of it, popping irresponsibly into being as something that might be defined as life. Perhaps it will cease to be, every bit as arbitrarily as it came into being. Perhaps it's just a mistake. Or maybe there have been others like it that came into being, moved around, then ceased to be, so that the substance of that single cell fell back into the soup. Why now, though? What's the purpose of it? This single moving cell can never be known or observed, so does it exist?

*

Far above, the land bakes under a merciless sun. The air is still. The far horizon in the Australian outback is crystal clear: no moisture, very little wind to raise the red earth, nothing to blur the atmosphere. In the evening, a light wind stirs and a single willy-willy of spiralling sand dances then settles to nothingness as the breeze dies. Night falls, and a glittering moon casts long shadows under each hill, each dune. The sky is brilliant with a million stars, with no competing lights to hide them.

In the cities at night, the moon makes shadows too. Between the buildings lie canyons deep and dark and mysterious, where no light penetrates. Proud tall buildings reflect the moon's brilliance, their glass windows making sheets of silver. In Sydney Harbour, the Opera House floats on sparkling water, its sails white and fluid as ever, posing against the starred sky.

The red and gold and blazing dawn comes again, lighting up the Opera House sails in washes of colour. A picture-postcard icon in its idyllic setting, with the Harbour Bridge boasting its constant arrogant counterpoint; but is the red of its girders just the glory of the sun? Or is the magnificent bridge now a filigree of rust?

In Paris, the Eiffel Tower too turned red, but now it lies crumpled like a child's meccano set from long ago. In New York, the Statue of Liberty holds aloft her lantern, which has toppled sideways, still attached. In London, Big Ben surveys his city with aloof pride, silently now; the great tourist attraction of the London Eye lies on its side, crumpled. Earth has not anything to show more fair?

Behind Sydney, in the Blue Mountains, the rising sun picks out each fold and dip, so that the hills seem as molten as when they were first pushed up and tumbled together like fabric in a careless hand. Far away in the Himalayas, Mt Everest lies astonished under the sun, free of its eternal snowy mantle.

Over the sea, salty and never-ending, the tides pull the saturated water endlessly around the planet. The world bakes. At the poles, some ice still lingers. Over the centuries, the winds ceased to howl and the currents slowed. There is a curious stillness, an ultimate peacefulness. That enormous island, Australia, seems untouched by the centuries. At its heart, the mighty rock Uluru dominates, unmoved.

Into the stillness came the rain…

     CRISETTA MACLEOD

In the towns and cities, at first it came as a few shy, secret drops, pinging on the iron roofs of the houses and gurgling among the gathered debris and dust, that now had rivulets to tease it all along, and there was movement and merriment chuckling into every drain.

In the desert, the first drops disappeared at once in the bright, brash, red desert cracked by many years of drought. The sun shone strong through the nimbus that brought these sly drops, so that a rainbow shone full and free, the whole promising arc of it building a new creation of unfettered colour as the rain became steady. Soon pools of water were filling every dip, every rocky crevice, and the rain splashed into them steadily and musically.

Before long the rain was falling generously, filling long-dry dams, bringing arid rivers to tumbling life, gushing boldly now in the gutters of the city so that it roared magnificently in underground clever waterways back to the sea.

Cars that stood in the streets, bright duco long smothered in red unrelenting dust, now had a wonderful restriction-free splashing and the colours sang out again, sparkling under the intermittent sun when the clouds parted. Backyard swimming pools, long forbidden, were filling generously now, making their own music. At the Waterworld playground, where the magical structures of slides and swooshes and fountains and waves had long since stopped functioning, the rain washed away the dust of disuse. Now water poured, chuckling down chutes, chortling over waterfalls, spraying and splashing as the children had once done.

As days went by and the rain fell generously, continuously, and the clouds that shed this bounty obscured the sun and the moon, the mighty Murray River stirred in its stagnant grave. Its waters had been pillaged and portioned, drained and desecrated until it could no long struggle to the sea, but now it woke, grateful and amazed. First a trickle here and a pool forming there, then, gathering from all the old irrigation ditches and ponds, a stream began tentatively to flow. Within days there was a river once more. Tethered houseboats, long disused, came alive and rocked to the music; abandoned aluminium boats on the shore were swept up and travelled joyfully, bumping each other and laughing. Soon there was a mighty river reborn, thundering, arrogant in its abundance, sweeping over dams and through drowned skeleton groves of long-dead trees to burst into the sea, colouring the water far, far out with the debris and good, red earth it gathered with its power. In the once dead, red heart of the continent, huge expanses of water made mighty lakes. Now at last, Australia had water everywhere, profligate, overabundant, omnipotent water.

When, after many days of steady downpour, the rain stopped falling at last, there was silence. Sometimes the wind blew and made its own soft susurrations, but mostly there was silence. In the desert, no willy-willies now, since the red earth was sated and steady. The whole world seemed to be holding its breath, waiting and watching.

Was this flooding rain too late? There had been no rain for a century and there had been no water left at all, except the salty unforgiving sea. Global warming had killed the planet and had long since extinguished any last trace of flower, fruit, animal or insect. Now Gaia had cooled her wounded self and, at last by some combination of changes, had allowed the water to lift once again into clouds, and then to fall copiously, forgivingly, throughout the world – sometimes here, sometimes there, but always renewed and fresh and restored to health. For so long, the atmosphere had been poisoned and polluted and any moisture that stirred only spread its poisons more thoroughly so that every last thing, every last living thing, had perished. Now after decades of sterilising barrenness, the rain was clean and cool again. It washed and comforted the wounded earth with clean forgiveness; it washed away the dirt and drabness, so that the world was newborn.

*

The fresh water stirred the sluggish sea into movement once more, as currents began to flow with the turning of the earth. The stagnant, salt-saturated, polluted sea began to dilute back to its ancient norms. It called and called for living things to enjoy its new freshness. All over the world, fragrant empty plains and mountains lay welcoming and waiting. But there were no seeds to answer the call, no grasses to refresh the air, no animals to leap and laugh; nothing to breathe in the new oxygenated air, nothing to photosynthesise and create the former wonderful cycle of circling, complementary gases.

     CRISETTA MACLEOD

It had taken millennia to create earth's paradise, with its balance of creatures and plants, with its emergent intelligence and love. It took only a matter of two or three centuries to ruin it, extinguish life forms one after the other and finally render the planet uninhabitable. Some of the polluters managed to leave the planet in ships that tore the last resources from the dying world; those left behind retreated to the poles and hid in caves and deep in cunning underground shelters, but it was too late. It was as if the sun winked out behind the clouds of filthy gases above the raped land – but not before it had burned the planet, sterilising it to barrenness. In deep dark holes, the last of humankind died miserably, drinking their urine and eating the meat from each other's bones until the last one of them gasped away. For a hundred years, there was nothing and nobody. That was the short time it took for Gaia to shake off her murdering creation and wash the planet clean – to try again? To lie empty, but free of pain and desecration?

Deep in that very deepest, dark crevice, that one single cell is moving. Is it the same one? How long has it been moving? For how long has it done this parody, perhaps this paradigm, of being alive? Is it a living being, then?

The currents are beginning to move where the fresh water has coaxed them back into life. Even at the very bottom of the ocean, there is an almost frolicsome stirring after such a long quietus. The plug of sand in the crevice is tempted and hops away grain by grain to join the fun. The new, fresh sea water explores the cavity below, playfully seeking how far down it can travel. It dilutes the soup in the cavity, which has been so long isolated.

Does that unicell, blindly moving in its small universe, feel surprise? Does it understand the concept 'different'? Perhaps there is no way to comprehend whether it has any awareness in any way at all; perhaps it is enough for it just to be, to exist, to move of its own volition. The water moves as the currents and the tides move; the unicell moves otherwise, dancing to its own tune. Perhaps it bounces its way up the crevice to the vastness of the dark seabed. Does it take nourishment into itself? What would it be that would nourish it? Will it perish, separated from its own soupy medium – will the fact that the soup is now diluted be the death of this arbitrary speck of life?

Questions, questions, when there can be no observations, no answers. Gaia stirs herself, feeling the tiny tickle as the unicell moves contrary to the blind mechanisms of gravity and rotational pull, or the now benign influences of the sun and moon.

The unicell divides.

 CRISETTA MACLEOD

THE FUTURE IS WOW

Sébastien Doubinsky

1.

'Attention! Attention! ETA in twenty-eight hours! I repeat, ETA in twenty-eighty hours!'

Super lieutenant First Class John Chen barely stopped chewing his synthetic chicken sandwich as the soft female autovoice repeated its message again and again. 'Man, can't they just chill for a sec?'

Super lieutenant Second Class Mita Jensen sighed. 'We know, we know... '

The other officers sitting around the table nodded and smirked. Everybody agreed with her, John Chen included. That voice was fucking irritating. As if they weren't stressed enough as it was. In twenty-eight hours, there would be chaos, pain and destruction in the name of order. They all knew that and the higher brass knew it too. So why didn't they stop the fucking robot and let them relax a little before the action started?

'Maybe we should send her to Victory 9 and use her as a demoralisation drone,' Under lieutenant First Class Avigor DaSilva said. 'I'm sure it would work just fine. Nothing for us to do but to get everybody back to their fucking huts, begging us to stop that horrible voice... '

They laughed heartily and John observed the faces of his fellow officers as they relaxed around what could be, for some of them, their last meal. He remembered a line in Homer's *Odyssey* where the guests couldn't stop laughing at a banquet, their faces frozen in anguish. Maybe Homer had experienced the same scene in a different setting. Man was man, after all. Only the clothes and the weapons were different.

John liked to read. Anything from the world classics to the newest bestsellers. He wasn't difficult. As long as the book taught him something or distracted him from his daily routine – this was basically the summary of his soldiering life. His classical culture had become sort of a trademark among his fellow officers and men. They had nicknamed him 'Caesar' Chen, first behind his back, but then he had adopted it himself, seeing it more as a compliment than an insult. If they had called him 'Octavius' or 'Hannibal' Chen, then he would have resented it. But Caesar had been an outstanding general and he had been murdered by the senators, not while running away from the enemy.

John washed down the last bit of his sandwich with some synthetic coffee and stood up.

'I need to relax a little,' he explained to the others, although he knew nobody really cared. Before hostile contact, everybody had his or her own routines. He knew Avigor would meditate and pray, and Mita would play a game of poker with some of the others. The fear of death had many faces; some young, some old.

'I'll go to the library and watch a movie,' he added, realising those words were part of his routine too.

Avigor and Mita nodded. Soon they would get up and do their thing too. Like he had said before: routine.

2.

Walking along the large *USS MacArthur Transporter* corridors, John couldn't help marvelling at the technology surrounding him. Synthetic soda and food dispensers, 3D projectors, personal hologram systems (PHS for short), health pills and whatnot. Amazing. Some of the stuff didn't exist when he was a kid. He wondered if the others had the same feeling of awe or if he was the only naïve idiot on board. Probably not, he thought, probably not. He would have to ask Mita, one of these days – and ask something else too. He felt a rush of heat in his cheeks and smiled involuntarily. Rangers had feelings too, as the bumper stickers said.

3.

The library was empty, as usual, so John had no difficulty finding a seat. He checked if the Visioreader worked and sat down. He looked at the list of available documentaries. He loved historical documentaries – especially the ones about past wars, of course. Whenever he had some time before a mission, he would watch a couple. Nothing better to boost your morale.

    SÉBASTIEN DOUBINSKY

He even thought about making it a mandatory requisite for new recruits. It helped you focus on the real purpose of every mission, to realise what you were really fighting for.

He chose the Battle of Thermopylae and the American Independence War. Freedom and democracy – that's what they were defending. The words could bring tears to his eyes. Seriously. Freedom and democracy. So much had been accomplished; so many people had regained their dignity. His father had been a cop in New Petersburg and had taught him the essential values of life. That's how he had been able to join the Officers' Academy – a whole different story than those ex-cons who enlisted in the Assault Sections. He hadn't joined to free himself from a despicable past. He had joined to convey the essential ideals of life.

He reclined comfortably as the first images of the documentary appeared in his Visioreader. As the Greek landscape began to unfold, he realised that he had actually never been to Earth. When his next long leave came, he would be sure to go and visit the Parthenon, first thing. The marble pillars of Democracy and Freedom.

4.
'Oh shit.'

Mita's voice in the speakers of John's helmet summed up the situation perfectly. The sight was terrifying. It looked as though a tornado with blades had torn the small village apart. Ironically, only the pole with the Red Cross flag was left standing.

'Okay, company, advance with caution,' John said into his mike. 'Bravo Section, recon the right side. Charlie Section, recon the left. Delta, stay here as support. I'll recon the center with Alpha.'

Now that the small Red Cross village had been wiped out, the jungle surrounding it appeared even more threatening. John regretted not having watched a documentary about the Vietnam War last night; he might have learnt something useful for today. Or maybe not. If he remembered correctly, the USA had had their arses kicked.

As he slowly progressed through the wreckage, he could see the horror of what had happened. The small school was a smoking ruin. The sleeping quarters had been levelled to the ground. The tiny supermarket looked like it had exploded, its colourful guts spilling all around in the form of various foods stripped of their wrappings. But the worst was the dispensary; it was still smoldering, invaluable medicine crushed or smashed on its walls and floors.

He saw Mita, leading the Bravo Section, kneel down to examine the body of an NGO worker. The head detached itself from the body as she turned him around. John turned his head and swallowed tepid air. The natives hadn't been nicknamed the 'Beastmen' for nothing. He scanned for survivors with his LifeSign module, but nothing came back on the tiny screen apart from the green dots of his own section.

Something caught his eye and he crouched to pick it up. It was a storybook for kids, stained with blood. The Beastmen had taken their kids back, destroying and killing everything in the process. Why?

John stood up again, staring hard at the jungle. They had come to Victory 9 in peace. They had offered the Beastmen medicine, progress, education ... and now this. John knew what it meant. There would be war. For real. This massacre was the last straw. They couldn't tolerate such barbaric behavior. No more mister nice guy. No more development programs. No more useless treaties with the natives. These people respected nothing.

Reaching the end of the main street of what was left of the plywood village, John stood for a long moment scanning the area. The jungle started about a hundred feet away, dark, thick and smelly. Why did these savages want to live there? What was so attractive about enormous insects, feral creatures and murky water? His thoughts filled with the image of a refrigerator, a huge one, filled with real milk, real fruit, real beer, meat, fish, yoghurt, you name it. The bright colours almost blinded him and he could hear the gentle humming of electricity running behind his closed eyes.

Then a large television set materialised, flashing ads and sports programs. The weather man appeared, pointing at various lands and regions. Rain, sun, wind. And the news; the news... A reassuringly middle-aged anchorman, greying at the temples, presented the night's stories looking concerned, but

   SÉBASTIEN DOUBINSKY

not the least worried. The voice of reason.

And films. And highways and roads. And fabulous urban landscapes. And kids reciting the Pledge, hand on heart, face lifted toward the rising sun.

Freedom and democracy. He couldn't suppress the tear stinging the corner of his eye. How could anyone run away from that?

He turned around and gestured to Avigor, who came running with the portable communication unit. 'Contact HQ. Tell them everybody's dead. Ask them for reinforcement and the authorisation to use maximum force.'

Avigor nodded and began typing the message.

The image of the open fridge, the TV set and fabulous highways slowly faded in John Chen's mind. He could focus again. He would show the bastards. He would show them that democracy and freedom weren't just empty words.

EUROPE IS NOT A COUNTRY

Bwesigye bwa Mwesigire

He is thinking of her. His face can't hide it. Put beside me, you cannot tell the difference between his face and mine. Of course, his face does not wear the cream paint that I wear, but it is as emotionless as I have forever been. Ever since he started renting this house, ever since he started paying for me to watch his every move, he has sunk into this emotionless being. I have to wait for him to turn on his computer for me to figure out what he is up to. His life is his computer. I long to be his computer. I would know him better. The computer knows him in and out. I know only what I steal from the computer.

The past tenants of this room wrote on me. One particular one used to write his girlfriend's name on me every night, even when she visited. The landlady had to paint me afresh to erase all the scribbling of Laura on me. I inherited Laura's name, in fact. It is that man who gave it to me. Maybe I am the only wall with a name. How would I know about other walls, beyond the other three of whom make up this rectangle for a room?

He enters. He throws books on the shelf. He switches on the light. He goes to the desk. He turns the computer on. His life begins. He heads one way: Programs, Mozilla Firefox, Facebook. The next step is: Programs, Skype. As Skype does the 'vooooooooom' sound, a click sounds from Facebook. We will be here for a long, long while. I have my eyes on the desktop, the chat window. He types...

Nsimbi Morris, 27 February 2036 at 19:43:
    'Hey.'
Nakie Rue, 27 February 2036 at 19:43:
    'Hello love.'
    'Hey.'
    'How are you?'
    'Hey, I can see that you are online, but cannot see your responses. What's up?'

'Really? I can actually see your *heys*. Let me restart the computer.'

I search his face for at least some sign of emotion showing his frustration, but I find nothing. He restarts the computer and resumes typing.

'Damn this internet connection; it is not stable at all. Love, can you see me now? I have restarted the computer.'

'Yes, precious, I can see you. *Smiles* How is Kampala?'

'Kampala is fine, my love. The taxi operators are on a sit-down strike today.'

'That is not fine. Strike after strike is not fine. Has the traders' strike ended? The Monitor website seems to suggest that it is still on.'

'It is on, of course. But this is normal. Strikes happen everywhere all the time.'

'But they never used to happen when I was there.'

'Come on, when was that? Maybe you never used to know about them.'

'I remember everything about Uganda, by the way; you would be surprised. A little more than a decade of being away is not forever.'

'The years you have been gone could be a lifetime, you know. Lots of things have happened while you have been away. You have grown breasts, have had your hips enlarge and... '

'Stupid you! Throughout these years, I have even grown more love for my heartthrob!'

'*Blushing*'

I search his face to see the blush, but I see a stone expression, emotionless. Isn't he lucky he has no webcam for Facebook Chat? How would he deceive that he is blushing and smiling, when he is not? They continue their chat. She teases him for being the eternally shy one. He denies, and she dares to prove him wrong when they meet. They agree to a gazing test when their meeting finally happens.

'Give me a minute, love,' he types.

'Okay.'

He stands and dashes out of the room. From the way he moves, it could be that he is going out to ease himself, to make himself easy, as the past tenant used to tell Laura, but I can't be sure. He may as well be on his way to buy a bottle of beer. I stay, looking at the computer and Rue's picture staring at me.

*

From the picture, I think Rue is more beautiful than Laura. I wish Morris would write her name on me, so I can change my name. But since he chooses to write her name on the desktop, the computer has the name. Isn't that the 'in thing' for this room? Doesn't it rule Morris's life? Doesn't Morris rule us, the lifeless walls? Do we have a voice to tell him what we like? Do we? My other three colleagues have no name! Shouldn't I be excited that the former tenant gave me a name?

He was a nice guy, that one. Whenever Laura did not come to sleep over, he always entertained us. He may even have been a poet or a rapper, a singer, a politician, or all those things rolled into one. How I wish I could chat to the other walls about the legendary moments we shared with that dude!

'What the hell are you doing on TV, Mr President?' he once shouted, out of the blue. The president was addressing the nation. The speech was boring; I did not catch much of it. But I did not miss the questions fired at the TV, in reaction to the president's monologue:

'In 1986, you said it was liberation. In 1996, it became stabilisation. In 2006, reconstruction. In 2016, modernisation. In 2026, transformation. What the hell will you say next year? Do you have any *tion* left?'

This type of conversation with the TV was different from what we were accustomed to. When the song videos by Nigerian singer Asa came on, we used to see him kiss the TV screen. He sang along to 'Mr Jailer' whenever it came on. In fact, whenever 'Mr Jailer' came on, the TV set's volume was turned up. When the neighbours started complaining, he bought a complete Asa album and played it through his DVD player, turning up the volume louder and louder. The neighbours' complaints turned into rounds and rounds of shouting matches.

'It is my freedom ... do you want to make my room a jail? That is why I must continue to turn up the volume, so you know my room is no jail. *You* are the Mr Jailers!'

That was the last of him we heard. A crowd, with many people we had never seen, ransacked and looted his property. Some of them were the neighbours, we could connect the voices and faces, but some were total strangers. Or maybe not. There were two men in particular who gave us, the walls, a part of the pain. We were kicked! Those men must have been soldiers. They were very ruthless. Why did they have to kick me more than other walls? Because Laura's name was scribbled all over me? If I had blood, I would have flooded the room with red. Lightning slaps can't be heavier than the kicks I received! I will ask the iron roofing sheets, which have been slapped by lightning, about the experience.

Laura came by that evening. She came about five hours after her boyfriend had vanished. The door was wide open; there was nothing useful left in the room. Almost everything had been looted. The only things left had been smashed on me and my other colleagues, and lay in their useless state on the dirty and messy floor. She kept pressing the keys on her phone, putting it to her ear and waiting. The phone connection was not going through. Her eyes told of a more sad state than mere confusion. She was carefully examining the ruins in the room, when her eyes landed on the broken pieces of a heart-shaped diamond crystal that she had given to him for his birthday. She bent to pick up the pieces she could find. Tears were flowing unceasingly. She put the pieces in her purse and, seeing the stains on me, proof of the kicks I had received from the soldier men, gave her body to me in an embrace I will never forget. If I had tears, a river would have sprung from the room, through the door and out to the world.

The landlady came the next day with painters and cleaners and, as Laura's name was rubbed from me, I kept telling myself that there was more I shared with Laura than what the painters and cleaners could take away.

*

      BWESIGYE BWA MWESIGIRE

Morris returns, wiping his hands on his trousers. He finds the computer screen dim. He touches the mouse and it springs to life.

'I am back, my love.'
'Welcome.'
'Thanks.'
'That took a while.'
'I was – er, er, er... '
'You were what?'
'Never mind.'
'I mind.'
'Nothing important.'
'Really? Stop the games, tell me.'
'Don't you know that everything is monitored nowadays? It is something I can't write here.'
'I know they tap phone calls, they hack into emails and other intrusive things, but Facebook Chat?'
'You never know. Facebook itself does not guarantee that it won't pass information to third parties, you know.'
'I want to know.'
'Just let it go, love.'
'Anyway, Uganda has never had a good government; even seventy-four years after independence.'
'Not about the government.'
'I give in to you. Do not tell me for your security!'
'Hmmm. The situation is, by the way, not as scary as you are saying.'
'I do not want to lose you, my love.'
'If you were to lose me, it would not be due to the government – surely.'
'Whatever it would be for, I do not want to lose you.'
'Are you sure about that?'
'Why do you doubt?'

*

Knock, knock. The knock is hard.

'A minute,' Morris says, rushing to the door. He opens it, and two men push him aside to enter.

'Who are you to force yourselves into my room?'

'Tell us who you are, young man,' says the taller man.

'But this is my room!'

'This is the country's security,' says the shorter man, as he looks at the computer.

'But, but ... privacy!'

'Identify yourself,' says the taller man, calmly turning to a now teary Morris.

Morris picks up his identity card, birth certificate, baptism certificate and other identification documents from the bedside drawer and shows them to the men. The taller one scrutinises the documents and passes them to the shorter one, who gets off the computer and, without bothering to check the documents, says to his colleague: 'He is not the one.' They leave at once.

Morris closes the door after them and, turning the key in the lock, he switches off the lights. He walks carefully, not making a sound, and climbs onto the bed. He inserts himself under the bedcover, not bothered that he is sleeping on top of the blanket. He is careful not to make a sound.

Rue has been sending messages on the chat window.

'Meanwhile, my neighbour gave birth yesterday. The baby is so adorable! I was thinking of what ours will look like when we have one.

My love?

Morris, sweetheart?

Morris...

Love?'

Incoming Skype call: Rue is calling on Skype!

'Shh—' Morris pushes the bedcover off himself and, in one go, jumps onto the computer. He declines the Skype call, signs out of Facebook, shuts down the computer and slips into the bed again. He goes deeper, now in between the sheets. He starts snoring an hour later.

*

Morris rarely snores. When he does, something uncommon happens to him in the morning. The last time he had snored,

BWESIGYE BWA MWESIGIRE

he had gone to bed frustrated after a chat with Rue. They were talking about fleeing to Europe to live with Rue and, somehow, it must have come up in his dreams.

'Does the world rotate around fleeing our homes?'

'Face it. Uganda sucks.'

'And doesn't Europe suck?'

'Not as much as Uganda!'

'Cleaning toilets! Refugee camps! Drug addiction! Suicide rates!'

'In Uganda, you have a much higher rate for all that.'

'You are saying I should bring my degree to clean toilets?'

'So, will you eat it in Uganda?'

'I can go and dig in the village, but not to tell lies so I can come to Europe.'

'Are you saying all Africans in Europe are liars?'

'Is that a secret, Rue?'

'What?!'

'Yes! Don't many say their genitals were mutilated, that they are being haunted by witchdoctors and other ludicrous things?'

'Come on!'

'Do you want to deny?'

'Hmmm ... no words for you!'

'I do not know your story, but I do not see why you would flee Uganda, why you fled.'

'So, my happy Ugandan, do the newspapers lie?'

'What do you mean?'

'Isn't there insecurity in Uganda?'

'The same as other countries, including Europe.'

'Really? And by the way, Europe is not a country!'

'Who cares whether it is a planet?'

I do not remember who ended the spat, but it was heated. Morris kept swearing in bed: 'Shit! Self-hating Africans! Good-for-nothing!' He kept reciting the same words until the invocation-like swearing turned into murmurs and finally disappeared, soon replaced with snores that could provoke the most dumb of walls.

*

There is something about the snoring following an awful experience before one goes to bed. Morris's snoring is so loud tonight. Louder than I have ever heard from him. It has to do with the magnitude of terror served by the mean looking, identity-less men asking for his identification.

'Nooooooooooo! Nooooooooooo!' He is shouting, sweating profusely as he jumps out of bed. He walks straight to the switch and turns on the lights. It must have been a bad dream. Why is he turning on the lights when it is already morning? Is he still dreaming? Does he sleepwalk? I know he talks while dreaming: dream-talking. I have heard him before having conversations with himself at night, while in sleeping. Take, for example, that night when his voice could even be heard from outside the boundaries of us, the four walls.

'I like your pawpaws! Let me swallow them all at once! Let me eat your lips off your face... Look me in the eye... Laugh with me.'

He was laughing, giggling like a smitten, young girl the better part of the night. I wished I could have followed him out of the room the next day, to find out where that happiness had come from. In fact, I wished I had followed him the previous day, so I could see the excitement building before it climaxed at night. In the morning, he had to soak his bed sheets. He had to bathe – something he did very rarely. When he returned that night, he went straight to the computer, to Facebook Chat. Because I was sure Rue was not the cause of the previous night's excitement, I wondered if he was going to tell her about it.

'I dreamt about you last night,' he typed.

> 'Really? So sweet. What exactly was the dream about?'
>
> 'We were making a baby.'
>
> 'Hahaha! You are making me blush.'
>
> 'A sweet and chubby one, actually.'
>
> 'Speaking of babies, when will we make a baby in reality?'
>
> 'I do not know. When should it be?'
>
> 'Of course, we have to first meet and live together for a while.'

     BWESIGYE BWA MWESIGIRE

'Like ants on a mission: live together, performing duties – wink, wink.'

'Hehehe! They call the process the *manufacturing of a child*. Hehehe, we are stupid!'

'We are ambitious, not stupid. To think of producing a child, is to be more forward looking than stupid.'

'I know; stupid in a good way – you know.'

'Things are moving fast. Just how long and we are talking about kids?'

'We have related for seasons, not mere days.'

'Sure? How many seasons?'

'Three, if my mathematics is not faulty.'

'Indeed, your mathematics is faulty! We started relating as long as we have known each other.'

'Hehehe! We were not relating when we were kids, we were just playing.'

'Sure? Playing? Hmmm. Don't you remember the several times we kissed?'

'Of course I remember! And we did not stop at kissing; I remember what we did and where.'

'So, you see, our relationship is more than a decade old! Hehehe!'

'We have always been meant for each other, you know. Even when we got separated for so long. By the way, speaking of separation, which was inevitable because we immigrated to Europe, why was your mother spreading rumours about my mother?'

'Which rumours?'

'You know, all the trash the women were saying after my father's death?'

'I do not know. What were they saying?'

'Stop the pretence. I know you know, because they still say those things now.'

'I have only heard that your mother was involved with someone who is suspected to have killed your father. And I did not hear this from my mother.'

'Will you tell me the truth, Morris?'

'I am telling you the truth.'

'Anyway, let us not talk about this for long. But just so you know, I do not want to come back to Uganda until such talk totally disappears.'

'Rue, let us get things clear: we were friends, me and you, before you left, weren't we? We were in love, weren't we?'

'That was not love. We were so young. Your tail was as small as a finger.'

'Okay, I am not talking about the size of my tail. I mean, our families may have had their differences, but you and I were friends.'

'How could you be my friend, when it is your father who masterminded the murder of my father?'

'What are you talking about?'

'Yes, your good-for-nothing father is the one who killed my father.'

'Rue, calm down.'

'I calm down, for what?'

'Let us deal with this delicately.'

'How delicate, when you want to extinguish our family?'

'Is this Rue or is someone using your account?'

'So what if someone is using my account?'

'We could ignore the bad things meant to separate us again and talk about the baby-making.'

The Ugandan electricity monopoly, UMEME, must have known that the talk between them had turned from happy babies to sad mothers, and relieved them of the conversation. The heaviness of heart, that night, was audible through the snoring that followed. I can't help thinking that this snoring is a sort of peace for him. I can't help thinking he is talking back with his snores. At least, he is booing the bad things and showing them that he is better than them.

*

28 February 2036: some minutes past 7.00 am.

The rays of the sun cut through the closed window. Morris

 BWESIGYE BWA MWESIGIRE

sits on his unmade bed, his head in his hands. He has just undressed, having spent the whole night fully-clothed, except his shoes. He looks at me; for the first time since renting this room, he looks at me. I itch to tell him all I have seen. All the stories of past tenants. I itch to tell him about Laura, about my name. I itch to tell him that he should open up to me more, that should not limit his life to the computer.

He gives me a hard slap. What have I done to him? Has he heard my thoughts?

'Why me?' he asks.

It is not only you, I want to tell him. He slaps me again and, leaning forward to rest his head on me, he fails and instead falls on the bed. He starts to sob. He curses. He looks at the ceiling and I imagine he is looking through the ceiling at the sky, probably daring God. He closes his eyes and gradually slips into sleep. About four hours later, he wakes up, takes a shower and leaves the room. He can't be going to school. He is much too late.

WHEN THE BIRDS COME

Emily Riches

Monday morning in Spring Gardens and the sky flared with red. Screams rent the air as they always did; a dawn chorus of shrieking that woke old Nell from dreams of dust and fire and reminded her to put the kettle on. She shuffled to the kitchen on swollen feet, slow as a beetle with her bent back and a constant ache in her marrow.

Already, the heat was palpable. Dark against the sky, a row of hulking shapes lined the branches of the crooked gum outside her window, their harsh voices grating like metal on metal. Nell knew they would fly down soon to scratch at her windows and leave her verandah streaked with droppings and ragged feathers.

'Miserable birds,' she muttered, shaking her head. As she filled the kettle, a flash of white through the window caught and held her eye. Leaning forward, she gripped the sill with quivering hands and peered down the street. A white van, silent and slow, emerged from around the block, the words *Spring Gardens Medical Vehicle* splashed across its side. The reflective windows were black and impenetrable, glazed with sunlight. She sucked in her creased cheeks, heart twisting in her chest like wrung washing. Someone else must have died in the night.

If her husband were there, she would have buried her face in his shoulder. But as the white van rolled past, she had only herself for comfort. She began to hum an old advertisement for flour that played on the wireless when she was a girl. She kept singing until she made sure it had turned into the next street.

The screeching of the kettle drew her attention back to breakfast.

*

With a plate of dry toast and tea, Nell sat out on the front verandah. Already, the black cockatoos had flown down. Perched around her railing like dark spirits, they ruffled their shaggy wings and turned their heads on the side, squinting at her out of rolling red eyes. They once scared her with their wild stares and monstrous beaks, curved and tough as fingernails. She used to chase them, brandishing a dusty broom as she tried to match their shrieking voices with her own. But then the vans came to quiet her down. And she learnt not to do that anymore.

This morning, however, she was almost indifferent to their brooding presence. It was Monday: visiting day. And Alan was coming.

The tea cup trembled in her misshapen hands. Lumpy and twisted, they gave the impression of having been moulded from damp clay. Her swollen knuckles bulged and slipped sideways under loose skin, pitted and pocked with age.

Everyone in Spring Gardens was old. Doddery, slow, invalid. *No longer capable of self-care*, said the pamphlet that came around when the communities were first being erected far outside the city limits. 'Vegetables,' Nell's husband had hissed, furious. The houses were all pale and similar as eggs, the entire community set into a grid and ringed with a tall barbed fence. The streets were patrolled by the vans, whose white-masked drivers sometimes entered apartments and wheeled out crinkling life-sized bags on steel gurneys.

On these days, Nell would always shut her eyes.

*

This was after Nell and her husband were forced out of the city. After the first images of waves swamping the coastline were beamed into their lounge room; news of cliffs crumpling like paper and spilling million-dollar mansions into the sea. After the city was drowned in a panic that rose as fast as the sea levels. After the heat became unbearable and the air almost unbreathable. After people vacuum sealed themselves in air-conditioned apartments and no longer went outside. When the city became a radio city, irradiated and radiant. A city plugged in. Turned on. Tuned in. A thrumming hive of interconnectivity. Interfaces, databases. At the time, Nell could barely keep up.

But then when the young people began dying, no-one knew what to do. Sudden tumours, sprouting spore-like in the brain, wiped out hundreds then thousands.

    EMILY RICHES

Nell's husband was bitter: 'Pumping all those signals through their heads, no wonder they're dropping like flies.' His voice quavered as his own pacemaker ticked like a bomb inside his chest.

So the elderly were deemed an unnecessary drain on the system. Irrelevant and outdated. The new government initiative shunted them out of the city into these small, purpose-built communities at the edges of everything. From the verandah, Nell could only see the city at night, a dull smudge of light on the distant horizon.

Spring Gardens offers you a safe and friendly environment where you can enjoy your retirement in maximum comfort. With professional expertise and round-the-clock services, you can be assured of receiving state-of-the-art care that will improve your quality of life.

But after the white vans took her husband away and turned his body into ash, her contact with people stopped altogether. No nurses, no doctors. Even her neighbours stayed indoors, locked into their television screens. All except Alan. His visits were the reason she pushed through the empty hours. Today, she would have liked to put on make-up; daub her face with white powder, apply a faux blush to her cheeks like she did when she was young. But her cosmetics were as dried up as she was and, besides, she hadn't much faith in the accuracy of her gnarled, slipping fingers. Tipping back her head, she laughed at the thought of her lips smeared with haphazard colour and the startled birds shifted on their perches, snapping their beaks.

*

She couldn't remember the last time it had rained. The bare expanse behind her house had once been the flourishing golf course that had given Spring Gardens its name. But the wind and the heat had stripped the grass to dust and the trees to husks. The fields were now all solar panels and wind turbines, mechanically operated, sprawling for kilometres producing the energy that lit the city and pumped the distant artesian water. The panels, an iridescent black, would turn to the east as the sun came up and follow it across the sky like flowers; a sight that sometimes made tears crawl down Nell's wrinkled cheeks.

Nothing grew, nothing changed.

So Nell marked her days by the Monday visits. The rest of the week she waited. Time pressed down on her with a weight that made her bones ache. Night brought the dreams of dust and fire punctured at dawn by the metallic shrieks of black cockatoos.

It was in the mornings, when the sun hung just above the horizon and the birds began to gather, that Nell felt the lowest. When the voice of her husband seemed to stream in with the dry breeze and make the dead grass whisper like hair. The smell of hot ash reminding her of the moment she scattered his body to the wind and he dissipated into the particles of dust that even now stung her eyes and eroded her skin as though it were stone.

Nell sighed and rubbed a hand over her bald head. She flicked a dry tongue over her lips, collecting fugitive crumbs in the corners of her mouth. The cockatoos became restless, shouldering each other and clawing at the railing. On other days, she pretended to take no notice, but today she detected something almost pathetic about these monstrous birds waiting for an old woman to finish her morning toast.

'Shoo, you beasts,' she felt brave enough to say, brushing crumbs onto the tiles. They paid her no attention and stretched out their necks, red eyes narrowing.

Nell kneaded her bent hands together, shooting a last quick glance down the street. Surely Alan should be here by now. She could already hear his quiet voice, so soft and gentle through the white mask, asking her how she was feeling today. His shining case full of needles that turned her bones to treacle and switched her nerves on until she felt like singing. Pills she swallowed like candy, easy as you please. Pills that made her forget time itself, if only for a while. For this, she could even forgive his arriving in one of those horrid white vans.

As she laboured to her feet, all restraint holding the birds collapsed: they surged, uncontrollable, towards the table. Nell raised withered arms over her head, trying to force her way inside through the sudden storm of beating wings. Breathless, she watched from behind the screen door as they lashed out at their neighbours, beaks and claws tearing and flashing. Even with her hands over her ears, she could hear their high piercing cries deep within her body, resonating and fanning out beneath her breastbone.

   EMILY RICHES

The meagre crumbs disappeared within seconds. With a muffled roar of flapping wings, the birds rose in a dark cloud and heaved themselves into the sky. Nell shivered despite the heat, clasping her elbows close to her body. As she turned away, the echo of their departing screams seemed to follow her, carrying and whispering like the voices of old ghosts.

MARTY AND THE MOON

Bronwyne Thomason

Nature never did betray the heart that loved her.
British poet William Wordsworth, 1770-1850.

We learnt about flow-dreaming from the internet. It takes a bit of practice, but after a while you can dissolve the boundaries of your physical body and become one with the world around you. If you do it right, you can achieve anything you can dream of, but first, you have to recall your deepest positive emotional moment and use the energy of that moment to propel you into the flow.

'For me, it was our first time,' I said.

Marty was quiet for a moment longer than his usual contemplative pause and I was about to repeat myself when he spoke. 'In my bedroom?'

'Yeah. It was perfect.'

'Really? But I thought... '

'Marty. It was perfect.'

His pause was shorter this time, the usual. 'Do you ever get there? Into the flow, I mean? All the way?'

'Sometimes. I think I do. I'm floating around like atoms in the air. Sometimes... it feels right.' I wanted to believe that it really could work. I wanted to believe it for Marty's sake.

'Mmm... What do you wish for?'

'To be with you forever, Marty. What about you?'

'Same.'

I kissed his foot. 'That's sweet, Marty.'

He kissed my foot back. 'If I'm on the moon, does that count? Would that mean we're together?'

'Sure.'

'Well that's where I go in my flow-dream. I'm on the moon forever, drifting around it, watching everybody down here on Earth. Not caring.'

'What's your positive moment?' Marty didn't answer that. I

knew why. We settled into silence for a while as I drifted in and out of sleep, but it couldn't have been more than an hour before Marty spoke again.

'There's a mark on the moon tonight,' he said.

Marty and I had been dating since we were fifteen and by the time we were seventeen we already knew we were destined to be together forever. Two years after that we knew we had already accumulated a lifetime of experience and there was nothing we didn't know about each other, nothing we hadn't shared.

It was our birthdays. Like perfect Gemini twins we lay on a blanket on the damp grass, head to toe, him facing the sky, me plucking blades of grass off their stems at the end of the picnic blanket.

'I've never seen a shadow like that before.' He shifted his hand that was resting warmly between my naked thighs, leaving a patch of dampness to go cold in the chilly air. I couldn't see, but I knew he'd be curling his chest hairs around his fingers, as he had a habit of absently doing while he thought about deep things. Then he dropped his hand again and gave my butt cheek a squeeze.

'It's really black. It's *ugly*. Can't you see it?' Marty loved the moon, especially when it was full. Sometimes we sat up for hours; watching until it moved beyond the stars. Sometimes I fell asleep. I'd wake up with his arm still hugging my thigh or his cheek against my foot.

But me, I was into poetry. I could see poetry in everything: in every situation and in everyday speech. I teased his foot with a blade of grass and tried to change his mood: *'There's nothing so lonely as a white moon – with a black scar – like the profile of a pirate ship sailing – full mast – a ship-shaped shadow on the moon.'*

'That's not right, Sooz.' He always called me Sooz. Never anything else. He was the only one I would allow to. It was special. Something just between us. 'Look at it,' he said.

'Therefore, let the moon shine on thee...'

'In thy solitary walk and let the misty mountain winds be free. Yeah, yeah. Wordsworth. But look. Shut up and look.'

Marty once tried to learn some of my favourite poems and recited them just to please me. He did alright, remembered every word of 'What Lips My Lips Have Kissed', but could only

       BRONWYNE THOMASON

remember the moon lines in Wordsworth. I told him: poetry is like music. You can't just learn it off by heart and then say the words. You have to *live* the words, *breathe* the words.

'Remember? *These beauteous forms*? Makes me think of breasts all white and sweet and tender, like little crescent moons. See. Soft. You want to... '

'Moooon. Look at the mooon, woman. It's got a mark on it.'

I could always tell when Marty was getting frustrated with me. He would condescendingly stretch his words. If I wanted to, I could be attentive and he'd talk without stopping for at least half an hour. Usually it was nice, interesting stuff, particularly when he talked so passionately about the moon. He knew the names of the craters, he knew everything there was to know about the moon and, when he ran out of information, he just made stuff up – philosophical stuff that I could really get into. But that night, I just wasn't in the mood to sit and listen while the air got stiff and cold around me. I was cold. I wanted to cuddle.

I said, 'These have marks too. Little roundish, pinkish craters. You wanna explore?'

I really blew it that time. Marty was more serious than I realised. He cutely smacked my bottom and then jumped up, comically scooped up his clothes as I twisted around, resting on one elbow to watch him. He bent over pointing his bum toward me.

'Explore this!'

'Aw, Marty. You really know how to spoil a romantic moment, don't you?'

Anyway, that was the last time I ever saw him. The last part of him I ever saw was his pimply, white bum in the moonlight. I wish I had paid attention to what he was saying that day. It was probably meaningful.

When his naked form had disappeared around the corner of the cowshed, I felt contrite, but I hung back for a while staring at the stars. The Milky Way. The Southern Cross. Then I noticed the moon. He was right. There was something unusual, but by the time I'd got my daft head together and run after him, he was long gone.

'Marty. Marty you left one of your socks behind ... Marty? I'm sorry, Marty.'

But it was too late. Marty was gone. And I never saw him again. Nobody did.

It was a strange night from the outset. For starters, the full moon came on our birthday, which wouldn't have been so strange if it was to have come about on the proper day. The moon had somehow undergone an extra revolution and the full moon was one day early. It had sped up.

We watched the big, yellow moon come up behind the phone tower and, at one point in time, it seemed to be impaled like a pickled onion on a fancy toothpick. That was the other strange thing. We sat on our blanket where we always did – so often that a square of grass was flattened and pale on our spot. We had watched so many full moons rise from that spot that we could have closed our eyes for half an hour and then opened them again and be staring at the moon exactly where it was in the sky. But on the night that Marty disappeared, the moon was in a different place. We had never before seen it sitting so perfectly, neatly atop the phone tower. Marty was worried. 'I don't like it at all,' he had said.

We had made love, as usual, but Marty had kept turning around so often to look at the moon that I eventually threw him over on his back so he could stare and get on with it at the same time.

'Good girlfriend,' he told me, pushing me sideways so he could see around me. I didn't mind too much, but I thought he was being oversensitive. I suppose that's why I mostly ignored him when he told me the moon had a shadow. I wish I hadn't. He might still be here if I had listened to him.

That's when the third strange thing happened – when I was on top of him. 'Whoa! Have you got fat, Sooz?' I would have smacked him if my orgasm wasn't so close, but then I understood what he was talking about.

'No, the ground's got soft. I think.' My knees were digging through the blanket making potholes, but it wasn't just me. Marty was sinking too. We were sinking into the ground.

'Soft? I think you're right. Like. Quicksand.'

We struggled off the blanket, lifted it up and shook it. But the grass and the earth beneath it were flat. Marty stretched out a foot and toed the place we'd been laying on, as if testing the temperature of a swimming pool. Then he put his foot down,

     BRONWYNE THOMASON

slowly at first, and then stepped onto our square of grass. Then jumped.

'Solid?'

'Solid.'

We spread the blanket a little way away from our usual place. 'I'm worried, Sooz.'

'Worry when we've finished,' I told him and we both forgot for a little while. The next thing I knew, he was curling his chest hairs, squeezing my bum and telling me about a shadow on the moon. And then he was gone. Gone forever.

*

'Martee. *Marty*. Where are you? Dammit, Marty, come back. I'm sorry.'

For someone who felt so empty and sad, at the time, my body felt incredibly nice. As I sat on the blanket and pulled on my jeans, I noticed that the blanket had gone all spongy again, and the tightness was gone from my jeans. The metal button on the fly was squishy, like play dough. I bent it and watched it spring back into shape.

'Marty? You've got to check this out,' I yelled. But Marty didn't answer.

'Ma. Ma. Ma.' I tested my voice. There was a kind of echo, but not outside of me, it was an echo like when you hear it on a phone line. It was right inside of my head. As a breeze swished past me my voice went up like The Chipmunks and then down again, like Darth Vader. 'Maaaaaaaa. Teeeeeeeee.' I played around with it for a little while and started laughing. The oscillation between chipmunk laugh and Vader laugh had me all the more hysterically giggling and ho, ho, ho-ing. Anybody watching would have thought I'd gone seriously troppo. God, I wish Marty could have seen it.

And I tingled too. I tingled like a Christmas tree covered in tinsel and fairy lights. I was thinking I was having another orgasm, but my God, this was better, and it wasn't stopping. It was like ... as if ... every nerve in my body was being tickled at once. I wanted it to go on forever – it was like that feeling you want to hold on to just before you come. Then, there was a spreading sensation, as if something inside of me was pushing outwards, pushing my body into a different shape, but it didn't hurt. The breeze blew through me and made me tingle all the more. It just felt really, really good.

I caught myself standing there, in one spot, not thinking, not trying to move. I wanted to just *be*, to exist in the moment forever, but every once in a while, there was a kind of interference, like the way static from Dad's power drill interrupts the television signal. It reminded me of the time Marty and I watched the *Dockers* and the *Eagles* and Dad used the drill every time Jacko was about to kick a goal. It was like that annoying jolt you get when you're in a deep sleep and for some reason your body decides to twitch and wake you up. It was like being almost asleep, but slipping back and forth, in and out of consciousness, where you're half dreaming, half knowing; where images tease you into thinking they're real, but they're not, they're dreams and you wonder for days afterwards whether it was a dream or not. That's how it was, standing there. Remembering Marty.

*

We had fallen in love on our way out of a Year Ten English class; literally as we stepped out through the door.

Me standing at the door as Marty held it open: 'Thanks, I'm Susanna.'

Marty had followed, halfway through the doorway: 'Marty. What's your assignment on?'

Me, on the outside of the door: 'Moon poems. You?'

Marty, closing the door behind him: 'Yeah. Me too.'

The English question was to put together a collection of poems on any theme on Earth. I argued with Marty that the Moon isn't on Earth, but he just said, 'Is.'

I stared at him, feeling slightly annoyed that somebody else had thought of my idea. I couldn't believe he hadn't just said that to piss me off. And then he said, 'Well. Part of Earth. It's Earth's Moon.'

And that was that. We were in love.

*

'Ah. What the hell was in that beer?'

I was half talking, half thinking, looking around for my t-shirt, but I could barely move. Every part of my body was

　　　　　BRONWYNE THOMASON

slow. The voice thing was starting to get annoying, as it was interfering with my real thoughts, as if my thoughts and my voice were the same thing. When I found my shirt, it was a pink smudge on what used to be the grass. In fact, I think my t-shirt was in the grass or the grass was in my shirt. Whatever the case, I couldn't pick it up because, for starters, I couldn't bend down properly and, when I finally got my toe to it, I couldn't separate the pink from the dark green. Whatever was wrong, was wrong with everything, not just me. My body was spread out loosely, the edges of my skin blurred and blending in with whatever I was touching: the grass at my feet, my clothes. That's when I started to get scared. I tried to cry.

'Marty.' That annoying echo. I didn't feel like being a chipmunk when I was in distress. 'Where are you?' Or Darth Vader.

There weren't any tears coming out of my eyes. There was no relief. It must have been how Marty felt sometimes. He had told me how he didn't have any tears anymore. He couldn't make them come out. It was like when you feel really sick and need to vomit, but it won't happen and you lay in bed wishing you could throw up because you know it would make you feel better. Marty told me that's how it felt when he couldn't cry anymore.

I was sixteen before Marty invited me home to his place. I understood as soon as I walked in through the slamming screen door to their kitchen and was hit with the smell. Cigarettes, stale beer-breath, bottles, empty brown bottles everywhere and Marty's mum with a bruised face.

'Who's this then? Your girlfriend?'

Marty mumbled my name.

She started to sing then. 'Oh Susanna, don't you cry for me ... '

Immediately, I had felt pity and hatred for her. I wanted to snatch that brown bottle right out of her hand and tip its contents down the sink. I wanted to throw her in the bath, clean her teeth and wash the hair that would have been beautiful before she let it go grey and stringy. I looked away in disgust. Marty took my hand and led me to his room.

'She's thirty-two,' he said. 'Doesn't look it, does she?'

'She was sixteen, then? When she had you.'

'Mmm-hmm.'

'Is that why you live with your granddad?'

'Mmm-hmm.'

Marty had, at the time, rubbed what was then his hairless chest through his shirt, twisting the shirt material around his fingers. He sat on his bed and reached out to me. It was the first time for both of us. He used his shirt to wipe my blood and then kissed me there.

'Sorry, Sooz. It didn't hurt, did it?'

'A little.'

'Sorry.'

*

I was jolted back to 'moon shadow night' when I heard a strange moan coming from the cowshed and realised that the milking cow was still inside. We were supposed to let her out, but we forgot. I wondered if she was as frightened as I was or if she was getting lost in the tingly sensations, but the moaning sound was the low-pitched bellow of a confused cow. Poor thing.

As I was thinking of the cow, I felt my awareness shift towards the shed. There was a breeze, only a soft wind, but the loose corrugated iron sheet on the roof waved soundlessly like a flag. The edges of the tin shed were clearly defined, but the wooden fence posts that led to the shed were smudges against the moonlit sky, and yet, the wire between them was a clean black line. I had moved closer to the fence.

There was a powerline that drooped downward from a power pole, between the branches of our ghost gum, to the corner of the shed where it was hung in a loop, then draped downward to the fuse box. I concentrated hard and found I could move very slowly if I imagined I was walking.

I could see inside the shed where the cow, a brown and white blur, seemed to be walking upside down on the ceiling. I wondered what she had been thinking. I wondered if she was thinking the same thing as Marty's mum had been the day we found her there two years ago, suicide note stuffed in the pocket of her blue dressing-gown, dressing-gown belt slung over the rafter, bare feet bump, bump, bump against the milking stall.

I had held her legs while Marty climbed up to cut her down. Her body had folded over the top of me; unprepared for her weight, I buckled at the knees and fell sideways. I ended up

 BRONWYNE THOMASON

with her bare, dead stomach in my face. It was cold, stiff and clammy. Marty rolled her off and wrapped up her nakedness with the gown. He found the note, and, sitting on his knees, read it through in silence. Then handed it to me. We were seventeen.

We laid her body out flat on her back, crossed her hands and prayed for her soul. Then we sat for a while, arms hooked in each other's arms.

He told me: When I die, Sooz, I'm going to the moon. I'm going to go right up there to the moon. I'll shine down on thee ... '

'I*n my solitary walk...* '

'*And I'll let the misty mountain winds be free.* Wordsworth? Right?'

'Yeah.'

'That's all I got right now, Sooz. I can't cry no more.'

'Then don't.'

*

I didn't understand back then, when his mum did that, how it felt to not be able to cry. At the cowshed, looking at that stupid animal hanging off the roof, upside down, I really wanted to cry too, but I couldn't. The breeze blew away my tears.

'Marty. My Marty. I'm so sorry.'

I moved out to the tree and stood by its foggy outline, concentrating hard on lifting my hand to touch it. My fingers went right into the trunk. It pulled my arm upwards, my body followed, up into the branches. I could feel its strength, sucking me along in its current, up, up into its leaves. I felt the inside and outside of every leaf. I felt its veins. Then. I touched the powerline.

'Fuck!'

Like a bolt of lightning, I was dragged along the powerline. Whack, through the power pole, slung around and around the loop and smashed into the fuse box. A brief pause. Then up again, along the wire, along the rafter and whoosh, out through the light bulb and, bang, exploded into the air and dissipated around the ceiling. I felt my body, frantically searching for its parts, zooming, zigzagging around the shed, collecting molecules and body parts. Is that how it feels to be dead? Better than being alive? Like Marty's mum wrote in her note.

Marty had wanted to kill his grandfather after that. After we sat beside her body, breathing and Marty scratching his chest, Marty had got up slowly then ran. I followed, running.

Holding the note in his fist, Marty found his grandfather pulling yabbies out of the pink dam in the early evening. He smelt grey, of mud.

'What did you do to her?'

'Oh no! What has she done now?'

'What did you do to her, Granddad?'

'Sit down, boy... You! Piss off.'

'She stays.'

I stayed. I wished I didn't have to know what I found out then, but I was glad I stayed. Marty vomited. Orange into the pink mud. We went back to the cowshed, climbed up into the tree and watched speechless as the ambulance came and went away, as the police came and went. We watched into the night as Marty's granddad/father paced alone around the cowshed and clawed his eyes.

'You have to cry, Marty.'

He didn't cry. Not that day. Never since. Instead, we spread a picnic blanket out behind the cowshed. Marty never got used to his granddad being his real father after all.

*

I pulled myself together after shooting out through the light bulb. The flesh on my hands and feet came back. I sunk down towards the floor of the shed. The cow fell. Thump. My jeans fell on top of her. I fell into a bail of hay. The tingling sensation left me instead with an ache all over. I could cry. I was crying. Hard. Pulling on my jeans, no knickers, wet, cold, tight. The cow was dead. I couldn't face death in that shed. Not again. Not even a cow.

I ran outside. The moon, with its shadow, wavered like the sun in a heatwave, directly above the phone tower.

'Oh, God. Marty. No.'

My legs, heavy as logs, carried me, shirtless, to the phone tower. I climbed its steely rungs, higher, up, up toward the moon. There, at the top, hanging like a white flag, a victory: Marty's other sock.

*

Even before his mother died, there was always just me, Marty and the moon. But since Marty disappeared, it's just been me. Sometimes when the wind picks up and sets my skin to shiver against the cold as my body keeps it out, I remember how it felt to be free and I think of Marty; all particles tingling and floating around the universe. In the flow. I wonder if he made it to the moon. I wonder, sometimes, if he is still trying to scale the phone tower, waiting for a bolt of lightning to throw him into the heavens.

I have moved the blanket to a place where I can line up the moon so it sits like a pickled onion skewered on a fancy toothpick and, when it's big and yellow and full, I stare at it and wave.

GAMIL YANAAY WALAYBAA: NO GOING HOME

Marcus Waters

Eyes open, then close.
A moment caught between time and lost in emotion...
A heart beats...
Eyes open and then close...
A heart beats...
Time to be born again.

*

The sound of two voices – not human. They are ancient, even older than time itself, belonging to a consciousness dating back as far as you can imagine... and then even further.

Voice One: 'I didn't mean to let you down and I meant no harm.'

Voice Two: 'You have left me tired – and it was your people and family, not me, who you let down.'

Voice One: 'I wanted you to leave my head and never return. I wasn't well... '

Voice Two: 'First, you are warranted an explanation of who I am ... before you go.'

Voice One: 'No, it is you who must leave... '

Voice Two: 'And then what? You think all this will be over and suddenly you can sleep?'

Voice One: 'Everything you say and do is but further deception.'

Voice Two: 'When else have you felt so alive, connected? You, of all people, must trust me.'

Voice One: 'Not just another trick to let you in?'

Voice Two: 'No, just the truth. The unconscious, unsustainable truth... '

Voice One: 'Again, playing with my mind. How can truth be unsustainable?'

Voice Two: 'Because all around you, Warrangun, is a lie...'

And in speaking the name, Warrangun, consciousness of one of the identities is revealed.

The Warrangun were soldiers of what Western culture would refer to as God. This is a conversation taking place between worlds, as timeless as imagination itself.

It is a place embedded deep in the reality of us all: what my people, the Kamilaroi First Nation People of Australia, refer to as the *Burruguu* or Dreamtime. It is a place of pure consciousness inhabited by the *Maran Dhinabarra* or Ancestral Beings, of which the Warrangun were one of the oldest.

The Warrangun replies, 'And there it is ... again, you ensure your own survival through words of deception.'

'Except that some, like you, are chosen, Warrangun. You see the truth against all its opposition, no matter the consequences,' says the Voice.

'Even if, in the end, it sends me mad ... insane?' demands the Warrangan.

The Voice remains calm, though assertive. 'It is for what you possess in your heart, by which you were chosen.'

'And what of justice?' asks the Warrangun.

'Yes, Warrangun – what of justice?' replies the Voice.

The Warrangun almost spits back his reply, 'How the delusions of a poor, sick people, abused as children, have trespassed upon my sleep? No more. I must cast you out!'

'Again, Warrangun, this is not about your victims. This is about you!' says the Voice.

BEAT

'One last time and then I will let you sleep. No more bad dreams ever again...'

'Another trick...' replies the Warrangun.

'We would finish, I would leave you. You would never see me again,' promises the Voice.

BEAT

'I need you to be telling the truth...' pleads the Warrangun.

The Voice replies, 'All over in an instant, I give my word. And then I will be gone.'

BEAT

'You cannot start and not finish, Warrangun. That, I assure you, will send you mad,' confirms the Voice.

'Please, I need to sleep...' pleads the Warrangan again.

'A Warrangun was never meant to sleep... so, what have you done that you cannot face being awake?' questions the Voice.

Unheard by man, tears begin emanating throughout the universe from deep within the Warrangun.

'Nothing is going to happen, other than what you want to happen. You're not going to say anything to me, but what you want to say. Now, it's time to relax,' calms the Voice.

The tears become deeper in their own insurrection, as the Warrangun is overcome with emotion.

'Thousands of years are running through my head,' says the Warrangun, crying as he speaks.

'Hundreds of thousands of years are running through your head!' corrects the Voice.

The tears stop. 'In truth, I did enjoy it, you know... going back,' says the Warrangun.

'In truth, you let your urges overcome you into becoming human and things were done that you are not able to leave behind,' states the Voice. 'I have often thought what I would do if given the same opportunity: never having to set foot in this realm again to live a normal human life.'

'But, you are forever?' asks the Warrangun.

'Which, at times, is far too long, even for me. Eternity is never-ending, the suffering becomes tiresome, the loneliness extreme.' There is an unavoidable sadness in the tone spoken by the Voice.

'Where do you go after this … once I leave?' asks the Warrangun.

'Home,' replies the Voice.

'The beginning?' enquires the Warrangun.

'No, before the beginning – there is a beat, a rhythm of thought that I love. The only compensation for the never-ending time,' confirms the Voice.

The Warrangun asks, 'Consciousness?'

'No, before consciousness. Before all else: a time before the beginning … gamilu bidi-wii.'

BEAT

The Voice continues: 'A moment caught beyond time. This, Warrangun, is Heaven.'

BEAT

The Warrangun asks, 'You were there?'

'Biami – Buwadjaar … God does not lie,' says the Voice.

In using these words, the Voice reveals itself to the universe and all its surroundings. In the teaching of our Kamilaroi law or binangarrangah, only those of the highest understanding are allowed to refer to the creator as Biami.

Instead, others are to refer to the word, Buwadjaar: the Spirit of all creation, born from Biami's own consciousness.

The Warrangun cries again, as the universe expands.

'It's time… ' states Buwadjaar.

     MARCUS WATERS

The Warrangun asks, 'Will I remember any of this ... afterwards?'

'No, nothing,' replies Buwadjaar.

'So much knowledge lost...' pleads the Warrangun.

'The sacrifice that comes with mortality and sin. I mean no interference,' says Buwadjaar.

'Then why do you do it?' asks the Warrangun.

'Only because you are so unhappy,' says Buwadjaar.

'As are you...' wails the Warrangun.

BEAT

'Sorry, I didn't mean that.'

'I still love you,' confirms Buwadjaar.

The Warrangun asks, 'Is that a sign of my becoming sick, things slipping out without my meaning?'

'Yes. That is how it all begins,' replies Buwadjaar.

'I'm ready to go back...' confirms the Warrangun.

'You have to know that last time you broke law ... Aboriginal law,' warns Buwadjaar.

'We were lost. You abandoned us,' pleads the Warrangun.

'I cannot control your will. You trespassed on sacred grounds; ceremonies you didn't understand,' commands Buwadjaar.

'Our land, our ceremonies!' states the Warrangun, in his defence.

'You initiated things you did not understand,' replies Buwadjaar.

The Warrangun begins to chant: 'Gamilaraay! Gomeroi, Gamilaroi, Kamilaroi... yammaa yaani yilaagi... Yaawuu!'

Again, Buwadjaar speaks with warning in his tone, 'This is a sacred dance you play with, Warrangun. And like all things ancient, they have a source — there are consequences.'

BEAT

'Tell me, Warrangun. Who taught you this?'

*

Eyes open, then close...
A man, in and out of deep sleep, not quite conscious.
The eyes open again, just long enough to show fear...
Then close.

*

A rainforest clearing: a group of Aboriginal people in traditional dress. It's the early colonisation of Australia, the 1800s. We are at the coalface of ancient and modern worlds colliding. There are only women and children protected by teenage boys, all moving as one group.

No men.

They come to the outskirts of the rainforest. And stop. They focus in on a teenage boy, who appears to be leading the group. There is a frightened anticipation. Suddenly, we hear the sound of a horn. Everyone runs out of the rainforest towards chaos.

The boy runs back to the cover of the forest in self-preservation – no time to think of the others.

The antagonists are revealed. Three Aboriginal warriors, fully naked, their bodies painted in traditional ochre. The men are warriors riding on horses with nets, nulla nullas (traditional clubs) and killer boomerangs. They start riding through the mob, rounding them up like sheep.

The sounds of wailing and screaming as the horsemen begin a random killing spree, clubbing women and children alike, while rounding up others in nets.

The boy zigzags past two of the horsemen, who then turn in pursuit with an open net.

He jumps over an exposed tree trunk. The two riders, in hot pursuit, are thrown from their horses as their net becomes entangled on the enormous trunk of the tree.

The boy makes his escape into the sanctuary of the rainforest.

*

He looks back from the security of the bushes to observe the survivors being herded away. He begins to follow them, but keeps a safe distance.

The boy is now watching the same three Aboriginal men,

 MARCUS WATERS

who are still covered in blood as they make camp by a lake bed. The men start to clean themselves as they throw the bloodied nulla nullas and killer boomerangs into the water. There are no survivors. The water becomes red as the nulla nullas and boomerangs float to the top.

The three men are laughing and joking among themselves.

A non-Indigenous infantryman in colonial, regimental uniform is seen walking down from up above the men, through the trees and towards the lake. It is Sergeant Colin Maxwell of the Brisbane regiment.

He does not look happy...

'What have you done?' Maxwell confronts the leader of the three men.

The leader's name is Make-A-Light: tall, elegant and athletic, the epitome of the noble savage. Make-A-Light puts up a hand, gesturing for Maxwell to wait. He picks up a native police uniform placed safely in among the foliage.

He begins to unfold the uniform meticulously.

As he dresses himself, Make-A-light makes Maxwell wait a little longer. Something in the bushes has taken his notice.

He sees the young boy hiding.

He and the boy make eye contact. Make-A-Light draws a finger across his throat, as if having his neck cut.

The boy does not move, he is frozen with fear. A wry smile comes over the face of Make-A-Light.

Maxwell has had enough and won't wait any longer.

'You disgust me you heathen,' he says gesturing around them, the water and weapons soaked in blood.

Make-A-Light snarls at the Sergeant. 'Heathen?' His tone is both questioning and threatening.

Sergeant Maxwell replies, 'You blaspheme God's book. You are no soldier of God, Queen or country. You kill with no mercy or feeling.'

Make-A-Light lifts up a nulla nulla towards the face of the Sergeant. 'No, I am no soldier ... just as you, sir, are no Christian.'

Maxwell bats the nulla nulla down from his face.

'How dare you challenge me! If only I had my way... '

Make-A-Light stares back at the Sergeant, growing ever more hostile with each word. 'But you don't have your way, do you Sergeant?'

Make-A-Light pauses as he looks over Maxwell's shoulder at the boy, who is still unmoved and frozen with fear.

'I have come to an understanding that, in war, the innocent die, Sergeant, and my only concern is survival,' he spits.

He takes his eyes off the boy to eyeball Maxwell.

'I am not torn by the same moral judgements and God that you face, Sergeant. One day, the white man, too, will bleed and, due to my actions now, my children will live to witness their demise.'

'You're speaking gibberish, the devil's language ... you make no sense,' replies Maxwell.

Make-A-light looks away unrepentantly towards the boy.

This time, the child is gone.

A lone branch moves slowly from side to side.

In my mind, I can see it all coming to an end, Make-A-light thinks to himself.

He turns to face Maxwell. 'I find it strange that you find our methods so brutal, Sergeant. The land has been cleared as I was instructed and the surviving rebels found and punished.'

Sergeant Maxwell shakes his head. 'Good Christian lives these savages were meant to be given, not this... '

He moves in towards Make-A-Light, almost whispering his contempt. 'I will never understand you, Make-A-Light. How you can turn on your people so.'

'You don't have to understand me, Sergeant. Just know that, due to your intervention, I have become a god. My people cannot hide from me and you cannot win this war without me,' replies Make-A-Light, now fully dressed in his native police uniform.

Maxwell turns his back and walks off. He knows Make-A-light is right – he has become unstoppable.

BEAT

*

Eyes open, then close...
Inner city, park, trees, Aboriginal people in modern dress.
It is the year 2014.
A man, in and out of deep sleep, not quite conscious.
He is Aboriginal and struggling for breath. The man is forty years old.

There is a paramedic and an Aboriginal health worker trying to resuscitate him, as a group of police watch on.

A crowd of people watch from behind.

His eyes remain closed…

*

It's 1852, Brisbane, Australia – night-time. The same, young boy, Wollombi, who survived the native police raid, watches on as an Aboriginal male, dressed in native police uniform, collapses to his knees. The man's neck is bound tight, held like a dog by another Aboriginal man, Dundalli.

It is not Make-A-Light.

'No, please, brother … we cousins … mob!' pleads the man.

Dundalli looks across at Wollombi. The man is now crying, shaking, begging for his survival. 'Please, brother … please … '

Dundalli leans forward and cuts the man's throat with a sharp blade.

The man collapses to the ground, limp.

The next morning, Dundalli walks into a blacks' camp with Wollombi. Both are carrying a number of kangaroos – Dundalli has two and his young apprentice carries one. Both with a coolamon each – a traditional instrument used to carry berries, nuts and indigenous vegetation.

They are both greeted by a number of women and children who appear from the shadows. First one, then two and then suddenly they are surrounded by a number of families.

Dundalli is in his late twenties, but he is given the respect of someone much older.

Sturdy and elegant, he demands respect, a benign king to his people. Wollombi is embraced, loved by both the women and children alike.

Hours later, after having provided a feast for his mob, Wollombi covers up the hole in the ground used for cooking the meat and vegetables. It slowly disappears into the indigenous landscape.

Their food stocks replaced with grain, sheep and meadows.

'Leave that,' Dundalli calls to Wollombi.

'Almost finished,' replies Wollombi, moving quickly.

The hole disappears among a mound of dirt.

Soon there would be no evidence that anyone was ever there at all, enjoying such a feast.

Dundalli smiles as he moves towards the dense growth of the bush. 'You a good boy, Wollombi. Come when you have finished.' Dundalli walks off.

Dundalli, now out from the other side of the dense scrub, is sitting on top of a mountain peak. Behind him, on the other side of the scrub, lays a perfectly secluded hiding place for the families, from any unwanted predators.

He is joined by Wollombi who sits down beside him. Together they look out over the landscape: a natural forest dotted with spasmodic attempts to clear the dense, indigenous foliage, replacing it with flat, lifeless plains and sheep. Smoke rises from intermittent chimneys within this new world.

Dundalli speaks first in a rich, cultured and authoritative voice, gesturing down to the meadows below. 'How can these people be our ancestors?'

Wollombi looks deeper into the landscape, hanging off every word spoken by his mentor.

Dundalli continues, 'It's gotten so big ... so fast ... our people are losing their way.'

Wollombi now looks directly at the man who has taught him all he knows. He wants to speak, but he is aware that a lack of knowledge and life experience prevents him from doing so. He remains silent.

'The smoke is burning from wasted food – food that has fed us all for thousands of years. The land is cleared, and for what? Sheep. The meat makes you tired and lazy ... also hard to shit ... bad shit, not good ... you have to push it out of you. Something wrong, something broken.' Dundalli looks over at Wollombi.

'Where's the understanding of custodial governance here? Where's the knowledge of land and country? This is not life as we know it, son. Nobody lives down there.'

The last of the light begins to fade. The fires are put out below, one after the other.

Dundalli continues, 'What right do they have, pushing all the families out, killing our children and grandchildren? Ripping the guts from our land and mother, how can you kill something yet to be born? What evil is this?'

He is not really asking Wollombi, so Wollombi doesn't answer.

'This is the way it is now: you can't find the heart of logic within anything they do.' Dundalli stops, looks away from Wollombi and stares into space.

He looks back, directly into Wollombi's eyes. 'There's something I want you to do...'

*

Eyes open and then close...

Inner city, park, trees, Aboriginal people in modern dress. The year is 2014

A man, in and out of deep sleep, not quite conscious.

He is Aboriginal, forty years old and struggling for breath.

He is observing himself, as if flying above a scene from earlier in the day. He is approached by two police officers.

'What language do you speak?' asks one of the officers.

'I don't understand,' says the man.

'Do you speak English?' asks the officer.

'I'm speaking English now... ' replies the man.

'It seems we have to speak to you everyday. Do you enjoy that?' asks the officer.

'I don't understand what you're saying,' answers the man.

He has been badly beaten.

There is a paramedic and an Aboriginal health worker trying to resuscitate him, as a group of police watch on.

He can't make out numbers, just uniforms.

There are more than just the first two who approached him, much more.

A crowd of people now gather and watch from behind the police. The man is dying, his eyes remain closed...

*

1850s Australia: Dundalli sits imprisoned in a dark cell. The only light seeps through the bars of a small window, slowly engulfing the room.

He is buttoning a white cotton shirt, when a deep inaudible voice is heard from beyond the cell.

Dundalli adjusts his collar.

'Uncle... ' booms the voice.

Dundalli continues to do up his buttons and starts to roll up his sleeve, ignoring the call.

'Please... ' pleads the voice.

Dundalli turns to face a tall, handsome, dark and beautiful Aboriginal man. It is Make-A-Light, dressed in full native police uniform.

Make-A-Light walks into the light as he and Dundalli face off, separated by the cell bars.

He takes a deep breath.

BEAT

The sound of keys echoes throughout the room as Make-A-Light opens the cell door. Dundalli stands back to allow his nephew space to enter.

'You don't want to join me out here?' asks Make-A-Light.

Dundalli just shakes his head as Make-A-Light joins him in the cell.

'I should have killed you as a child,' says Dundalli.

Make-A-Light takes another step in towards his uncle. 'My revelation was to do whatever it takes. I dream of a world where our family will live through this, to still be here at the end of days.'

Dundalli looks his nephew up and down. 'You have fallen for an adulterer, nephew, one who has you crazy with lust and murder of your own people.'

'I have no pact with Queen or country,' replies Make-A-Light.

Dundalli looks through the barred window. He is looking at a noose hanging in the distance. 'No, but Queen and country has a pact with you.'

Make-A-Light walks into Dundalli's vision. 'You are fighting a battle we cannot win. Why won't you listen? Through me, your bloodline will live through this. My kids, your family, will survive this. Through my actions now, they will still be here at the end.'

Over Make-A-Light's shoulder, Dundalli keeps looking at the noose swaying ever so slightly as it hangs in the breeze.

He looks back at Make-A-Light.

'There was no reason to go after the women and children.'

'I couldn't let anyone survive. One tongue to tell tales and

     MARCUS WATERS

people would not fear me as they do. My hand was forced,' replies Make-A-Light.

'You show concern only for this physical world. You forget our Burruguu-ngayi-li: our Dreaming goes beyond this world. You will have to answer for what you have done,' warns Dundalli.

'Have you seen what these people possess?' asks Make-A-Light. 'Muskets and inventions we could only dream of. Survival is my only concern.'

Dundalli replies, 'I, too, have made friends with some of these people. Our boomerang is far more advanced than anything they have understood. This, my nephew, is mathematics of such a high degree, which they can never muster. A simple stick, carved from hand, that returns when thrown, goes far beyond all that has made you sick and so obsessed.'

'And what of our people sneezing, their eyes red before dying? Even their magic is stronger than ours,' argues Make-A-Light.

'This, I still do not understand. But by allowing you to take me in, I will soon be seeing our ancestors.' Dundalli looks out at the noose again. 'And I will find the source of this evil.'

Make-A-Light spits back his reply, 'Unlike you, I have made no friends with the mogwi, but I do listen. Our ways are backward, primitive, and their world has found us – nothing more.'

'These people live like birds of passage: they have no interest in what is best for the land they dwell in, only what suits their most primeval needs of power and greed. When they arrived, we were free: clean water, plentiful food, children laughing... now the water is poison, our food gone and the children are dead or in hiding. In choosing their ways over and above our own, your children and their children's children are already dead.'

BEAT

'It is in my blood that you have condemned their fate,' curses Dundalli. He then turns his back on Make-A-Light.

'Now leave me to die... '

These are Dundalli's last words to his nephew.

*

It's now dark, becoming night.

The Aboriginal man has his shirt off, revealing bruising from being beaten.

The Aboriginal health worker talks with the paramedic.

'How is he doing?'

'Calm, but not out of trouble.'

'Is he awake?' asks the health worker.

'No,' replies the paramedic.

'He looks like he is waking,' says the health worker.

'It's his reticular activating system, it triggers the brain into arousal,' states the paramedic.

'English?' asks the health worker.

'It's what we call a fight-or-flight reaction. It spreads through his sympathetic nervous system. He has massive internal injuries and is going into shock,' says the paramedic, as he and the Aboriginal health worker look up at the police.

They have now moved into the crowd, stopping people from taking pictures with mobile phones, threatening arrest.

The paramedic checks heart monitors as the Aboriginal health worker checks blood pressure.

'Shit, he's starting to spike,' says the paramedic.

He pushes down on the man's chest. 'We're losing him… '

*

An old colonial blacksmith's cabin – night.

The cabin belongs to Richard Thomas, a Welsh blacksmith. He is sorting through a number of nulla nullas with custom-made lead darts, which he has attached to the ends, making them lethal weapons. Like missiles that can be thrown from a distance.

An Aboriginal woman, earthly and motherly, walks in holding a small child of mixed race. She kisses Thomas on the cheek before retiring to bed. Thomas returns to bagging the nulla nullas separately, in readiness of being picked up.

The door flies open, it is Dundalli.

He stands staring at Thomas and the nulla nullas piled around the room. Thomas, sensing Dundalli's despair, walks towards him, arms out to console him.

Dundalli pulls away with his hand held up to Thomas.

     MARCUS WATERS

'Before we are buried, brother, we will have our revenge,' says Thomas.

'That's what you say, but this goes beyond our lives. This is an unimaginable evil and we are trapped. I have given word and some of the boys have taken the women and children away. Only men left to die in a final battle,' answers Dundalli.

Dundalli steps towards Thomas, picking up one of the nulla nullas off the floor and pressing it against Thomas's throat.

Thomas doesn't show any emotion.

'Will you stand with me till the end, brother?' asks Dundalli.

'As we agreed... I have Aboriginal seed, born from my own blood, and family to watch over, Dundalli. For now, that is all we can do,' says Thomas.

Dundalli presses the sharp point of the nulla nulla even deeper into Thomas's throat, causing it to bleed. Thomas doesn't resist, but continues to eyeball Dundalli.

Both men are frozen on the spot.

Suddenly, Dundalli releases the nulla nulla from Thomas's throat. He walks away with his back turned to Thomas. His concentration is taken by a cockroach, which slithers across the floor before disappearing under the boarding against the wall.

He looks around, noticing more cockroaches hidden around the room.

'Your people are like cockroaches: they are everywhere,' he says.

The sound of cockroaches scurrying across the floor can be heard. It is gradually getting louder, magnifying as the cockroaches disappear under the floorboards against the wall.

The sound becomes louder and louder until it's deafening – timeless and embedded into the same consciousness as the Warrangun when speaking to Buwadjaar.

*

Nightmarish, close-up. The magnification of cockroaches eating on the other side of the wall is interspersed with dialogue from the modern-day police approaching the forty-year-old Aboriginal male.

'Get on the ground with feet out in front of you ... feet out in front of you! Put your hands on your knees … your fucking hands on your knees!'

Another cockroach reaches the others – they are devouring a dead insect. The noise is disgusting.

'See my fists? They're getting ready to fuck you up,' says the policeman, as the noise of cockroaches eating, crunching and scurrying gets louder and louder.

The sounds of the Aboriginal man, screaming for help as he is being beaten, are immersed with the disgusting, magnified noises of the cockroaches eating the insect.

'I'm sorry, I'm sorry … please … help … please … I'm sorry… '

'Get your hands behind your back … your back! Get your hands behind your back!'

'I'm sorry… '

'Lay on your stomach … your fucking stomach!'

The images and noises are unsettling … disturbing.

*

Dundalli squashes another cockroach with the tip of a *nulla nulla*.

'We did not have these disgusting insects before you arrived.' He looks towards Thomas for an answer, but it is not what he wants to hear.

'You have no idea what is coming, they will not stop, no matter how hard you fight. It will never end, but you can't ever give up. Trust me, we must fight until the very end,' says Thomas.

Dundalli takes a deep breath before he replies, 'I was not born a killer, but I have been labelled as such. I accept that I am to die as a criminal and a thief in defending my land.'

'You will be remembered, I promise you, and not as a criminal. It is they who lie, cheat and steal, not you, my friend,' says Thomas.

Before Dundalli can answer, the front door flies open.

Dundalli stands with the nulla nulla ready. Thomas has picked up a musket. Both are armed and ready for what comes through the door.

The door flaps against the wind. The noise and anticipation is eerie.

Finally, Wollombi makes his way out from beyond the shadows and comes through the door.

 MARCUS WATERS

A tired, exhausted, young, withered face.
'Make-A-Light ... he's here!'

*

The paramedic is trying desperately to keep the Aboriginal man alive.

'It's a heightened physiological activity.'

Another paramedic has joined the scene, moving the Aboriginal health worker to the side as he joins the first paramedic.

'We're seeing a high increase in emotions, together with a reduction in cortical functioning.'

The man's body starts to seizure, held tightly against the bounds trying to keep him alive.

'Is he okay?' asks the health worker.

The first paramedic prepares the man's arm for a needle.

'His conscious control is being lost to trauma.' The paramedic injects the man through the arm. 'This should calm him down.'

'Is he going to survive?' asks the health worker, looking back at the police who appear to have increased in numbers – still keeping witnesses with mobile phones at bay.

The activity increases as the two paramedics work together frantically.

'We're losing him, we're losing him!' screams one of the paramedics.

*

A moment caught between time and lost in emotion.
A heart beats...
Eyes open, then close.
A moment caught between time and lost in emotion.
A heart beats...
Eyes open, then close.
A man, in and out of deep sleep.
His eyes spring open.
Then close...

*

Across time, images of Dundalli, Wollombi and the police beating the Aboriginal man merge into one as all feelings become lost, disorientated. As the images become one, time somehow merges and the past, present and future also become one.

Anxiety and fear so close, it has no boundaries.

A blinking pulse beating with a rhythm of antiquity, timeless within the electric darkness of space.

Coursing with phosphorous light, burning beneath the derma of lost consciousness, is something living and breathing.

A voice from an ancient past.

'Hello?'

Data now flashes across the man's memory; data long before having ever breathed, lived or felt – life.

He sees Wollombi hiding in the bushes, the dead piled up around him.

He can see the cell holding Dundalli, before his execution by hanging.

'I'm inside. Not able to engage?' It's a woman's voice.

The forty year old dying man is Make-A-Light. The Warrangun, but in another time. His sins having finally caught up with him.

Another voice: this time even older than the first. Again, breaking through time and space.

'Object has crashed.' It is Buwadjaar.

All thoughts fill with racing columns of numbers. Shimmering like green, electric rivets, they rush towards the beginning of time and space.

'He doesn't remember us. We're wasting our time, he is gone,' says Buwadjaar.

The numbers suddenly freeze, motionless, timeless. The first three numbers become fixed, then darkness.

'Alright, we try again.' It's the woman's voice.

'No, not again. We have lost him, it's over,' says Buwadjaar. 'The trauma and consequences of his last life were too much to bear – even for him.'

'He's not coming home?' asks the female voice.

'No,' confirms Buwadjaar. 'It's over, but trust me when I say, his sacrifice has not been in vain.'

Anxiety and fear so close, it has no boundaries.

                    MARCUS WATERS

A blinking pulse beating with a rhythm of antiquity, timeless within the electric darkness of space. Coursing with phosphorous light, burning beneath the derma of Warrangun's own consciousness, is something … slowly … burning … out …

'Good bye, old friend.'

And Buwadjaar is gone.

*

A moment, again, caught between time and lost in emotion.

A heart beats…

Eyes open, then close.

The Warrangun closes his eyes for the very last time, finally allowed to sleep.

A heart stops.

*

The paramedic looks up.

'We lost him, he's dead.'

*

Two police officers have been charged with second-degree murder, involuntary manslaughter and the use of excessive force on a forty year old, homeless, Aboriginal man. Both are pleading not guilty. The trial will centre on video footage released on YouTube by witnesses with mobile phones. The footage shows the Aboriginal man struggling with six police officers, who hit, knee and jolted him with a stun gun, as he lay on the ground calling out for help over and over again.

The case highlights how modern technology is being used around the globe to document police brutality against citizens, with a number of cases now appearing on social media. Never before have people had access to free media in the protection of civil liberties. Everyone now, due to modern technology, is walking around with a video camera on their phone. Within hours, these events are being uploaded to social media and are seen by millions of people worldwide. This changes everything.

BIOGRAPHIES

BEN BROOKER is a writer, editor, critic and playwright. He is the author of many published short stories, poems and reviews and has had his work featured at the Short + Sweet short play festival in Sydney. He has also written for *New Matilda, New Internationalist, Overland, dB Magazine, RealTime, Fringe Benefits, artsHub, The Daily Review* and his blog *Marginalia*. In 2013, his first full-length play *The Lake* was produced by award-winning independent theatre company five.point.one in Adelaide.

BWESIGYE BWA MWESIGIRE was born in 1987 in Kigezi, south-western Uganda. His work has appeared in literary and academic journals, magazines, national newspapers and in other places, including the Short Story Day Africa, *Uganda Modern Literary Digest, New Black Magazine, Saraba, Readers Cafe Africa, Daily Monitor* and *AFLA Quarterly* among others. His book, *Fables out of Nyanja*, a collection of short fictional rhythmic narratives of childhood was published by Kushinda (2012). He blogs at orwaari.blogspot.com

THAM CHUI-JOE is a sixteen-year-old A-level student at The Alice Smith School, Kuala Lumpur, Malaysia. She likes reading, writing and listening to music. She has a penguin with forty different personas, an imaginary dragon that is obsessed with rhyming, and a sister who is also a hedgehog. Her favourite subjects are English and History.

CRAIG CORMICK is an award-winning author and science communicator. He has published over 100 short stories, including eight collections as well as novels and non-fiction. His writing awards include the ACT Book of the Year Award and the Queensland Premier's Literary Award. He has been a Writer in Residence at the Universiti Sains Malaysia, and in 2008 received an Antarctic Arts Fellowship to travel to Antarctica, a trip he documented in his 2011 book *In Bed with Douglas Mawson*. His latest book is a young adult speculative fiction novel *Time Vandals*. When he grows up he wants to be much younger (at heart).

JEANNETTE DELAMOIR taught at Central Queensland University for eleven years, and completed a PhD in media studies at La Trobe University in 2002. Currently she lives in Sydney and is working on a non-fiction project about the 1913 visit to Rockhampton, Queensland, by a travelling vaudeville company.

SÉBASTIEN DOUBINSKY was born in Paris in 1963. Having spent a part of his early childhood in America, he is bilingual and writes both in English and in French. An established writer in France, Sébastien Doubinsky has published a series of novels, covering different genres, from classical literature to crime fiction, as well as a few poetry collections. He currently lives in Århus, Denmark, with his wife and his two children.

JOHN FULTON is the author of three books of fiction: *Retribution*, which won the Southern Review Short Fiction Award, *More Than Enough*, a Barnes and Noble's Discover Great New Writers selection, and the collection of novellas and stories, *The Animal Girl,* which was shortlisted for the Story Award. His short fiction has been awarded a Pushcart Prize, cited for distinction in the Best American Short Stories, shortlisted for the O. Henry Award, and published in numerous journals, including *Zoetrope, The Southern Review,* and *The Sun*. He is a professor of creative writing at the University of Massachusetts, Boston, where he directs the MFA program in creative writing.

LUCY GREENWOOD lives in a housing collective in the town of Kwoorabup (also known as Denmark) on the south coast of Western Australia. The area attracts many visitors to its beautiful forests and wild coastline. Lucy is re-learning to live close to nature as a way to find peace and renewal. Now in her sixties, she feels it is time to gather together her abandoned dreams and bring them home. Perhaps it is that time for the world, as well."

ABIR HAMDAR is a lecturer in the School of Modern Languages and Cultures at Durham University. She has published articles, short stories and plays on gender, illness/disability, cinema, exile and Islamism. Her play *The Silicone Bomb* was performed in Beirut, Alexandria and Amman. She is preparing a monograph on female illness and disability in Arabic literature and a co-edited collection on Islamism and Arab Cultural Expression.

TABISH KHAIR is the author of various critically acclaimed poetry collections, studies and novels. Winner of the All India Poetry Prize and fellowships at Delhi, Cambridge and Hong Kong, his novels *The Bus Stopped* (2004), *Filming: A Love Story* (2007) and *The Thing About Thugs* (2010) have been translated into several languages and shortlisted for major prizes, including the Encore Award (UK), the Crossword Prize, the Hindu Best Fiction Prize, the DSC Prize for South Asia (India) and the Man Asian Literary Prize (Hong Kong). Khair now lives in Århus, Denmark.

CRISETTA MACLEOD has been French horn professional, experimental psychologist, clinical psychologist, church minister (failed) and now, a writer. She has had six short stories published, and won six assorted awards. She writes reviews, interviews and non-fiction articles for *Aurealis* magazine, the flagship Australian sci fi and fantasy magazine which went online at the beginning of 2012.

EUNICE NGONGKUM holds a PhD in African Literature from the University of Yaoundé where she presently teaches in the Department of African Literature and Civilizations. She has a good number of scientific articles in national and international peer-reviewed journals. Her short story collections, *Manna of a Life Time and Other Stories* (2007) and *Wen Men Nte* (2012), were published by Editions Clé and Miraclaire Publishing, respectively. Her short stories have also appeared in *The Spirit Machine and other New Short Stories from Cameroon* (Ed. Emma Dawson, Nottingham: Critical Cultural and Communication Press, 2008) and *The Ngoh Kuoh Review*, 2011.

TIM RICHARDS is a Melbourne-based script assessor and screenwriting teacher. His stories have been widely published in Australia, the UK, the USA and Sweden, and he is the author of four books: *Letters to Francesca, The Prince, Duckness* and *Thought Crimes*. His work has appeared in a number of anthologies, along with journals including *Heat, Meanjin, Overland* and *The Sleepers Almanac*. Six of his stories have been re-printed in *Best Australian Stories*.

EMILY RICHES creates a world not so different from the interior of our own minds – insular, surreal and vaguely terrifying. She feels that 'the end' really comes down to what we miss, and what we long for.

LEONE ROSS is a Jamaican/British award-winning writer, editor and lecturer. Prior to publishing and teaching fiction, she worked in print media and television. She has taught at the City Literary Institute in London, Cardiff University, the Arvon Foundation, as an International Fellow at Trinity College Dublin and for the British Council. She is the author of three novels and her short fiction has been published in the UK, France, Eastern Europe, Canada, the USA and the Caribbean. *Wasafiri* magazine named her second novel, *Orange Laughter*, one of the most influential books written in the last 25 years. Ross works as a senior lecturer at Roehampton University in London.

A graduate of Harvard College and Harvard Law School, USA, **JOHN G. SHULMAN** is a visiting professor at the National Law University, Delhi, and an internationally recognised expert in negotiation and conflict resolution. John has written numerous books and other publications on negotiation and conflict resolution. He has also written a children's book, entitled *The Lama, the Snow Leopard and the Thunder Dragon*, and co-wrote and directed the award-winning human rights movie *Justice*.

DIRK STRASSER has written over 30 books for major publishers in Australia and has been editing magazines and anthologies since 1990. His speculative fiction novels – including *Zenith* and *Equinox* – were originally published by Pan Macmillan in Australia and Heyne Verlag in Germany. His science fiction story 'The Doppelgänger Effect' appeared in the World Fantasy Award-winning anthology *Dreaming Down-Under*. Several stories have appeared in Best of anthologies and lists in Australia and the USA, and in the Gardner Dozois' Year's Best Science Fiction Honorable Mentions. His short fiction has been translated into a number of languages. He founded the *Aurealis Awards* and has co-published *Aurealis* magazine for over 20 years.

LEAH SWANN's short stories and poems have appeared in *Best Australian Short Stories, Award Winning Australian Writing, The Review of Australian Fiction, page seventeen, Masthead* and *Reflecting on Melbourne*. Her first book, *Bearings*, a collection of short stories and a novella, was published by Affirm Press in 2011, and was shortlisted for The Dobbie Award. Her second book, *Irina The Wolf Queen*, the first of a children's fantasy trilogy, was released as a print and e-book in 2012 by Xoum Publishing. Leah Swann has worked in public relations and as a journalist, and lives with her family in Melbourne.

BRONWYNE THOMASON is a writer and part-time tutor at Deakin University. She has earned a Bachelor of Arts (Writing) with First Class Honours from Edith Cowan University in Perth, holds a Master of Fine Arts in Writing from Swinburne University in Melbourne and is currently a PhD Candidate with Deakin University in Geelong, Victoria.

MARCUS WATERS is a Kamilaroi First Nation Australian writer and language speaker. Married to a Maialwali Karuwali and Pitta Pitta First Nation Australian woman, together they have six kids. Marcus is currently teaching at Griffith University, Brisbane in the School of Humanities.

JEANETTE ZISSELL is a PhD candidate studying medieval literature at the University of Connecticut. In addition to her academic work on the vernacular theology of fourteenth-century England, she has also pursued creative writing throughout her scholarly career. Having published works of short fiction, creative non-fiction, and poetry, she received the Connecticut Writing Project prize in fiction in 2009 and the Edwin Way Teale award in 2012. She lives with her husband, pets, and a prodigious pile of books in a quiet corner of rural Connecticut.

THE EDITORS

PATRICK WEST is author of the short story collection, *The World Swimmers* (2011), and numerous other stories in publications such as *The Penguin Book of the Road, The Best Australian Stories, Going Down Swinging* and *Southerly*. The *Australian's* reviewer wrote that *The World Swimmers* contains 'incredible insight into the human condition throughout.' Patrick's stories have been successful in many writing awards and competitions, and his writing practice extends into creative nonfiction, poetry, reviewing, exhibition catalog writing and film scriptwriting. Patrick is a respected writing teacher and supervisor of postgraduate writing projects, and is currently based at Deakin University. He resides in Melbourne with his partner and their two children.

OM PRAKASH DWIVEDI is assistant professor in English at the University of Taiz, Yemen. He is the editor of *Literature of the Indian Diaspora* (2011); *The Other India: Narratives of Terror, Communalism and Violence* (2012); *Changing Worlds/Changing Nations: The Concept of Nation in the Transnational Era* (2012); and *Postcolonial Theory in the Global Age* (2013). *Tracing the Indian Diaspora*, a collection of essays, is forthcoming.

Also from
SPINELESS WONDERS

SINGLE-AUTHOR

Stories that illuminate the ordinary - told with humour and generosity.
'O'Flynn's faultless ear for laconic Aussie parlance, his wry ability to turn a story in a moment from comedy to tragedy and back again, his exhilaratingly deft range... all this makes him one of a kind, in my opinion. A hugely enjoyable collection.'
CATE KENNEDY

In this short story collection, travellers on highways and trains are preoccupied with the lives of the dead, with lost children or with parents. A woman searches a suburban deadland for her missing mother. A rural family struggles on a land that fails to sustain them. A young man's attempt to leave the strictures of family life ends in violence.
'A talent to watch.' WALTER MASON

In these seventeen stories, Melbourne writer, Mary Manning, looks at the ways people are shaped, or damaged, by their circumstances. The results may sometimes be humorous, sometimes tragic. Whether set on a tram, along a highway or on an Outback road?it is the journey, the characters and the telling of the tale that will capture your attention.
'Tart, tight and compulsively readable.'
PADDY O'REILLY

COLLECTIONS

What makes a man? In this collection of short stories, Pierz Newton John moves through the full range of masculine experience, with an openness not afraid to show men at their most lonely, sexual, loving, sometimes vulnerable, sometimes abusive.

'A startling collection…sly humour and memorable characters.'
CHRIS WOMERSLEY

This entertaining collection includes a romp of a novella as well as short stories and micro fictions all set in and around contemporary Melbourne. Sometimes serious, sometimes seriously playful – always written in breathtakingly beautiful prose.

"Be careful. These stories might cut you.'
RYAN O'NEILL

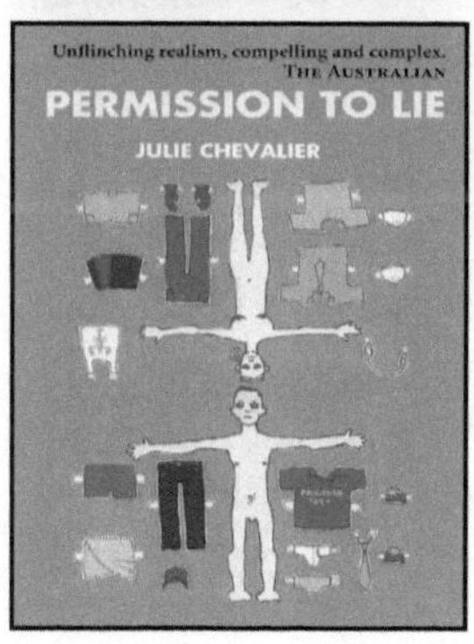

In *Permission to Lie*, Julie Chevalier casts a curious eye into many different worlds. Her characters ride the citybound bus route, spend the night in a nudist colony and wait tables. Quirky and beautifully-written, these stories provide insights that ring with integrity and compassion.

'A new voice in Australian fiction, wry, gritty, knowing and true.'
FIONA MCGREGOR

SHORT FICTION ANTHOLOGIES

In this anthology, our editor, Angela Meyer, pays tribute to the undeniable cultural influence that American TV programs such as Twilight Zone and Outer Limits have had on our lives 'down under'.

'These TV dramas,' Meyer says, ' were often metaphors for equality, justice, the nuclear threat and more. Though they were just as often pure, spooky fun.'

Due for release Dec 2013

If you like your genres with a bit of edge, you'll love this diverse collection of stories from Spineless Wonders. Features award-winning writers such as Ryan O'Neill, Jen Mills, Andy Kissane, Louise Swinn, Julie Chevalier, A.S. Patric and Kim Westwood as well as stories chosen by Sophie Cunningham in the inaugural Carmel Bird Short Fiction Award.

'Quality short fiction, packed with surprises. Prepare to be transported.'
MARION HALLIGAN

THE Carmel Bird AWARD

PROSE POEM & MICROFICTION ANTHOLOGIES

What do our best wordsmiths have to say about Australian icons? This anthology takes a fresh look at everything from the HIH collapse to crocs, Margaret Olley, bush burials and the ABC. We visit a post-apocalyptic Opera House and spend Saturday night in downtown Byron Bay.
'A celebration of the many things Australia can mean to us.'
NEWTOWN REVIEW OF BOOKS

Here are short and clever pieces by thirty contemporary Australian writers on topics ranging from the eroticism of mash potato, parenting as magic realism and a tongue-in-cheek history of the Cyclops bicycle. Includes award-winning writers Michael Farrell, Keri Glastonbury, Judith Beveridge, Peter Boyle, Kent MacCarter, Erin Gough and Charles D'Anastasi.
'A treasure trove.' READINGS MONTHLY

THE *joanne burns* AWARD

Dear Writer Revisited

DEAR WRITER REVISITED is about writing and the imagination is essential reading for any writer, emerging or experienced. Re-released with new material and updated advice for the Twenty-first Century writer.

"Carmel Bird has updated her brilliant guide to those who are perplexed by writing. *Dear Writer Revisited* is a dazzling, humane and witty book which will be enlightening for anyone who picks it up, however experienced she or he may be. This is a classic account of how to write. I know of nothing that equals it."

PETER CRAVEN

'I first read *Dear Writer* as a nervy, secretive scribbler-in-journals 20 years ago. Reading this revised version I'm struck again by its practical generosity on technical matters - but am also inspired by the deeper, more complex conversations I think I missed in those early readings: about courage, about the urgency and mystery and self-discovery of the writing process. *Dear Writer Revisited* may masquerade – convincingly – as a book for beginners, but its lessons are mature and wise.'

—CHARLOTTE WOOD
THE WRITER'S ROOM INTERVIEWS

Cracking the Spine
Ten short Austrlalian stories and how they were written

'Cracking The Spine is the most innovative resource in Australian literature I have seen in many years. An anthology of contemporary short stories, each with a commentary by their authors, the collection breaks down the wall between the creative and discursive, the imagistic and the expository. Filled with cutting-edge, innovative writers and armed with an expansive definition of what it is to be an Australian, Cracking the Spine will be at once accessible to undergraduate students and informative and challenging for their teachers. What a thrill to see a work like this come about!'

NICHOLAS BIRNS,
Editor, *Antipodes*

'Cracking the Spine is not just a deftly curated overview of the contemporary Australian short story, including pieces by ten of the best practitioners at work today. The auto-critical essays that accompany each work gesture even more widely. Literature, life, landscape, history: the whole gamut of Antipodean experience may be gleaned from its pages. An ideal resource for those interested in Ozlit, Cracking the Spine is also a pure pleasure to read.'

—GEORDIE WILLIAMSON
THE AUSTRALIAN

EARWORMS

Earworms are those songs with unforgettable hooks that get stuck in your head but Spineless Wonders brings you short Australian earworms—stories by award-winning writers that you definitely won't want to forget.

Stuck in a queue? Don't stress. You can listen to our selection of funny, political and thought-provoking prose poems and microfiction from our anthology, Small Wonder.

Got a pile of washing-up or ironing to do? Housework's not a chore when you can listen to short fiction from our anthology, Escape.

Commuting every day? Traffic jams are not a problem when you can listen to the latest in contemporary short fiction from Spineless Wonders.

Prices range from $0.99 to $2.99. Gift vouchers available. Listen to our audio trailers at
www.shortaustralianstories.com.au/audio

**FIND OUT MORE ABOUT
SPINELESS WONDERS**

www.shortaustralianstories.com.au

www.ingramcontent.com/pod-product-compliance
Lightning Source LLC
Chambersburg PA
CBHW051301210726
48287CB00002B/608